TEXT WARS

AN ACCIDENTALLY IN LOVE STORY BOOK 3

WHITNEY DINEEN

MELANIE SUMMERS

THE ACCIDENTALLY IN LOVE STORIES

BY WHITNEY DINEEN & MELANIE SUMMERS

Text Me on Tuesday
The Text God
Text Wars
Text in Show (coming June 2021)
Mistle Text (coming Fall 2021)

ALSO BY WHITNEY DINEEN

Romantic Comedies

Love is a Battlefield

Ain't She Sweet

It's My Party

The Event

The Move

The Plan

The Dream

Relatively Normal

Relatively Sane

Relatively Happy

The Reinvention of Mimi Finnegan

Mimi Plus Two

Kindred Spirits

She Sins at Midnight

Going Up?

Non-Fiction Humor

Motherhood, Martyrdom & Costco Runs

Conspiracy Thriller

See No More

Middle Reader Fiction

Wilhelmina and the Willamette Wig Factory

Who the Heck is Harvey Stingle?

Children's Books

The Friendship Bench

ALSO BY MELANIE SUMMERS

ROMANTIC COMEDIES
The Crown Jewels Series

The Royal Treatment

The Royal Wedding

The Royal Delivery

Paradise Bay Series

The Honeymooner

Whisked Away

The Suite Life

Resting Beach Face (Coming Soon)

Crazy Royal Love Series

Royally Crushed

Royally Wild

Royally Tied

WOMEN'S FICTION

The After Wife

The Deep End (Coming Soon)

DEDICATION

This book is dedicated to space geeks of all kinds.
Your curiosity makes you cool,
W & M

ONE

Serafina

As a Libra, I'm "all about the balance." I've recently begun to sing my astrological motto to the tune of Meghan Trainor's song "All About That Bass" because — why not? Every morning I stand on one foot with my eyes closed and both arms outstretched like I'm trying to touch the opposite walls in my airy SoHo loft. I do this for five minutes on each foot and like to keep myself entertained in the process.

The problem with being the scale of the zodiac — our symbol really is a scale — is that other star signs often have a hard time grasping a Libra's need for equilibrium. While we all have our quirks, this fundamental necessity for balance can be a real bear. Especially when others don't play along, which is *a lot* of the time. Since I started making my living with my *Live for Your Star Sign* app, I've butted up against all sorts of people who couldn't care less about harmony. But harmony is the secret to my success. That, and sweet treats to keep my creative juices flowing all day long (and sometimes into the night).

Understanding trends and knowing how to position your app as *the one* with the answers to life's biggest problems (all for the bargain price of $4.99/month) is a full-time gig, and I've sunk so much time and money into this business, I need it to succeed, no matter what I have to do to make that happen.

As I get to the part of the song where I belt out how I'm bringing booty back, my front door slams open and the best assistant/programmer/neighbor to ever inhabit the body of a fifteen-year-old girl charges into my inner domain, upsetting the tranquility of my early morning routine. I lose my balance and tip sideways, landing on the bean bag chair to my right with an unceremonious thump.

"Sera!!! You won't believe it!" Charley yells while waving a piece of paper in the air and hopping around like her shredded jeans are on fire. "I got into Yale!"

"Are you serious?!" I ask, scrambling to get up, but somehow managing to get caught in the zipper of the faux fur cover.

Charley gives me a look of concern. "You okay?"

"I'm good." Miraculously, I manage to free myself and stand up. "Commence celebrating."

We jump up and down and squeal before I ask the all-important question, "What did your parents say? Will they let you go?" I hold my breath while working to contain my excitement. I'm worried they're going to say no, as their daughter *is* only fifteen.

Having said that, Charley is a certifiable genius who took the GED and graduated from high school in the middle of her sophomore year ... during her fourth suspension. She has a penchant for repeatedly breaking into the school's computer system and renaming the students according to her personal thoughts about them. For instance, her arch nemesis, Madison Parker, most recently became Butt-Face McGee. Her crush Jacob Fein was awarded the moniker, Hunky Pants McHottiestein.

I know I shouldn't find it funny. I am, after all, an adult, but at twenty-eight it's pretty easy for me to slip back into teenage Serafina and want to stick it to all the mean kids. While Charley and I found the monikers highly entertaining (not to mention justified), Principal Fox didn't share our enjoyment.

"My mom says I can't go anywhere until I prove I'm mature enough to handle myself," Charley groans while collapsing on my overstuffed butter-colored sofa. Her mother, Martha Jenkins, is an esteemed heart surgeon with a limited sense of humor. In fact, now that I think about it, I can't actually recall the sound of her laugh, which is pretty shocking since they've been my neighbors for three years.

"What does your dad say?"

Lorne Jenkins is a play-by-the-rules circuit court judge who is always at odds with his fiery daughter. As her advanced calculus teacher Mr. Banks pointed out on multiple occasions, "A bored Charley is a bad Charley." Not a particularly kind thing to say about a teenager, but then again, Charley had just hacked into the school's computer system and renamed said teacher Bad Breath Banks.

As much as Lorne and Martha love their offspring (and they really do), they don't "get" her, which is probably why she started hanging out with me in the first place.

Charley's eyes twinkle. "Dad says that if I can keep my job with you and stay out of trouble, he'll let me start next year when I'm sixteen." She looks up at me hopefully and asks, "Can you keep me employed for that long? Please say yes, because if you don't, I will probably *accidentally* hack into the government's computer system and rename all of the senators or something."

I sit down next to her and reply, "I'm pretty sure my *Live for Your Star Sign* app will keep us both busy for at least that long." In addition to *Dress for Your Star Sign*, *Eat for Your Star Sign*, *Work for Your Star Sign*, and *Decorate for Your Star Sign*, we're in the process of adding a *Date for Your Star Sign* feature. I tell Charley excitedly, "We've had over a hundred local test subjects sign up for our trial dating feature, can you believe it?"

"Of course I can!" she says enthusiastically — I love this girl's raw excitement about life. "When will we know if it works?"

"As soon as you upload everyone's info, we'll set the algorithm loose and see what happens."

Looking around at my silvery grey walls with sharp pops of colorful artwork, Charley replies, "I'll do it today. I hope you're going to fill out a questionnaire too. God knows you have no social life."

"I am. I figure it would be irresponsible of me not to participate."

"Plus, you'll finally get to go on some dates." My young friend always tries to push me into the dating world, which, frankly, has not been on my radar at all. When you're busy launching the most comprehensive lifestyle app to ever hit the market, other aspects of your life suffer. My social life, for instance, is practically non-existent.

Charley pulls at a handful of micro-braids that frame her gorgeous brown face. "I think your letter of recommendation is what got me into Yale. You were such a superstar when you were there."

"My endorsement only got you so far, my friend. I'm pretty sure your near-perfect SAT and ACT scores are the basis of your admission. Yale is big on prodigies." Before I can comment further, my phone rings. Not recognizing the number, I pick it up and say, "May your stars be in alignment today. This is Serafina." I know, that's a little out there, but trust me, this stuff works.

"Um, hi," comes the hesitant voice on the line. "My name is Waltraut Hemper. I'm a producer at *Wake Up America!* here in New York."

First of all, Waltraut? I know it's a German name, but in my esteemed opinion, it's an unfortunate one as it brings to mind one of those singing stuffed fish that people used to hang on their walls. "Hi, Waltraut. What can I do for you?"

I put her on speaker phone so Charley can hear what's being said.

"We're looking to do a 'Shoot for the Stars' episode here at *Wake Up America!* We came across your app and thought it might be fun if you came on and hosted a segment on dressing for your star sign."

Hal and Lacey have been a staple in my morning since I was in college. It's all I can do not to scream my excitement. A segment on *Wake Up America!* will launch my app into the stratosphere! I sit-dance in my spot while I say, "That sounds doable. When would you like me to be a guest?"

"One week from today. Will that give you enough time to get your models and their wardrobes ready?"

Charley is typing away on her laptop and turns the screen toward me to show an animated gif of a cheer-leading squad jumping up and down. Then she hops off the sofa and imitates the movements herself.

"That should be fine," I tell the producer. "How many looks do you want for each sign?"

"We'll only have time for one, but we'd like you to cover everything from casual to formal depending on who will wear it best. We'll give you a budget to pay for the models. Most stores will either give you the clothes or let you borrow them if you mention their name during the segment."

My body starts to vibrate in anticipation of my first-ever national television appearance. I feel all floaty, like my essence is lifting out of my form and hovering some-where above myself. Before it can float to Brooklyn, I say, "Sounds terrific. If you send me all the details, I'll make sure to give you the best fashion segment you've ever had." I don't know how, but I manage to keep my compo-sure and not sound like I'm about to eat my first hot fudge sundae after successfully losing twenty pounds. Well done, me.

"Great. And FYI, we have someone coming from NASA the same day. We thought it might be fun if you gave him some fashion tips, as well."

"Absolutely! If you ask me, those scientist types could use a little input on the more sensory applications of life."

Waltraut says, "We really want to play up the juxta-position between the scientific and the popular culture views of space."

"The two aren't mutually exclusive," I tell her. "Just because science doesn't give credence to astrology doesn't mean astrology isn't a relevant science of its own."

"That's exactly the kind of thing we want you to say on air," the producer tells me.

Buoyed by her enthusiasm, I add, "Astrology has been practiced for over two thousand years, far longer than most scientific fields. If you think about it, two hundred years ago, people didn't even know enough about germs and viruses to realize that washing their hands was a fundamental deterrent to illness."

"I'm so glad I called you. I think this is going to be a real winner of a segment."

"I'm sure it will." After I hang up, Charley and I stare at each other for a full second before we both dance around the living room, screaming like fools. Once our initial burst of enthusiasm is over (there will be more), I suggest, "Celebratory donut?"

"This calls for two," she says.

Oh, to have a fifteen-year-old's metabolism. But you know what? Who cares about calories because I just got the best news in the two years since I launched my app. We hurry out of my apartment and take the elevator down to the main floor. Charley chats away about how sick this is going to be. (Apparently, sick is the new cool.)

As I listen to her, a tiny seed of worry starts to grow in my belly. Diehard astronomers don't generally mix well with people from my world. In fact, scientists usually disregard astrology as a parlor game. As such, there's a very good chance that if I don't get the upper hand with this astronomer right out of the gate, he may very well try to make me look like a moron on national television.

Which is pretty much my worst nightmare.

TWO

Ben

"...And then Chewy scooted his butt across the living room rug for ten minutes straight while Don complained about how my dog was ruining his nineteenth century Aubusson carpet. As if it's *my* fault the little guy's anal glands keep getting impacted. What do you think, Ben?"

I think I wish you would stop talking.

Carla Jameson, our senior data analyst — and, according to the mug she carries everywhere, "World's Best Dog Mom"— has not stopped talking since she walked into my office twelve minutes and thirty-six seconds ago. I swear the woman has mastered the art of keeping up both ends of a conversation even while doing the kinds of calculations that would cause the average physics student's head to explode. If you don't answer her in a speedy fashion, she'll answer for you. Her mouth moves non-stop, all day long.

There are six of us in total on NASA's Earth II

TRAPPIST-1 Exoplanet Research Team. I was tapped to lead our little group of geeks as we analyze the habit-ability of the seven rocky planets in the TRAPPIST-1 solar system. Five of our team are introverts (including me) and the sixth is currently nattering on about her Labradoodle's hind quarters like I'm thoroughly invested in the topic. Which I am not.

While some of us occasionally lack social awareness — ahem, Carla — we are all exceptionally bright, and get along well considering most of us would rather be crunching numbers and hypothesizing about growing food on another planet than actually conversing with other humans.

As the team leader, I'm lucky enough to have walls and a door to my office that I can shut when I need silence, like I do right now. I've had enough of Chewy's bodily functions and fluctuations to last a lifetime.

Picking up my phone, I tell the imaginary person who hasn't called to, "Hold on a sec." Then I shoo Carla toward the door with an apologetic look. "I've got to take this. Could you please shut my door?"

As she turns to walk off, she's still talking about her dog, but now the unlucky victim is Alec Maestas, one of our junior analysts, who is about to get his daily Chewy update. I sit back in my chair, holding the receiver to my ear and nodding for good measure in case she looks back. After all, I don't want to hurt her feelings, but I'm liable to scream if I hear the words "anal sac" again.

Through the glass wall, I see Alec giving me a dirty look as Carla descends upon his desk. I offer him a satis-fied smile, then type *Sorry, not sorry* in our private chat. He sends back a middle finger emoji in return.

I'm about to reply with a GIF of Han Solo shrugging when my boss, Dev Grover, walks in and shuts the door. "Good God, you'd think she would just take the dog to the vet already. Wow, just wow," he says, sitting down on the opposite side of my desk. "Speaking of wow — I've got the opportunity of a lifetime for you."

"Really?" I ask, not liking the look on his face, which is a cross between trepidation and excitement.

Giving one firm nod, he says, "You know how we're always lamenting the fact that we missed NASA's glory days, when the entire nation would stop everything to watch a shuttle launch?"

"Yes ..." I already hate where this is going.

"And you know how, when you took this position, I mentioned you'd be the face of our department when we needed to drum up publicity?"

"I also recall you saying that particular scenario would likely never come to fruitition since no one is interested in space exploration anymore." I don't know why I think pointing this out will change what he's about to say, but I suddenly feel exceedingly nervous.

"Yes, well, it turns out, all of that is about to change!" he says with a wide grin. "A Caelum Supercluster-sized opportunity has popped up and we've finally got a chance to earn back the love of the masses." His face morphs into something more sinister as he adds, "We might actually be able to steal some of the attention away from those Mars bastards."

Dev's a little bitter that he wasn't put on the Mars team when it got started. He's been one of NASA's top astrophysicists for close to thirty years, so he should have been a shoo-in for the team. Somehow, a certain congressman's son-in-law was given the last spot, so Dev wound up here in New York working at the Goddard Institute on a project that will likely not be completed in his lifetime. Or mine, possibly. People think marathons are long, but they've got nothing on space exploration.

I wait patiently for my boss to tell me exactly what this huge opportunity is. "You, my young friend, are going to be a guest on *Wake Up America!* next week." Raising and lowering his eyebrows like an old-time comedian, he says, "Exciting, right?"

There are a lot of words I'd use to describe what he's asking me to do — most of them are four letters and not considered polite. Exciting is not one of them. "Why not get Carla to do it?" I suggest.

Dev tilts his head in a *you must be kidding* sort of way. "We need someone with stage presence. Charisma!"

I take off my glasses and rub the bridge of my nose. "Have you ever heard anyone describe me as charismatic?"

"Me. Just now," Dev says. "Remember the speech you gave at Clarissa Henderson's retirement party? You had 'em rolling in the aisles."

"That was because a bee landed on my hand and I screamed like a little girl for ten seconds straight."

"Hmm ... I don't remember the bee, but I do remember the laughter."

"So do I. That's why I'm not going to do the show." I glance out at the bullpen and say, "Pick someone else. Ewan would be great. He could do his C-3Po impression. The audience will eat it up."

Dev turns around and looks at the team. They're all tapping away on their keyboards, looking totally engrossed in their work. Ewan picks up his nasal spray, parks it halfway up his nose and takes a whiff. Turning back to me, Dev says, "Him?"

"Maybe not, but also ... not me."

Dev makes a little clicking sound with his tongue. "Sorry, my friend. You're the best-looking one of the bunch, and if there's anything we know about regular humans, it's that they're far more likely to listen to good-looking people."

Sliding my glasses back on, I contort my features, doing my best to look less attractive. "What about you? You're good-looking-ish."

"Tell that to my wife," he answers with a wry grin. Then, shaking his head, he adds, "Can't be me. The top brass wants young and hot. I'm over fifty and when I sit, you can see my love handles spilling over my belt. That doesn't play well on television."

My palms feel clammy at just the thought of appearing on television.

"If you go on the show, I'll give you my ticket to Florida for the next launch."

Oh, that bastard. He's offering me the one thing he knows I want most in the world: the chance to go to the mothership — the Kennedy Space Center — and be part of the excitement of a launch. Only department heads get invited to those and it's the most thrilling thing anyone in the astronomy world can do. Not only is there a tour of the facilities and front-row seats at the launch, but there are parties for days afterward. Wild ones — apparently with poker, booze, and hot women. Although that could just be an urban myth like Bigfoot or girls who love geeks.

I'm about to say no, when Dev stands. "Good. Glad that's settled."

"Dev, is there anyone else?" I ask, my stomach squeezing at the thought of going on live television.

"Nope. You're my guy. And don't worry because you'll be fine. In fact, you'll be better than fine. You're going to be the next Neil Armstrong because you're about to make one giant leap for nerd-kind." With that, he walks out, leaving me to stew in my own juices.

They say that which doesn't kill you, makes you stronger, but I'm guessing *they* didn't try to increase their adolescent popularity by running for junior class president. I still have nightmares about standing in front of an auditorium full of pubescent humans who jeered their way through my speech about my bad boy math club antics. Apparently, you can't win over a crowd of high school kids with stories of that time you pretended you solved all four of Landau's problems. Weird.

Anyway, as a thirty-one-year-old man, I've forgotten most of what I said, but the dawning awareness that I was committing social suicide is something that will always feel fresh.

I suppose the "what doesn't kill you" people are referring to things like sore muscles from an extremely hard workout or perhaps going through a temporary-but-difficult time, such as your parents' divorce. (I was seven when that happened —and as much as it sucked, it doesn't accompany you everywhere you go for the rest of your life like a fear of public speaking does.)

Forget public speaking, I don't even do small talk with strangers. In fact, I once sat beside a beautiful woman all the way from L.A. to Sydney, Australia, and didn't say one word to her, even though she smiled at me several times throughout our twenty-two hours and twelve minutes together. Not one. I wasn't even bothered by the awkward silence because for me, it was far more pleasurable than trying to come up with even one conversation starter.

Being on *Wake Up America!* is going to be like competing in the Olympics of small talk. And I'm going to come in dead last.

THREE

Serafina

Everything I know about modeling I learned from watching *America's Next Top Model*. Luckily, that should be enough to get me through hiring models for my upcoming television segment.

Yesterday, right after getting the call from Waltraut, Charley and I spent the day shopping in Herald Square. Turns out department stores practically bend over backwards to loan you whatever you want if you'll mention their names on national television. I kind of wish I'd known that little tip when I was young and broke, not that anyone would have believed my claim that I'd be promoting them on television...

Since this week has been one of the hottest starts to July on record, we decided to go with twelve summery outfits. They vary wildly in style from each other, but I wanted to make the differences very obvious to viewers.

When we got home, buried under a mountain of bags,

I called several local modeling agencies and set up auditions for models. I requested all kinds of women from a size two to a size twenty, all ethnicities, a variety of ages, and I even asked for short women, which in the modeling world means five feet, seven inches. Rude, I know.

Charley is currently sitting at my kitchen counter snacking on mixed nuts — typical Scorpio, craving salty over sweet. I sit down next to her and grab a donut. We Libras are the opposite. Give us a sugary treat any day and we'll be your best friend.

"The models should start arriving in a few minutes. Are you excited?" I ask my young employee.

"I guess. Although I'm totally annoyed by what the mainstream thinks of as beautiful. The standard seems to be set to make normal women feel bad about themselves."

After savoring the remnants of Bavarian cream in my mouth, I reply, "Yeah, but I'm the one picking the models. Don't worry, I'm not going to exclude anyone. In fact, I was thinking I could use a fifteen-year-old goddess for the Scorpio outfit. What do you think, are you game?"

"For real?" Charley jumps up in excitement and starts to catwalk around my loft. After one pass, she sings, "I'm too sexy for the stars, too sexy by far ..."

"Right Said Fred couldn't have sung it any better himself," I tease her.

"Who's that?"

"The guy who sings that song."

"Oh, I only know it from TikTok."

"Ah," I say with a nod. Sometimes I forget Charley is part of a whole new generation that I don't quite understand. Twenty-eight isn't old, but in the presence of a teenager, it often feels that way.

Not five minutes later, the buzzer starts ringing and doesn't stop for the next several hours.

The rest of our day is spent deciding which models to hire after seeing them in a variety of outfits. To say I'm exhausted is an understatement. I'm starting to regard Tyra Banks as something of a superhero.

When the last women leave, Charley collapses on my sofa and declares, "I'm pretty sure I'd hate being a real model. We can only hire eleven of those ladies and the others get a 'thanks, but no thanks.' Talk about always feeling rejected."

"The Universe has much better plans for you, my beautiful genius, but for one day, you get to strut your stuff on the runway," I say with a wink. "Now, as to what you're going to wear ..." I hurry to the clothes racks at the back of my living room area and pull out a gorgeous and shockingly bright red dress. I bring it over to the couch where Charley is sitting and declare, "Bold and dangerous are in your DNA. What do you think about this?"

Sitting up, she studies the vibrant slip dress. "Maybe if we pair it with some leopard heels and purple belt or something."

"I leave it in your hands," I tell her. Then I literally put it in her hands.

My phone rings a minute later. It's the producer for our segment on *Wake Up America!* I put her on speaker before saying, "Hey, Waltraut, what's up?"

"I just did a little research on our NASA guest, Dr. Williams, and discovered he's a Gemini. I thought it would be fun if you could bring in a sample outfit that would be suitable for him."

"Oh ... I could." I sit down on a huge bean bag chair

that's positioned across from the couch Charley is lying on. "I'd need to know what size Dr. Williams wears."

"He won't have time to try it on or anything. I thought you could bring in a male model for the Gemini outfit."

"Sure!" I try to sound excited even though that means the bright yellow jumpsuit I already picked out for Gemini won't get seen. Poop. "I've already chosen the models so I don't think I can switch any others out for men, but let's face it, most of your viewers are probably women."

"Seventy-nine percent, so we're fine with only one male model. I'm really excited about this episode, Serafina," she tells me. "If it goes well, we'd love to work with you in the future on other segments."

Holy. Crap. The key to all business success boils down to marketing and there is *no tool* as effective as getting your product in front of a large audience. And free publicity? Well, there's nothing better than that. I'm willing to do whatever it takes to impress Waltraut. I want to do all kinds of segments for her.

"I'm excited too!" I tell her. "I'm always up for a new adventure."

"Great. We'll see you on Monday then. Have your models arrive by five a.m. so we can make sure everything is ready to go by airtime at seven. When they check into security, they'll be sent upstairs to the dressing rooms to meet with you and get ready."

"Super!" I hang up, no longer annoyed that I have to get a male Gemini outfit and a new model. Being that yellow is the Gemini color, I'm hoping to find a yellow suit or some chic yellow cropped pants that I can pair with a smart pair of saddle shoes. I'm going to make sure my Gemini outfit will be the star of the show.

My segment has to go perfectly, which of course means getting on Dr. Williams' good side. Waltraut needs to be impressed with me enough to have me back again and again. The good news is that Libras are very social and get along with everyone, so this should be an ace in the hole for me and the future of my app.

FOUR

Ben

My alarm goes off at four a.m., and for a moment, I'm completely disoriented. I allow a nano-second of thinking that I can go back to sleep when my eyes spring open. Today is my segment on *Wake Up America!* with Hal and Lacey, which means I'm going to humiliate myself on live television. Full-tilt boogie panic ensues.

Throwing off my covers, I sit up, displacing my tabby Mr. Spock, who was nestled under my arm. He opens his mouth to hiss but holds back, then snuggles himself back into the blankets. Mr. Spock is like the feline version of the Incredible Hulk — always ready to lose it. I wouldn't be surprised if his temper is what landed him in a shelter in the first place.

My phone rings and I see it's my mom calling. She lives outside of Portland, where I grew up.

I swipe the screen to answer while stumbling into the bathroom to brush my teeth. "What are you doing up?" I ask her, even though I already know.

"I was worried you'd oversleep," she says. My mom still thinks I'm a kid incapable of setting an alarm.

"So you got yourself up at one a.m. to wake me?"

"It's no trouble," she answers. "I wanted to tell you I know you'll be brilliant today, just like you are every other day."

"Thanks," I tell her. I truly love my mom, but she puts the mother in smother. At some point, I hope she'll realize I'm a competent adult. Based on the facts before me though, I'd say there's a low probability of that ever occurring.

"Don't be nervous. You'll be great."

"Thanks. How does one go about not being nervous?" I ask sarcastically.

"Slow steady breathing," she answers, ignoring my rude tone. "I checked with Marsha and she said this appearance is going to change your life."

"Marsha?"

"My new psychic. She said to tell you that after today your life will never be the same."

"Mom," I groan before continuing. "Is this news supposed to relax me? Because so far, it's failing miserably. Also, a psychic? I'd hoped you learned your lesson as far as psychics go."

I'm referring to the time she went to a fortune teller at the county fair who told her that she was about to meet her Prince Charming. Phil showed up a week later and, believe me when I say, he was as much of a prince as I was a prom king. Phil lived with us for a year before leaving with Mom's entire life savings — paltry as it was — along with the car they bought together but he conveniently kept in his name. While you'd think this would have put my mom off charlatans who predict the future for a price, it actually jump-started her interest in all kinds of crazy things like tarot cards, seances, runes, chicken bones...

"You're such a party pooper, Ben. I don't know how I ever had a child who was so closed-minded about the sixth sense."

"I don't know either, Mom. Wait, maybe it's because you let other people make your life decisions based on what they see inside a crystal ball."

"Please. No one uses crystal balls anymore," she scoffs.

"Thank you for the wake-up call, Mom," I tell her, realizing that she will never hear the truth of my words. The woman who gave me life is a die-hard lover of woo-woo nonsense that will likely bilk her of her savings and have her moving in with me by the time she's sixty. "Why don't you go back to bed for awhile," I suggest.

"No way," she says. "The girls are coming over in a bit to catch your big national television debut. I'm making my famous cornflake casserole."

The girls are my mom's two best friends, Lita and Lynda. My mom's name is Lydia, so together they're the L-Triad, sort of like a gang of middle-aged women who wear yoga pants and drink a lot of wine. They've known each other for a whopping fifty-one years now. When my dad left, it was Lita and Lynda who picked up the slack and helped get both of us through the fallout. "Tell them hi for me."

"I will. Oh, and Lita said to tell you to break a leg."

"I'm sure I will." I immediately have a vision of tripping over my own foot and shattering my tibia on national television.

"And call me as soon as you're done so we can celebrate over the phone!"

"Okay, Mom. Love you."

"Love you too, my big TV star son!"

I get to the studio precisely twelve minutes early, which I've determined to be the right arrival time for any occasion. Fifteen minutes is too long because I get panicky and want to leave right around the fourteen-minute mark, whereas ten isn't quite enough for me to acclimate myself to my new surroundings.

The tired-looking security guard gives me a visitor's badge and points down the hall. "Take the elevator to the fifteenth floor and someone will meet you."

By the time I get there, my tongue feels like it's transformed from a human-sized into a giant cow's tongue. I'm about to choke on it. Well, that's going to help me speak coherently, isn't it?

When the elevator doors open, I follow the signs that lead to *Wake Up America!*'s dressing rooms. As soon as I arrive at my destination, I'm stunned speechless by the brightly lit room filled with gorgeous women. They are way too beautiful to be average, everyday people. I check the floor number again to make sure I'm at the *Wake Up America!* studio and unfortunately, I am. Great. Beautiful women. This is the last thing I need.

"You! You there!" a woman with a clipboard and headset yells. "Are you our Gemini?"

I glance around and realize she's talking to me. "Pardon?"

She rolls her eyes. "Did the agency send you?"

I've never heard NASA referred to as "the agency," but I suppose it fits. "Yes."

"Okay, we don't have a spot for you yet because we can't put you in the dressing room with the other models ... unless you're gay. Are you gay?"

All the other women stop what they're doing to listen to our conversation, which causes my anxiety to shoot up to the mesosphere. Okay, I'm exaggerating — more like the troposphere. My mouth suddenly becomes so dry, I can't speak. I shake my head to indicate that I'm not, in fact, gay. Although I'm still not sure why that matters.

Apparently, my sexuality is a real irritation for her because she rolls her eyes. "Wait over by the wall and I'll get someone to find a room for you."

I nod, then do as she says, glad to be standing in a corner away from all the action. Grabbing my cell out of my suit jacket pocket, I pretend to be reading something riveting to avoid the possibility of anyone striking up a conversation with me. Also, to avoid actually looking at these women because there's no way I'll be able to concentrate around any of them.

A few minutes later, the gorgeous crowd is ushered through a door that says *Green Room*. That's when a young man with a headset comes out to greet me.

"I'm Justin, the unpaid, under-appreciated intern." He looks me up and down, and says, "Man, I know you guys end up wearing some pretty odd outfits, but the pants they picked for you..." He pauses and makes a clicking sound with his teeth. "It's really out there."

What uncomfortable outfits is he referring to? Space-suits? I'm about to tell him I'm not an actual astronaut, but really, what's the point? It would only lead to questions I don't want to answer.

He turns and leads me through a set of double doors

and down a long hall as my mind races to figure out what exactly is going on. "What's wrong with what I have on?" I ask. Navy sports jacket, light blue button-up shirt, and tan slacks. The man at the store told me it's a classic look for any occasion.

"Personally, I think you look great, but apparently they want everyone wearing clothes for their star sign. Are you really a Gemini, or is that just the outfit they're giving you?"

I pause for a moment, aggravation scraping my insides at the very mention of anything to do with astrology. My mom religiously tracks her horoscope and has been known to cancel vacations if Mercury is in retrograde. If Mars or Venus go into retrograde, she refuses to leave the house. I tell the intern, "I was born on June twentieth, if that's what you're asking."

"They *really* are going for authenticity, then." He stops in front of an open door and points to the clothes rack. "You might want to try it on and make sure it fits. Those pants look, well, like they were bought in the boys department."

I stare, my mouth hanging down, at a pair of bright yellow pants, a white button-up shirt and a green sweater vest. Justin's gone before I can tell him there's no way I'm wearing that ensemble on national television. Then an image of me sitting front row at a shuttle launch pops into my mind. Maybe it won't be so bad. If I end up behind a desk, no one will even see my legs. I hope, because if not, I'm about to renew my membership in the geeks and freaks club.

Glancing at my watch, I see it's only five, so I doubt Dev will be up yet. To prove what an exemplary NASA employee I am, I take a shot of the ridiculous clown outfit they want me in, then send it to him with the hashtag: #totallycommittedteamleader

If I'm going to humiliate myself like this, I'm going to damn well be at that launch.

FIVE

Serafina

This morning is super hectic, but even so, it's gone much smoother than I expected. The only fly in the ointment so far is that the model wearing my Gemini outfit hasn't shown up yet. I didn't personally audition the models for that spot; I just called the agency and got access to look at online portfolios. The guy I picked was supposed to be here a half an hour ago and I'm starting to feel a bit panicky about the fact that he's not here.

Once all the other models, including Charley, are ready to go, I look for Waltraut to see if she's seen my Gemini model. I can't find her though, so I stop a youngish looking guy in a headset. "Hey, there. I'm Serafina Lopez from *Live for Your Star Sign*. Have you seen my male model?"

He nods his head quickly. "Yup, he's in dressing room three." He points down the hall.

I hurry to the correct door and knock lightly before walking in. The model is standing there in his boxer shorts staring at the yellow pants I picked out for him. He looks up at me with panic in his eyes. I see the problem immediately. I smile nicely even though I'm ready to kill him for being so late. "They're skinny legs so you'll have to go commando or the lines from your boxer shorts will show through."

"Commando?" A blush covers his gorgeous face. This guy looks *so* much better in person than he did in his photos. His hair is darker, and his eyes are green instead of blue. Huh, weird. But no problem because he is yummy!

"You know, take your underwear off." I gesture that he should get going.

"I-I'm not getting naked in front of you." He looks like he's never been ordered to strip down before.

I turn my back to him and say, "Of course, sorry." I'm pretty sure I would have turned away had he actually started to take his underwear off in front of me. Maybe not though. We Libras do like our eye candy.

Still facing the other direction, I ask, "Are you ready?"

"Almost," he says as I hear the rustling of fabric as he pulls his pants up. I turn around just as he gets his zipper up.

"You look great!" I tell him. Actually, great is an understatement. His chest is bare and, while he's not musclebound, he's definitely ripped. My hands itch to reach out and touch him but I manage to resist the temptation.

The sight of him is a painful reminder how much I miss dating. I've just been so busy with work this last year, I haven't had time to go out and meet people. Seeing this hottie without a shirt on makes me excited about trying the new dating feature for my app. We'll have to run a few months of trials before it goes live, but who knows, I might have met my match by then. Maybe I'll even get matched with a guy who can rock the tight pants and no shirt look like this guy. Phew! Somebody get me a fan.

My Gemini puts on his white shirt and asks, "Why can't I wear my own clothes?"

Seriously? Does he not know how modeling works? I'll have to make sure I state that I have a preference for dating men who aren't dumb as rocks when I enter my profile. There's no way I'd ever have anything to talk about with someone as thick in the head as him. "You have to be astrologically correct for this segment. It's a whole outer space thing, you know?"

Looking down at his feet, he says, "I have to wear bright yellow pants that are three inches too short?"

"They're cropped pants." Then I instruct, "Take your socks off. I picked up a pair of penny loafers for you to wear, but not with black socks. Barefoot is best. Also, don't forget the green sweater vest and the plaid bowtie."

"You can't be serious."

Who does this guy think he is? I'm tempted to tell him he's a glorified mannequin and to just put the clothes on and zip it, but as a rule, I try not to start arguments before seven in the morning. "Of course I'm serious. It's the Gemini look. Studious and smart with a playful edge."

I watch as he buttons up the shirt, then tugs the vest over his head. Glancing at my watch, I realize we're going to run short on time, so I swipe the bowtie off the dressing table and start to put it on for him. He stares at me, those green eyes of his making my knees go a little weak. Maybe I could be the smart one in the relationship. Surely, I could talk to this guy about something ... like body-building or Archie comics.

Swallowing hard, I force my gaze back to the bowtie and get to work, trying very hard not to notice how incredible his aftershave smells. Actually, now that I think about it, talking is highly overrated. There are much more creative ways to enjoy a relationship.

Disappointment strikes when I realize I'm done with the bowtie. My brain tells me to step away from the male model, but my body doesn't want to listen.

My Gemini glances into the mirror. "These pants are practically painted onto me. You can see my..." He indicates the area around his fly.

Yeah, you can. "You look very manly," I tell him with my signature flirtatious Libra-ness. *Very* manly. "Now hurry up, I need to get you over to hair and makeup before we go on."

"Who are you?" he demands like I've been speaking a foreign language.

"Serafina Lopez."

"I'm supposed to meet a woman named Waltraut."

"No, you're not," I tell him. "Waltraut is *my* contact. You were supposed to report to me. Now come on, I want to get some gel in your hair and maybe style you with a pair of glasses frames."

"Can I at least wear my own glasses?" he asks.

"Let me see them."

He picks them up off the dressing table and slides them on. "Not bad, but they're a little dull."

"That may be, but I'm pretty much blind without them."

"The agency didn't tell you to wear contacts?" I ask.

"Why would they do that?"

Oh, wow. So, so dim. "For versatility."

He opens his mouth to argue, but in the interest of time, I say, "It's fine. We'll make them work."

I practically have to drag him along with me which is getting annoying. I thank my lucky stars the other models were nowhere near this high maintenance, because if they all had been, we wouldn't even have managed to be ready in time for the evening news.

As we walk toward hair and makeup, I tell him, "You're my only guy today so I need you to ooze sex. Seriously, shake your moneymaker like you've got rent to pay and you're a month late."

His eyes practically pop out of his head. I nuzzle up next to him and croon, "Pretend we're going out dancing and you're giving the audience a sneak peek at your moves." Then I squeeze his arm muscles a little and immediately feel swoony.

As soon as we reach the makeup chairs, I tell Tony, one of the hair and makeup people, "Give him a little highlighter to enhance his cheekbones and I want his hair gelled to give those waves some definition. Oh, and maybe a little color on those luscious lips."

"Will do," Tony says while getting right to work.

I hurry over to the mirror to touch up my own lipstick when I hear my Gemini say, "I'm putting my foot down at wearing lipstick. I won't do it."

Tony says, "No sweat, just bite your lips a bit for me. That'll bring the color up and make them a little bee-stung."

I've never worked with models before, but I know for a fact that Tyra would not let hers call the shots like this guy is trying to do. If the rest of my crew weren't all ready to go, I might call him out for being so difficult. But as it is,

I only have to work with him for a short time so there's no point in creating drama that would mess with my balance.

Waltraut rushes over and pulls me aside, "Dr. Williams hasn't shown up yet and I'm not sure he'll be here for the segment. Can you be prepared to talk more about each star sign should we need to fill time?"

"Do Scorpios snap? Do Leos think they're royal?" Her blank expression has me adding, "Of course. I can talk as long as you want me to."

"Good. Okay, meet me in the green room in two. We'll mic you and have you come out on set during commercial break so Hal and Lacey can talk to you for a few before the fashion show starts."

As she rushes off, I grab my Gemini and pull him off to the green room. My energy level is positively humming with excitement. All I need to do is get through the next half hour with everything going smoothly and I'm on my way to mega success.

SIX

Ben

Once I'm dragged off into the green room with all the gorgeous women, I sneak a peek at myself in one of the full-length mirrors propped against the wall. *Who am I?* And where is astrophysicist Ben Williams under all that hair gel and bronzer? This is going to be the single most humiliating experience of my life. Not only am I dressed like a banana for his first day of school, my manhood is on display like it's about to be auctioned off to the highest bidder. How is *anyone* going to take me seriously?

They won't. That's how.

Not to mention, everyone I know, including my co-workers, will be watching. NOOOO!!! I have to stop this. Panic starts to build inside of me until my chest cavity feels like it's about to explode.

The bossy woman who made me take my underwear off loudly declares, "You all look great! This is going to be an amazing show!"

I have no idea what she's talking about, but I don't

have time to ask because someone else comes in and says, "You're on next. Follow me."

I tug at these ridiculous pants in hopes they'll magically grow three sizes and turn black. Or a nice brown, even. That would be good too. Although I don't know if brown would go with this awful green vest.

Oh, for pity's sake, Ben, it doesn't matter! Your pants aren't going to change color so forget it.

Unless ...what if I change into normal pants? Yes, that's the answer. As we march down the hall, I decide I'm going to put on my own clothes no matter what anyone says. As I open the door to dressing room three, I hear Ms. Bossy Boots yelling at me. "Where are you going?"

She doesn't wait for an answer. Instead, she takes my hand and leads me to the third spot in line. "There. You're right behind our Taurus."

Grinning broadly, she says, "Okay, everyone, you look fabulous. Just get out there and strut your fine selves."

Strut my fine self? What in the world is she talking about?

"Listen, I-I think there's been a mistake," I call out to her.

"I know, the pants aren't exactly the right fit, but you can really get away with it, trust me." She boldly winks which causes me even more distress.

"No, not..."

That Justin intern rushes over and says, "Ms. Lopez, you're on!"

I try to get his attention, but he disappears, leaving me with no one to ask for help. I wait for what feels like forever, but is likely only a couple of minutes before Justin comes back and starts to lead us backstage. "When

I point to you, walk onto the stage, turn left at the X, strut down the catwalk toward the studio audience. Pause for a count of two, then spin back around and go out the other way."

He points to the woman in front of me. As she goes, I watch her carefully, trying to memorize what she's doing. Okay, that doesn't look so hard. It's just walking, right? I can walk. Do they introduce all of their guests like this? My confusion equals my horror. I should have watched an episode of this show, so I knew what I was getting into.

When the woman turns back my way, she's not smiling. Are we not supposed to smile? Do we pout? Yes, pouting seems right. How do you pout?

Turning to the woman behind me, I say, "Does this look right?" then I push my lips out and try to look like I'm really angry about something. Which is actually true because I'm going to lose it on Dev when I see him.

She wrinkles up her nose and answers, "You look like you're trying to poop."

Well, that was rude. I'm trying to learn here, I could use constructive feedback. I give her a glare and she snaps her fingers. "Perfect! Now you've got some serious smolder going on."

"Gemini Guy! Gemini Guy!" Justin whisper-yells.

I spin around, realizing he means me. He points to the stage wearing a completely disgusted look. As I walk by, I hear him say something about models with rocks for brains into his headset.

Models? I'm not a model.

My heart is thumping like a rabbit surrounded by a pack of bears as I walk, trying to keep time with the music which is some airy-fairy crap that doesn't even have a beat. That bossy Lopez person is sitting on a chair next to the show's hosts talking ... about me ... it turns out.

"Geminis absolutely love to be the center of attention, almost to a fault. They're known to be intelligent, passionate, fun, but also sometimes unreliable and are even called flighty on occasion."

While I walk toward center stage, I glare at her instead of watching where I'm going. This causes me to miss the big X on the floor.

"As you can see, our model truly is a flighty Gemini. He just missed his mark," she says.

I hate this woman. I hate her with every cell of my being.

Hal lets out a chuckle. "Other way, buddy!"

"Wow, those are some tight pants!" Lacey inserts. "I can certainly see his center of attention!"

The audience laughs as I scramble to find the damn X. It's actually quite large and is in bright green tape, so it's pretty hard to miss. I stalk down the catwalk feeling like a piece of poorly-dressed meat. The audience — mainly older women — start to hoot and whistle and, I swear to God, one woman is waving a five-dollar bill at me.

How the hell did I end up here? I have my PhD. I work for NASA.

I head back toward the hosts while that awful woman talks about astrology. I'm so busy trying to make sure I land on the X this time I almost don't hear Hal say, "Geminis really must be flighty because our other guest, Dr. Ben Williams, didn't bother to show up for Star Day. I understand he's a Gemini as well."

I stop in my tracks and stare at him, sweat trickling down my back.

Hal looks at me while making a scooting gesture with his hands. "You can go now."

Astrology girl gives me an urgent head nod toward the exit. Now is my only chance to fix what has gone terribly, terribly wrong. "I'm Ben Williams."

All three of them stare at me like I've just said I'm from planet Zorbits. Lacey gives me a sympathetic look, as though she feels so bad for the male model who's so dumb he doesn't know his own name. "Um, no. Ben Williams is a rocket scientist. You're a model." She says this slowly like it's the only way I'll be able to understand her.

I wait while the audience has a good laugh at my expense. Off to the side, Justin and some other woman with a headset are frantically waving at me. "I'm not a rocket scientist."

Giving me a condescending look, Hal says, "We know you're not, buddy. But you're still special, okay? Now, off you go!"

The fashion show music stops, and the audience becomes so still you'd think they were waiting for me to perform a magic show. Out of the corner of my eye, I see two security guards at the ready. I swallow hard, then keep going. "There's no such thing as a rocket scientist," I say. "What you're thinking of is actually called an aeronautical engineer or an astronautical engineer. The phrase rocket scientist is a dumbed down label for the job."

"Wow," Lacey says, blinking at me. "You know a lot about rocket science."

I shut my eyes at her inane statement, then open them and say, "That's because I'm an astrophysicist."

The astrology "expert" (and I'm using that term lightly) seems to be the first one of the three geniuses to figure out who I am. "Wait, if you're Dr. Williams, why are you masquerading as a male model?"

Don't be rude. Don't be rude. Even though she's most likely the worst person on the planet, you're here trying to win fans for NASA. "Because ... the staff here wouldn't listen to me when I tried to explain who I was."

Hal's face fills with panic. "Well, we'll need to get you up here with us, then, Dr. Williams."

I nod at him. "Sounds good."

Lacey, the other show host, laughs awkwardly, before saying, "What a crazy mix-up! Can you believe it?"

"No," Hal answers, still chuckling even though his eyes say he's going to kill someone. "Why don't we take a quick commercial break so we can bring out another chair for our esteemed guest?"

"Why don't we?" Lacey says. "We'll be right back in a couple of minutes with astrophysicist, and part-time fashion model, Dr. Ben Williams from NASA. Don't go anywhere."

SEVEN

Serafina

"What did you do with my model?" I hiss at Ben Williams as soon as he's seated next to me.

He rolls his eyes. "Obviously I murdered him and stuffed his body in the closet so I could make my lifelong dream of appearing on national television as a complete ass come true."

Before I can slay him with a witty comeback, Lacey waves her hands frantically to shut me up. Then she turns to the camera and gushes, "Welcome back to *Wake Up America!* In case you're just joining us, we have astrophysicist Dr. Ben Williams on today, here to talk about NASA's Earth Two project. But before we get to Dr. Williams, Serafina Lopez, creator of the smashing *Live for Your Star Sign* app, is going to give us a fashion-forward look for *your* star sign."

Hal continues, "We had a surprise model in the form of Dr. Williams here. Tell us, Ben, are you really a Gemini?"

"I have no idea."

"According to our research, you are," Lacey hurries to say. "You'd think you'd know that, being a rocket scientist and all."

Dr. Grumpy Pants pauses, then slowly explains, "Science is the systematic, logical, and relentless pursuit of knowledge to help us better understand the universe and all things in it. Astrology is the pursuit of unsuspecting people's money through trickery, predictions so vague they could apply to anyone in any given location, and blatant insensitivity to empirical evidence." He glances at me, then turns back to Lacey. "For you to presume I should possess the knowledge of which utterly irrelevant category I land in based on my date of birth is about as useful as knowing which house I'd fit into at Hogwarts. It's meaningless. It's nothing more than a party game."

"A *party game*?" I blurt out. "I'll have you know that the practical use of astrology dates back to the third millennium BC. It is rooted in the calendrical system as a predictor of seasonal shifts and even helped drive the development of modern-day astronomy."

"Please, that's like saying the first grunt from an Australopithecus is responsible for modern literature."

"Australo-what-a-cus?" Hal asks, hamming it up for the audience.

"Australopithecus — the first ancestor of man."

I jump in, righteous indignation bubbling in my chest. "I *would* argue that the first grunt from an Australopithecus *is* the origin of modern literature and speech."

"You'd be wrong. Just because ancient astrologers looked into the sky, doesn't mean they had the first clue what they were seeing." He gives me a satisfied smile that I'm tempted to slap off his face. Then, turning away from me as if I've been dismissed, he leans closer to Lacey. He smiles at her and shrugs his eyebrows in a sleazy fashion. "What's your sign? Can I buy you a drink?"

Lacey doesn't seem to gather that he's being facetious because she winks back and answers, "How about if you take me for a ride on your rocket ship?"

"Okay, there, Lacey," Hal laughs nervously. "We don't want to get sued for sexual harassment."

"Then Dr. Ben shouldn't have worn those pants," Lacey says.

The audience laughs appreciatively, and one woman even calls out, "Stand up and show us your rocket ship again!" This of course leads to more hilarity.

Dr. Jerkface grins, before instructing, "Eyes up here, ladies."

Oh great, now they've burst into applause and are hooting. How did this become the Dr. Ben show? I need to take back control of this segment before I lose the viewers' interest in my app. So, I do the only thing I can think of. I stand up to draw attention to myself and loudly say, "If you'll start the music again, I'd like to introduce Cancer!"

The mystical flute soundtrack I chose for this segment starts to play as a fifty-something model with long silver hair and rose-colored sunglasses sashays out. She's wearing a flowing batik-patterned summer dress, "Our celestial hippy chick likes to be comfortable while showcasing her innate psychic abilities. Just don't cross her or she might pinch you like the crab from her astrological symbol."

Lacey gushes, "I would *so* wear that dress! I love how you paired it with sandals that lace up the calves. Really chic."

"Cancer thrives while displaying their carefree fashion sense," I tell her brightly.

"No, they don't," Dr. Jerky McIHateHimFace mutters. "Because that's not a thing."

"Yeah, it is," I tell him as my Cancer model finishes her walk. When she's offstage, I announce, "Leo is the royalty of the zodiac." My model is in her twenties, and she has bright orange curls that are slightly teased around her head like a lion's mane. She's wearing a gold lamé evening gown that only has one strap, the other shoulder is completely bare. "Leos love to strut their stuff, so if this is your star sign, going bold with your fashion is going to help bring you to your best life."

"I doubt that very much," Dr. Ben grumbles. "I can tell you for a fact I wouldn't be living my best life in these ridiculous banana pants."

When my Leo model reaches the end of the catwalk and walks back toward us, Hal growls like a lion while gesturing with his hands like he's the aforementioned cat about to pounce. "Rooooooar! I like that one. She looks like a queen!"

"Who's getting sued for sexual harassment now?" Lacey says with a phoney smile. I'm starting to wonder if Hal and Lacey actually like each other. I'm guessing a good deal of their success as a hosting duo is based on discord as it keeps everyone on their toes. Even so, I would absolutely hate to work with someone I couldn't stand on a regular basis. Talk about upsetting my sense of balance.

The highpoint of the show for me is when Charley comes out in her red dress and animal print pumps. She struts like she was born to the catwalk and I can tell that she's really feeling her power.

I do my best to talk up each outfit and get in the name of my app all the while trying to ignore Dr. Hateful's snide jibes. By the time the last model is leaving the stage, I'm ready to kick him right in his banana.

He definitely stole attention away from my segment.

Lacey smiles at the camera. "Star Day continues when we come back to chat with Dr. Ben Williams about NASA's Earth Two project." Turning to me, she says, "Why don't you stick around, Serafina? This has been so much fun."

I nod while forcing a wide smile to remain in place until the director calls out, "We're in commercial ..."

Dr. Ben stands up. "If you don't mind, I'm going to go change into my own pants."

"No time, buddy," Hal tells him. "Sorry about that. I bet those things are a real bear to sit in. Bunching up your junk and all."

"Hal!" Lacey hits him on the arm. "You can't say that kind of stuff."

"You saw the man when he came out, Lace. The whole world is going to be talking about it. I can only imagine the kind of hashtags that are already trending."

I suddenly have a great idea that will keep my app alive in the public's mind. I just have to find the right place to insert it into the conversation.

When the producer indicates we're coming back from commercial, Lacey says, "So, Dr. Williams, may I call you Ben?" He nods so imperceptibly I barely see it. "Ben," the hostess continues, "tell us when science thinks they'll find an Earth Two planet that can be inhabited."

"It's a long process, I'm afraid," he says. "But the hard part won't be finding the planet — we know they're out there. We need to increase our knowledge of space travel so we can actually get there in a reasonable amount of time."

"You mean like on *Star Trek* when they used to beam themselves up?" Hal asks.

"We're thinking more along the lines of creating a vehicle that will allow us to travel on magnetic waves. Hypothetically, if we can do that, we can travel a million miles in as little as an hour."

Now is my moment. I announce, "While I understand the science of that, Dr. Dogmatic, what are the chances you're going to be able to succeed in doing that in your lifetime?"

He glares at me with such hatred, I feel myself leaning away from him. "What did you call me?"

"I was just teasing because you're so blind to the possibilities of the Universe." I force a light tone. "But in all seriousness, don't you think it might be more beneficial to focus your energies on Einstein-Rosen bridges?" I turn to the camera and add, "Or wormholes, as they're more commonly termed."

Before Ben can have at me — and believe me when I say he looks like he's about to attack — Lacey interjects, "Wow, Serafina, it sounds like you know a thing or two about science yourself."

"I *did* graduate at the top of my class from Yale," I tell her.

"There's no way..." Ben starts to say.

I interrupt him before he can officially call my intelligence into question. "Just because I use my education in a different way than you do, *Dr.* Williams, doesn't mean I didn't get one."

"Yes, but..."

"In fact," I tell him, "It seems to me that science has only benefited when researchers keep an open-mind."

He scoffs, then says, "But astrology—"

"Is a science in its own right," I tell him forcefully.

"According to fortune tellers and genies that pop out of old lanterns." He rolls his eyes dismissively.

Before I have a chance to retaliate, Lacey announces, "I can't believe how quickly the time has flown! Unfortunately, we have to tie things up because it's time for the news."

Hal interjects, "Serafina, Ben, thank you so much for joining us this morning. Maybe, if we're lucky, you'd both agree to come back some time soon."

"Absolutely." I say enthusiastically before smiling at Ben. "What do you think, Dr. Dogmatic? Want to face off with me again?"

"I'm sure Hal meant separately," he says stiffly.

"I don't know about that," Lacey says. "It might be more fun if you came back together." Looking into the camera, she asks, "What do you think, America? Do you want to wake up with Ben and Serafina together or alone? Let us know on social media and we'll make sure to listen."

While I would rather run a 5K with my ankles tied together than be on this show with Dr. Know-It-All again, I'll do it if it means aiding a positive view toward astrology and promoting my app. The good news is that if Ben's constipated expression is anything to go on, I'll have the whole segment to myself. I am one hundred percent sure he won't come back to *Wake Up America!* Not if *I'm* a guest.

EIGHT

Ben

As soon as the director says we're on a commercial break, I stand, then shake Lacey and Hal's hands before making a beeline for my dressing room. I don't bother to acknowledge Serafina. *Dr. Dogmatic? I'm* the dogmatic one? I don't think so. She can kiss my banana pants.

Of all the infuriating, insane ways to waste my time, this one takes the cake. I'm going to march right into work and tell Dev this was the very last public appearance I'll be making. If NASA wants a spokesperson, they can hire one. I don't have time to argue with some airy-fairy nonsense-spreader.

Shutting the door to my dressing room, I remove the horridly tight pants, freeing my man parts from the confines of their holding cell. "Ahhhh, that's better."

Sorry about that, boys. It won't happen again.

I quickly tug on my underwear and pants, then strip off the shirt and vest. I must be allergic to some fiber in it because I'm itching like I've got a virulent case of the chicken pox. Once I'm free from the horrid costume, I take a moment to walk over to the small bathroom and splash some water on my face, trying to relish the fact that it's all over and I never have to do it again.

There's a loud knock at the door. I call for whoever it is to come in, expecting it to be Justin. Instead, it's Serafina Lopez. Her eyes land on my bare chest and she blushes a little, then she straightens her back and announces, "I came to get my clothes back."

"You can have them," I say with disgust as I gather them up and unceremoniously toss them to her.

"Thanks a lot." After she has them, we stare at each other a second too long, but neither of us says anything. I'm momentarily struck by how beautiful she is, which inevitably renders me mute even though I'd love nothing more than to keep arguing with her about her asinine beliefs.

Serafina opens her mouth, then shakes her head at me. "Nope, not worth it."

"My sentiments exactly."

She spins on her heel and leaves, slamming the door behind her.

"Good riddance."

When I walk into work, the entire team stands and starts applauding me. I look up and see my image in a freeze-frame on all the 80-inch screens that line the walls. I'm walking down the catwalk in my Gemini jumpsuit. "Very funny, guys," I say with a conciliatory nod. "Get your jabs in now so we can move on like grown-ups, okay?"

"That was epic," Ewan yells. "Fighting the good fight up there for the world to see."

"You certainly gave the world a lot to see," Carla adds, glancing at my nether region with wide eyes.

My cheeks heat up and I shift uncomfortably while the rest of the team starts in with their opinions. Their words all rush together, but I pick up phrases and words like "Dr. Dogmatic," "You got the best of her" and "pants" — lots of mention of the pants. I wait for them to finish, before saying, "We good now? Can we let it go?"

Alec whistles under his breath while shaking his head. "I'm pretty sure we'll be talking about this until we actually land on Earth Two."

Perfect. Just perfect. How the hell am I ever going to be taken seriously again? "Listen, the show is over, and will never be repeated. Once the top brass sees what a failure that ridiculous mission was, they'll never let any of us near a television camera again." I point to the screen and order, "Now, shut that off and get back to work."

I walk into my office and close the door while letting out a big sigh. I hurry to my desk and turn on my computer, wanting to dive back into the safety of work. My phone rings and I see it's my mom calling. My entire body heats up with renewed embarrassment as I realize the L-Triad saw my modeling debut. Might as well get this over with. "Hi, Mom."

"You were amazing, sweetie! Just amazing. While it's not exactly what Lita, Lynda, and I were expecting, you sure did make an impression. You could definitely be a male model if you wanted to, not that I think you should do that because you're wildly successful already, but you *could*. Lita and Lynda both said so." It's not that I expect my mom to be horrified by my television debut — she is my mother after all, and I can do no wrong. But you'd think she'd at least be embarrassed on my behalf.

"It was a ridiculous waste of time," I tell her. "I didn't even get a chance to talk about the project. It was just arguing with that ... that ... *astrologer*."

"Wasn't she wonderful?" my mom gushes. "I already signed up for her app. She has all kinds of information like how to eat, dress, and even where to *vacation* for your star sign. And did you know she's adding a dating app? Apparently, it's being tested in New York City now, but they hope to have it go national by next year. You should totally sign up!"

"That's a firm no, Mom. I am not interested in dating according to my star sign. I'd rather date based on my favorite M&M color."

"I think you're missing out on a wonderful opportunity," she says.

It's time to shut this down before we start arguing about her crazy beliefs. "Okay, Mom. Thanks for calling, but I really have to get some work done."

"Oh, yes, of course. You get back to searching for the next Earth, sweetie. Love you!"

"Love you too."

I spend the next two hours keeping my attention focused on my computer screen, in part because I really am swamped, but also to avoid making eye contact with anyone who walks past my office. While I would never admit this to anyone, I'm also trying not to think about Serafina Lopez. No matter how off-base her beliefs are, she's quite possibly the most attractive woman I've ever met. Talk about irony. The last person I would *ever* date is an astrologer, but she's the only one to catch my eye in what ... months? Years? Could that be right?

Yes, yes, it could. Pathetic as that sounds. While I occasionally gather the nerve to ask a woman out, nothing much has ever come from it. There aren't as many single women at NASA as you might think and, since I rarely do anything other than work, I don't have the chance to meet many potential dates.

My computer pings and I see an email from Dev (who thankfully hasn't made an appearance yet today).

Email from Dev.Grover@GoddardInstitute.com
To: Ben.Williams@GoddardInstitute.com

Subject: Wake Up America!

Hey Ben,

Caught your segment on Wake Up America! and apparently so did about thirty million other people. Waltraut, the producer, called me just now to say you're trending under the hashtags #DrBanana-Pants #DrRocketship, and #MarryMeDrBen. They've put your segment on their YouTube playlist and it already has over two million views. Anyway, they want you back on as a weekly segment, starting next Monday. Obviously, I said yes. The top brass said no more tight pants, but otherwise they loved it. Our project website has had ten times the views it normally gets on a Monday, so people are paying attention.

Well done, lad!
Dev

Email from: Ben.Williams@GoddardInstitute.com
To: Dev.Grover@GoddardInstitute.com

Subject: RE: Wake Up America!

No. Nada. Not happening. Never again. Not doing it.

Ben

Email from Dev.Grover@GoddardInstitute.com
To: Ben.Williams@GoddardInstitute.com

Subject: RE: RE: Wake Up America!

Atlas V Lucy Mission launches soon. Will you be there?

D

I storm past Dev's assistant, May, not giving her time to tell me he's busy. Without knocking, I open the door and walk in, too angry to bother with manners.

Dev doesn't even look up from his computer. He keeps typing as he says, "Yes, you are."

"No, I am not."

"Will you please read the words on the name plate on

my desk for me?" he asks, pointing to the triangular wooden plaque.

"Dev Grover, Department Head, NASA Goddard Institute."

"Right, and what does the name plate on your desk say?" he asks, looking up at the ceiling as though he's trying to remember. "Oh right, nothing because you don't have one. And you never will if you can't show up for the job you've got."

I swallow hard, trying to calm myself down. "Listen, Dev. They made a joke of me by dressing me up like a clown. NASA can't want us to look like fools."

"Actually, according to Waltraut, your willingness to play along made you very popular among female viewers in their child-bearing years."

"Is that really who we're trying to appeal to?" I ask, raising my voice a little.

"Other than seniors, stay-at-home moms are the other demographic most likely to have the television on during the day. If we can get them excited about space-related matters, we're going to see a lot more funding from our partners and from the Feds."

"So, you're just going to pimp me out like ... some ... space whore?" I ask.

"Yes, Ben. Yes, I am." Dev sits back in his chair. "I'd pimp out the entire team if it meant taking top-billing away from those Mars sons of bitches."

"Well, that's just perfect," I say, folding my arms. "Why don't we just pose shirtless with puppies like firefighters? We could make our own calendar."

"That's not a bad idea," Dev answers with a grin.

"I'm not serious!"

"I am. Times are tough, my friend. At any moment,

we could lose our funding completely and we'll all be out on our asses. I'm not sure if you know this or not, but there aren't exactly a plethora of places hiring astrophysicists," Dev says. "If you can be the key to us all having jobs, you owe it to the rest of us to make that happen. That's what being a leader is about. Sometimes you have to take one for the team."

My shoulders slump and I stare at him, scrambling to think of a viable counterargument. Nope. I'm totally blank.

"I'm going to make this very simple for you, Ben. Every Monday morning from now until the world gets tired of you, you're going to be at that studio talking us up. And if you do that, you'll get to come back here and spend the rest of the week doing the work you love," he says. "If you don't, you won't."

"You'd fire me? Are you serious?" I ask, my heart pounding.

"Don't think of it like that. Think of it as me safeguarding the continued job security of all of my employees, including you."

Shaking my head, I say, "Fine. I'll do it, but ..." I try to think of the perfect threat, but only manage to come up with, "I'm not coming to the Christmas party this year. Not if it's at your house."

There. I told him.

NINE

Serafina

"Six hundred dollars? You can't be serious?" Charley practically yells when I hand her a check for her modeling appearance on *Wake Up America!*

"Apparently the money is why models are so willing to go on auditions they might not get. Take it and enjoy, but *don't* fall for the lure of easy cash," I caution her.

"As if there's any way I could ever be a real model," she grumbles.

I remember all too well the angst associated with being a teenager and I feel for my young friend. "Can you imagine what they're saying about you at your high school right now? Because you *know* the word is out that you modeled on *Wake Up America!*"

"How could the word be out? I don't even keep in touch with anyone." She plops down on a bean bag chair looking more forlorn than I remember seeing her.

Winking at her, I pick up my phone. After going to the search bar and hitting the microphone and speaker buttons simultaneously, I say, "Call Eleanor Falls Academy in New York."

Charley's eyes pop wide open when she hears the secretary answer the phone. "Eleanor Falls Academy. How may I help you?"

Plugging my nose to alter the tone of my voice, I say, "This is Sera Martin calling from *The Post*, I'd like to speak to your principal, please."

"May I tell her what this is regarding?"

"I'm calling about Charlotte Jenkins. I believe she's a sophomore at your school."

"Not anymore," the secretary says snidely. "What has she done now?"

Charley looks like she wants to jump into the phone and do something that would really get her into trouble. I simply say, "She was accepted into Yale at age fifteen and just made her national modeling debut on *Wake Up America!*"

"What?! That can't be right."

"May I quote you in my article?" I ask.

She gasps audibly before saying, "No! I mean, I'd rather you didn't. Please hold for Principal Fox."

While I wait, Charley says, "You can't go telling them I'm going to be in an article in *The Post*. They'll be looking for it."

"Ye of little faith. My brother Zay's girlfriend's mother works there. I'll just call in a couple favors and see what they can do."

"Why would they want to write about me?"

"Because you, my young friend, are extraordinary and brilliant, funny and talented. You are exactly the kind of person people want to read about right now."

After a quick chat with Charley's old principal,

where I suggest she might want to line up some students and teachers to be interviewed for the upcoming article, I hang up and offer my young employee a bright smile.

"No one is going to say anything nice about me," she moans. "They'll say I'm a freak with a penchant for getting into trouble."

Shaking my head, I tell her, "No, they won't. Trust me, they're going to bend over backwards to look and act like they're your best friends."

"They'd be lying then," she grumbles.

"So what? You didn't like them anyway, and this is a fabulous way to exact your revenge."

Throwing her head back dramatically, Charley replies, "I do dream about that."

"I know you do, kid. And I'm here to help." Before I can say anything else, my phone rings with the ringtone I've assigned to *Wake Up America!*, George Michael's "Wake Me Up Before You Go-Go."

Charley sits bolt upright with a look of pure excitement on her face as I answer, "Hello, Waltraut. What can I do for you?"

"Have you been on social media since our segment this morning?" she asks.

"Not yet. I just got back to my place and haven't even had a chance to kick off my shoes yet." Meanwhile Charley has opened her laptop and is clicking away.

"Go to Instagram," Waltraut says. "I'll wait."

Charley hands over the screen and I say, "Okay, I'm on."

"Go to the *Wake Up America!* profile."

Click, click, click. "I'm there," I tell her. Then I start to read the posts.

When I don't say anything else for several beats, the

producer says, "You'll need a month to read everything. The long and short of it is that we want you and Dr. Ben to host a regular Monday morning spot."

My heart is pounding so hard I'm sure my blood pressure is reaching some kind of danger zone. "I would love to!" I gush before saying, "But I'm pretty sure Dr. Williams won't agree to it."

"NASA has already approved his participation."

"You're joking."

"I am not joking," she says. "The two of you were such a powerhouse duo that the world has fallen in love with you."

"But how? We could barely stand each other." And even though there was a brief moment where I thought about jumping the man's bones, those feelings went right away as soon as he opened his mouth.

"The world loves conflict, Serafina, and you and Ben brought that in spades. Now, do you have a pen? I'm going to give you Dr. Williams' number. I need you to contact him and pitch me three segment ideas by tomorrow morning. I'll pick my favorite, so you know which one to run with."

"Oh, wow. I mean, I thought I'd just come on and talk or something. This sounds like Ben and I are going to have to spend a good deal of time together."

"You'll be paid for your time, of course," Waltraut says. "Also, the publicity will do a lot to enhance both of your agendas."

Oh, my God! My app is going to go global! I make a mental note to investigate having it translated into other languages. It's already available in English and Spanish, but if I'm going to be on national television regularly, I can definitely parlay that exposure into more.

"Thank you so much for this opportunity," I tell Waltraut. "I won't let you down."

"I'm sure you won't. Now, give Dr. Williams a call. I look forward to hearing from you soon."

Charley has since jumped up and is hopping around my loft looking like she's performing some kind of tribal dance. When I put my phone down, she lets out an honest to goodness scream. "You're going to be famous!!!"

"I think you're right," I tell her, feeling every ounce as enthusiastic as she is. "But I have to work with that Ben guy."

"You mean Dr. Banana Pants," she bursts out laughing. "Did you see the hashtags they're using for you?"

I hurry over to the couch and sit down with my laptop. #SassyStarLady, #LaLaLopez, and #WhatsUrSign are the most popular. I click on the *Live for Your Star Sign* page and see that I have over eight thousand new Instagram followers since yesterday.

Picking up my phone, I add Ben as a contact while I tell Charley, "Dr. Banana Pants and I have some work to do."

Then I send him a text, because there's no way he's going to actually take my call.

> LibraGrl: Hey Ben. It's Serafina Lopez from the Live for Your Star Sign App. Looks like you and I have a new gig together. Waltraut wants us to pitch her three segment ideas by tomorrow morning. I thought we might consider an "Eat for your Star Sign" thing. I'd talk about interesting stuff and you could talk about Tang or something. Isn't that what the astronauts drink in space?

DrBananaPants: …

DrBananaPants: …

LibraGrl: I've rendered you mute with possibility, have I?

DrBananaPants: …

LibraGrl: Should we grab lunch or dinner and plan the other two pitches together?

DrBananaPants: …

LibraGrl: Earth to Dr. Banana Pants; come in, Dr. Banana Pants …

DrBananaPants: It's pretty rich that you're using that ridiculous moniker when you're the one who picked out those hideous pants.

LibraGrl: I thought you might find it funny since you're the one who called them banana pants to begin with. So, dinner? Drinks? How do you want to do this?

Dr.BananaPants: I'm absolutely not meeting you for anything. As for the segment, I'm going to use my time to discuss the first of the five current ways we're searching for planets. It's called radial velocity (there's a good explanation of it on the NASA Kids website if you'd like to read up on it). If you want to talk about star sign nonsense, that's up to you. Perhaps we can find out how many minutes we have on air and divide it proportionally based on importance.

NASA Kids site? Rude! I can go to the regular NASA site, thank you very much. "Charley, as fast as possible, find out what you can about radial velocity. I need this jerk to think I know what it is."

After about thirty seconds, she says, "It's observing changes in a star's light caused by a planet orbiting it. The planet and star have a tug of war going on that causes the star to wobble a bit ... blah, blah, blah ... gravitational pull ... Doppler effect."

"Thanks."

LibraGrl: Well, if you're talking about radial velocity, that'll be a great opportunity for me to discuss the tug of war between opposing star signs in the dating world. But in order to appear professional, we really should get together and hash out a plan. Unless you're afraid of me, of course. In which case, you should see if a braver nerd can take your spot on the show from now on.

DrBananaPants: There is nothing we can accomplish in person that we can't via text.

LibraGrl: Ah, so you *are* intimidated by me.

DrBananaPants: Obviously not. I'm just extremely busy with far more important things. However, in the interest of ending this inane back and forth, I'm willing to meet you at the benches on 103rd Street at Riverside Park at six p.m.

LibraGrl: Are we going to have dinner after that?
Where should we go? I hear there's a great new place
on Broadway and 107th. Should we meet there
instead?

DrBananaPants: We are going to sit on a bench and
spend a grand total of five minutes together and not a
second more.

LibraGrl: I just looked up the name of the restaurant.
It's called The Cove. I'll meet you there at six thirty.

I don't actually want to share a meal with Ben, but I do want to make two things abundantly clear to him from the start. The first is that he is not in a position of power between the two of us. The second is that I like to eat while I think.

I ignore his twelve other texts where he tells me that he's not going to meet me at The Cove and that he will be sitting on a bench in Riverside Park at six instead. He can text me all he wants. I am not losing this battle.

TEN

Ben

Alec: You're going for supper with her? Don't you hate each other?

ObiWan: Yes and yes.

Alec: Hmm … maybe she doesn't hate you. It sounds like she pushed pretty hard for a date. You know what they say about opposites attracting …

ObiWan: I assure you there's NO attraction between us. I'm going to meet her, have a quick appetizer, go over what we're going to talk about on the show, and get the hell out of there.

Alec: If I were you, I wouldn't be in such a rush. It's not every day guys like us get to sit at the same table with a gorgeous woman like that.

ObiWan: She might as well be a man. Honestly, there is no spark whatsoever. Besides, even if there were, she's an ASTROLOGER.

Alec: So what? She's hot.
ObiWan: You date her then. That is if you don't mind betraying everything you believe in for a chance at sex.

Alec: Dude, I'd betray my own grandmother for a chance at sex.

ObiWan: Well, that's where you and I differ. Gotta go. I don't want to be late for my non-date.

This is ridiculous. Possibly even more so than my accidental modeling gig. I'm currently on my way to some stupid restaurant to meet a woman I can't stand because she refuses to answer my texts. I hurry down the busy Broadway sidewalk as the sky grows darker, my sense of dread growing with each step.

The Cove is trendy and loud — the kind of place I avoid like the plague. I walk in and glance around, spotting Serafina at a table for two in the corner. She waves at me in a way that says *I won*, which she most certainly has not. Just because I didn't feel like acting like an adolescent, doesn't mean I lost. It just means I'm an adult. She should take notes on how it's done.

I weave my way through the tables, taking measured breaths and telling my heart rate to slow down, but it's really no use. Alec was right. Serafina Lopez is gorgeous. And strong. And, as much as I hate to admit it, she's smart. Completely wrong-headed, but intelligent, none-theless. When I get to the table, she smiles. "Hi there, thanks for coming."

I sit down across from her. "What can I say? I'm a gentleman." I decide to leave the burden of conversation on her shoulders. After all, she's the one who insisted we meet in person.

"The seafood paella is supposed to be incredible here," she says with a small smile. She looks almost unsure of herself, which throws me off a little. I need her to stay in full battle mode so I can do the same.

"I'm just having an appetizer, then I have to run."

The waiter walks up to our table with two glasses of water. "Hi, I'm Nathan. I'll be your server this evening. Can I bring you something to start?"

He glances back and forth between us to see who's going first. I gesture to Serafina to go ahead. "I'll have a glass of Viognier, the house salad, and the paella for my main."

"I'll have a pint of Stella and the crab-stuffed mush-rooms," I tell him, handing him my menu.

"And for your main?"

"Nothing, thanks," I say.

Nathan's smile fades and he grumbles, "Not again."

"Excuse me?"

"This is the third time this week that I end up serving the couple that's about to break up. Of course, that always results in a huge argument and no tip."

"Why on earth would you think we're about to break up?" Serafina asks with curiosity etched across her brow.

He shakes his head as though he's breaking bad news to her. "I've seen it a hundred times. Whenever a guy only orders an appetizer after his date orders a full meal, it means he's breaking up with her but is doing it in a public place so she won't freak out at him. If I were you, I'd walk out right now."

Then he looks at me and adds, "Spoiler alert: she's going to freak out. Sorry to ruin your great plan, but I just can't have another food fight, broken dishes kind of evening, okay, buddy? It's not fair to me, it's not fair to her, and it's not fair to the other people trying to have a nice evening out. Do it somewhere else."

"This is a business meeting," I tell him, while looking over the top of my glasses. It's a power move that I learned from my multivariable calculus professor.

A look of embarrassment crosses our waiter's face. "I'll be right back with your drinks."

As soon as he leaves, Serafina and I exchange amused glances. She says, "How much do you want to bet he's a Leo? Leo men have a tendency to jump to conclusions."

"I don't know anything about Leos, but he did go from A to Z without any stops in between." We both laugh, before I remember we hate each other, and that I want to get out of here as soon as humanly possible.

I pull a pen and a small notepad out of my jacket pocket and flip it open. "Okay, so we should get started."

Serafina nods as she takes a laptop out of her bag. Then she sets her cutlery aside and puts it down in front of her. Without realizing it, I let out a "Huh."

"What?" she asks, raising one eyebrow.

"Nothing."

"No, it's something," she says. "Are you surprised I brought a laptop with me? I bet you thought I'd pull out some tarot cards and do a reading to determine what we should talk about on air."

I let a grin escape my lips. "I was thinking a Ouija board. Maybe summon Dick Clark for advice."

Glaring at me, Serafina opens her computer. "Let's get one thing straight. I am a businesswoman — an extremely successful one at that. I probably make more in one month than you make all year."

I stare at her for a moment, quickly multiplying my annual salary by twelve months. I suppose it's possible. There are a lot of desperate people out there, and desperate people are easily parted from their hard-earned cash. Rather than getting into a pissing match over money (especially since I may lose), I tilt my head and ask, "Before or after taxes?"

She snort laughs. Not particularly attractive, but oddly cute in its own way. Not that I should be noticing.

Nathan comes by with our drinks. "This round is on me for accusing you of planning a cowardly break up."

"Thanks," Serafina and I both say at the same time.

"Your appetizers will be right out." He walks away, leaving us to our awkward conversation.

Serafina lifts hers in a toast. "To our blossoming television career."

I pick up my glass and lightly tap it against hers. "May it be over as quickly as it started."

We each take a sip, then find ourselves staring at each other for seconds too long. Boy, she is really pretty. I force myself out of whatever weird hypnosis has taken over by giving my head a sharp shake.

She turns her gaze back to her computer screen and says, "Radial velocity would pair well with a talk about my dating app. I'm going to come up with a whole thing about gravitational pull so when you talk about the tug of war between a planet and the star it orbits, I'll come in with my stuff about opposites ..."— she glances up at me and pauses, then quickly looks back down before finishing her sentence — "attracting."

ELEVEN

Serafina

"You have salad dressing on your nose," Ben tells me rather rudely.

"I like the smell of ranch so I like to leave a little bit on the tip of my nose to enhance my enjoyment." I wipe it off, totally negating the veracity of my claim.

Ben laughs. "I like a woman with a sense of humor." As soon as the words leave his mouth his eyes pop open so wide, he looks like he's about to have a seizure.

"Don't worry, Dr. Banana Pants, I'm not going to think you like me just because you gave me a compliment."

He clears his throat nervously before taking a big gulp of his beer. "I ... just ... well ... that is to say ..."

I love knowing I have the power to make a brilliant specimen like Dr. Ben Williams lose his ability to speak. Instead of sitting back and letting him suffer, I say, "Waltraut did ask for three ideas, and so far we've only come up with one."

"Yes, but it's a good one, at least my end of it is." He arches one eyebrow as though challenging me to a verbal dual.

En garde! Monsieur Snooty Pants.

Instead of slaying him outright, I mumble, "Ad astra per aspera." Then I wave our waiter over to order another drink.

"You speak Latin?" he asks in a super-insulting fashion.

"What, you think only astro-nerds know Latin?"

"I'm sorry," he says somewhat contritely. "I did ask that in a rather offensive manner."

"Did you know they put that saying on a plaque to memorialize the astronauts who died on Apollo One? 'Through adversity to the stars ...' It gives me chills to think of it used like that," I say.

"What did *you* mean by it?" he asks with a glint in his eye.

I exhale a great gush of air before answering, "If I can stand working with you for long enough, I'll see my app reach the stars. But, of course, you knew that ..."

He's grinning like a darn fool. "We both have an agenda for doing this show," he tells me. "While yours is entirely selfish, mine is to open people's minds to the possibilities of our infinite universe."

"You're such an ass. I'm willing to bet you weren't even given a choice if you wanted to go back on *Wake Up America!* It's my guess your bosses are making you do it."

His lack of answer confirms my suspicion.

"As to the other ideas we need to pitch," I continue, "I suggest we do a *Decorate for Your Star Sign* segment. You could talk about the interiors of rockets or something."

"I'm sure America couldn't care less about decorating rockets and, frankly, neither could I."

I shrug my shoulders. "It's not my fault that your part of the segment would be boring."

"How about if we talk about energy wave theory? I can discuss NASA's efforts in pioneering safe and efficient space travel while traversing electromagnetic waves. You could talk about the best mode of transportation for your star sign."

That's actually a great idea, but I'm not going to tell him that. Instead, I say, "Fine. We'll pitch Waltraut all three segments and let her decide."

When my paella arrives, I ask our server for an extra plate, then I dish half of it up and hand it over to Ben. "I have more than I need."

He looks like I'm handing him a plate full of poisonous rat pellets, but ultimately takes it. "Thank you."

We're halfway through my entrée when two women around my age approach our table. They stare at Ben like he's the Second Coming. The taller of the two says, "Hi, are you Dr. Ben Williams? My friend didn't think you were, but I told her I'd know you anywhere."

"I'm sorry, have we met?" Ben sounds so nervous you'd think he just got caught plagiarizing his thesis or something.

His fan clearly takes his answer to mean that he is who she thinks he is because she gushes, "I saw you on television this morning. Those pants made my day."

"Thank you," I insert into the conversation. "I picked them out for him to wear."

Dr. Banana Pants' somewhat excitable admirer turns to me and announces, "That segment was the highlight of my week. At least until coming here and seeing the man in the flesh." She's back to drooling after my dinner companion.

Ben looks intensely agitated. His face has turned a bright pink, and his jaw is so clenched you'd probably need a crowbar to pry it open. I decide to have a little fun. "Dr. Ben, are you single or are you seeing somebody?"

"I ... I ... I'm ... why does it matter?"

"I was just thinking that we could do a fun segment where I match you up with a viewer based on her star sign." I tell his admirer, "I'm adding a dating feature to my app. You aren't by chance a Leo, are you?"

"I'm a Libra," she tells me. "But I did some research after your segment and found out that Libra women do well with Gemini men." She looks at Ben from under her long flirty lashes.

"As flattering as this attention is," Ben says nervously, "I'm not currently on the market."

"You're married?" she asks disappointedly.

"No, just not on the market," he tells her.

After signing a cocktail napkin for both women, they eventually walk back to their own table. Ben looks relieved and furious at the same time. "If we're going to work together, you need to know I won't put up with being put on the spot like that." He sounds like a stern father about to ground me.

I'm a bit taken aback by his anger. "I was just brainstorming out loud. Plus, she was totally cute and super into you."

"Well, don't do it again," he says with a set jaw.

"Dude, relax," I tell him. "I just figured a good-looking guy like yourself might enjoy the social aspects of being a national television star."

"Oh, really? Would you like it if that were a couple of men interested in you?"

Hmm, probably not, but since he's being so rude about it, I'm not going to admit it. Before I answer, he continues. "Are you going to put yourself out there to date total strangers?"

"Not unless the retired crowd is interested in dating me. Men our age aren't usually watching morning television."

"That's sexist," he says derisively.

"It would only be sexist if it weren't true," I tell him. "But if men in their thirties were morning show people, I'd totally do it." I think about my sad personal life and once again get excited about my dating app.

"Sure you would," he says, oozing sarcasm.

"You don't know me, so don't pretend you do."

"I just find it hard to believe any woman would be willing to date some random stranger just because he saw you on TV. It sounds stalkerish."

"Everyone you don't already know is a random stranger. That's how dating works. You meet someone new and learn about them. Then you decide if you want to go out with them again," I say, before adding, "I'm surprised you don't know this."

His face turns slightly red, then he runs his tongue over his teeth. "Okay, fine. You're also a dating expert who knows the secret to happiness, and I'm a closed-off shut-in who has no idea about the opposite sex."

I stare at him, wondering if there's some truth to what he's saying. Nope. He's way too good-looking for that to be the case.

He holds up both hands in front of him like he's getting ready to catch a basketball. "It doesn't matter.

We're here to discuss the show, which we've done. Clearly, it's in both our best interests to keep our future interactions as brief as possible as we seem incapable of having a civil conversation."

"Um, okay," I say with more than a hint of derisiveness. "I thought we could find some common ground, but apparently that's not possible. Look, we don't have to be friends, but we do have to work together. We can either make the best of it or we can always be at odds. I think life will be more pleasant if we try to get along."

After a lengthy silence, he answers, "For that to happen, you can't make me look like a fool again. I will not wear any more clothes that you pick out for me and I will not allow you to try to set me up. Is that understood?"

"Perfectly," I tell him. Meanwhile his supercilious tone is almost more than I can stand.

Ben pulls his wallet out of his pants pocket and drops a fifty on the table. Then he stands up and says, "You can text me to let me know which segment Waltraut picks."

"You're leaving?" I ask as though we're playing out the scene our waiter earlier accused him of planning.

"We've completed what we came here to do. I see no reason to prolong this meeting," he states plainly.

"I'm not done eating."

He shrugs his broad shoulders. "So eat." Then he turns and walks away.

Try as I might to be conciliatory to that man, I will not stand for rudeness. No sir, If Dr. Banana Pants wants war, I'm happy to accommodate — starting with pitching Waltraut the very segment he's so opposed to.

We Libras like calm and balance, but if you get on our wrong side, you'd better watch out.

TWELVE

Ben

Email from: Serafina.Lopez@StarSign.Com
To: Waltraut.Hemper@WakeUpAmerica.com, cc:
Ben.Williams@GoddardInstitute.com

Subject: Segment Pitches

Dear Waltraut,

Dr. Williams and I had a productive meeting regarding the three segment pitches last night. The following three concepts will be weeks one through three:
1) I'll discuss decorating for your star sign and Dr. Williams will talk about the interiors of rockets. (We would both love to do this one first.)
2) NASA's use of radial velocity (gravitational pull/the tug of war between a planet and the star it orbits) will tie nicely into the upcoming dating

feature on my app. I'll use it to show how people with different star signs are often attracted to each other.

3) NASA's efforts in pioneering safe and efficient space travel while traversing electromagnetic waves. I'll pair this with the best modes of transportation for your star sign.

All the best,
Serafina

———

Email from: Waltraut.Hemper@WakeUpAmerica.com
To: Serafina.Lopez@StarSign.Com cc: Ben.Williams@GoddardInstitute.com

Subject: RE: Segment Pitches

Hi Serafina and Ben,

Sure, let's start with #1. Our viewers always love a good decorating segment. See you Monday morning at 5 a.m. sharp.

Waltraut

———

TEXT from ObiWan: Are you serious? You pitched her the idea I gave a hard no to?

StarNut: You're the one who walked out on our dinner. I figured you didn't want to be bothered making the final decision.

ObiWan: So this is some sort of petty revenge? I thought we'd decided on the traveling segment.

StarNut: I told you Waltraut wanted three pitches.

ObiWan: For someone who pretends she wants us to get along, you're certainly doing everything possible to see that this is going to be a disaster.

StarNut: Is that some kind of implied threat?

ObiWan: I'm merely notifying you of the consequences of your actions in order to assist you in making better choices.

I stare at our exchange, waiting for her to write back. *Forget it, Ben. Get back to work. You've got the final frontier to explore and it's not getting done while you spar with this woman. Your team is counting on you.* Although, should I really feel bad for wasting time on something that is apparently part of my job? After all, *I'm* not the one who got myself into this mess. It's Dev's fault.

Irritation courses through every cell in my body as it has since I walked out of the restaurant last night. I'm currently in the cafeteria, having a large coffee with extra cream and sugar to help get me through the afternoon. According to my smart watch, I only had fifteen minutes of deep sleep last night, which I'd say is accurate based on my level of exhaustion today.

I laid awake until well after three a.m., replaying my dinner meeting with Serafina, specifically the part when I tossed the money on the table and walked out. I've never done something so rude in my life, but honestly, that woman brings out the worst in me. I mean, it would be one thing if she were a half-wit. Then I could almost forgive her for clinging to these ridiculous beliefs. But someone *intelligent* spouting zodiac nonsense? That's just madness. "She has the mental capacity to know better. It's just such a ... waste," I mutter.

Alec sits down on the other side of the table, interrupting the mental tirade I've been repeating for the last eighteen hours. He breaks off a piece of his daily two p.m. cranberry-orange muffin and pops it in his mouth. Alec is nothing if not a creature of habit.

"What's up?"

He grins. "I couldn't help but notice you're talking to yourself, so I thought I'd eavesdrop."

"It was a private conversation," I tell him with a wry smile.

"Serafina Lopez has really gotten under your skin, hasn't she?"

"Of course not," I lie. "I just ... didn't sleep well."

"Riiight," he says, "and the earth is flat ..."

"I don't want to talk about it."

Throwing his hands into the air, he says, "Fine, I won't push it."

I give a firm nod, then have another sip of my coffee. "It's just frustrating because she could be doing so much more with her life. She's bright. *Really* bright."

"Not to mention good-looking."

"That too," I agree before I can stop myself.

"I knew you liked her," Alec says with a satisfied

smile.

"I could never be with someone like her," I say, bouncing my right leg so quickly my whole body starts vibrating. "I'd sooner date Dev."

"He's married, so ..."

"Ha-ha," I say with a roll of my eyes. "*She's* not what's got me all agitated. I'm pissed I have to do these stupid morning show segments. I didn't spend twenty-one years of my life in school just to be a performing monkey for a bunch of stay-at-home moms and retirees. I graduated at the top of my class at MIT, for God's sake. The very top!" I hold my hand up as though measuring height. "If I'd known this was what the team leader job was all about, I wouldn't have accepted it. It's bad enough that Serafina is wasting her brain, but now mine is being dragged into this idiocy."

"Must be awful," Alec says, pulling off another piece of his muffin.

"It *is*." It's nice to know someone understands.

"Spending time with a beautiful woman ... all those ladies online calling you the Astro-hotty ... What a nightmare," he adds, tossing the piece in his mouth.

"No one likes a smart-ass, Alec," I tell him.

"Suck it up, Princess. Your life's not that bad." He swallows before adding, "You know who else graduated at the top of his class at MIT? Me. And I did it three years before you. And I've been on this team for four years longer than you, but I still lost the team leader position to you which totally blows because if I were you, I'd be making the most of my fifteen minutes."

Guilt gives me a good whack on the back of my head. I shouldn't be complaining to Alec about this. "Sorry."

"What are you going to do?" he says with a shrug.

Scratching the back of my neck, I ask, "What *would* you do with your fifteen minutes if you were me?"

"Get women," he says, with an expression that says I should have graduated at the bottom of the class at flower arranging school for not realizing this on my own.

"You can't be serious."

"Why not? If Einstein could be a ladies' man, surely you can. This might be your only chance to be a bonafide player. I think you should go for it. I for one just signed up to help your co-host test her new dating app."

"Oh, my God. You've either completely lost your mind or you're joking," I say, in utter disbelief that one of the smartest people I know is going to try dating according to his star sign.

"Every nerd that ever got shoved into a locker dreams of being the object of adoration, pal. You may not think you need this now, but you should relish the attention if for no other reason than to seek retribution for your younger self. After all, revenge is a dish best served cold."

"Now you're quoting Pierre Choderlos de Laclos to me?"

"Remember how you once told me about that girl who turned down your offer to take her to senior prom?"

I nod my head in shame. I shared that story one night while he and I were tossing back a few. We were bemoaning the fact that nerds never seemed to get the girl in high school.

"Get up there and show her what she missed out on," Alec tells me.

He's got a point. I'd love for every person who hurt me when I was a kid to know that I'm not that guy anymore. I just don't want to have to go on national television to prove it.

THIRTEEN

Serafina

"He's such a turd!" I yell at my brother Zay. "I have *never* had another person talk down to me the way he does."

"You did make him wear those ridiculous pants on national television."

"Whose side are you on?" My decibel level keeps creeping higher.

"Look at me, Ser. I'm your four-foot, eleven-inch, fully-grown *older* brother. Sue me for being empathetic to other people's humiliation."

I decided to stop by Zay's apartment today for some sibling commiseration. "You have a pituitary gland issue. That's so much bigger than being embarrassed about wearing some tight pants on TV."

I plop down on the couch next to him while he says, "I'm sensitive to cruel nicknames, and the whole country is calling that guy Dr. Banana Pants. I assure you, the man did not spend all that time at university to have his hard-earned title reduced to a joke."

"Point taken," I say, somewhat annoyed that my brother isn't immediately taking my side. "But *he's* the one who put them on and joined in the fashion show. He should have said something so that the whole fiasco never happened."

"What happened to the real male model you hired? Did he ever turn up?" my brother asks.

"Yeah, he did. They put him in Ben's dressing room but didn't find out he wasn't the astrophysicist from NASA until it was time to send him out. At that point Ben was already on set, strutting his stuff."

"Well, it looks like it's all turned out for the best if *Wake Up America!* wants you guys on every week. The question is, how are the two of you going to keep from tearing each other's heads off?"

That *is* the question, especially if we can't even have a civil meal together when there are no cameras around. Pulling the afghan off the back of Zay's couch and wrapping it around my legs, I tell him, "I'm going to be lovely and delightful and stay on point. Ben can sink himself with his rude behavior for all I care."

"I'm willing to bet the man isn't half as bad as you portray him to be." My brother, the traitor!

"And how did you come to that conclusion?"

"Look, Ser, you're a flirt by nature. You flirt with men, women, dogs, pigeons in the park ..." The nasty look I send his way has him hurrying to add, "It's not a bad thing. In fact, according to you, it's a Libra thing. I'm just saying that whenever someone doesn't respond to your innate charm, or doesn't like you, you get really mad."

Ignoring a truth about myself I'd rather not address, I demand, "Who doesn't like me?"

My brother rubs his eyes before staring at the ceiling.

"Oh, I don't know, there was that girl Tiffany Taylor from high school, and then there was that guy Stanford Wellington in college ..."

He pauses for dramatic effect.

"Big whoop. Two idiots from my past didn't like me," I try to act like I'm not bothered by it, but I totally still am.

"You agonized about them both for years," he reminds me. "In fact, I bet you've started up again after meeting Ben Williams."

As if. The truth is, I've been so busy being mad at Ben that I haven't even thought of the miscreants from my formative years — but I will now. *Thanks so much, Zay.* "You act like I'm some kind of egomaniac or something." I can't help my pouting tone.

Zay gets up and walks to his kitchen counter to pick up a box of gingersnaps, which he tosses in my direction. "All I'm saying is that you like to be liked. And as much as it pains me to tell you this, not all people are going to like you."

"Why?" I hear the pathetic whine in my voice, and I hate it.

"Because not all people are smart enough to like you." I know my brother is placating me, but that's okay. As much as I enjoy people's adoration, I'm also amenable to appeasement when needed to maintain my emotional balance.

"Enough about Ben," I say. "I came by for a much more important reason. I was wondering if you could talk to Shelby about having her mother write an article for *The Post* about Charley."

"Charley, your child prodigy employee?" he asks.

"Do you know of another Charley?" Before he can answer, I say, "She recently got accepted into Yale, at fifteen no less, and she made her national modeling debut on *Wake Up America!* I thought she might be an inspirational person to write about."

He shrugs his shoulders. "I guess."

"Please ask her, Zay. As I may have mentioned, Charley had a tough time in school. It's hard to relate to people when you're so much smarter than they are, and, if you'll recall, high school students are not generally tolerant of those who stand out from the pack in ways they don't approve of or understand."

"Don't I know it." Poor Zay had a horrible time in high school. It wasn't bad enough that he never grew beyond a grade school height, but he's also genius-level smart which earned him a host of nasty nicknames like "Brain Dwarf" and "Pint-sized Poindexter."

"You *do* know it," I tell him. "So please help me help Charley exact her revenge."

"When you put it that way, of course I'm in. But you know Shelby, she can be a bit touchy when she thinks people are using her."

The truth is, my brother's girlfriend is not the most likable person on the planet. In fact, she was Zay's office tormentor before they got together. Shelby didn't tease him about his height or anything, rather, she complained that Zay got to work from home while everyone else had to go into the office. Eventually, she got her way and Zay had to quit hiding out and join the real world. While it was painfully hard on him, it all worked out for the best. After thirty-two years, my brother has learned to accept himself for who he is. Not to mention, he finally has a girlfriend who is really into him.

"How are things going with you and Shelby anyway?"

I ask. "Have you thought about introducing her to Mom and Dad?"

An actual blush washes over Zay's face. "If things keep going so well, I'll take her back to Miami over the Christmas holiday. There's no place like Miami when you're freezing your butt off in New York."

"God help her. She and Mom are both Capricorns who like to be in charge of everything. They'll either love each other or hate each other."

"Can you imagine Mom hating the woman who loves her son? A Cuban mother's sun rises and sets in the happiness of her children."

"Shelby loves you?" I'm so happy I feel tears of joy prickle behind my eyes. "Do you love her?"

Zay nods his head. "I do. She's so great, Ser. When we go out together, it's like she's actually proud to be with me, which I never in my life thought would happen. She's given me the push I needed to realize there's nothing wrong with being me."

"Thank God!" I tell him. "Although, it's not like your own family hasn't been telling you that forever."

"Yeah, but you guys are family. You *have* to love me. Shelby hardly likes anyone, so her love feels like a real prize, you know?"

I scoot over on the couch close enough to my brother so that I can hug him. "You *are* a real prize and I'm glad you're finally accepting yourself. Now, ask Shelby to talk to her mom, okay? I really want to give Charley a self-esteem boost. If she can stay out of trouble, her parents will let her go to Yale next year."

Zay looks pensive. "It's funny how the kids who peak in high school often don't make big successes of their lives as adults, but the ones who struggle can really fly."

"It all boils down to how hard you're willing to work," I tell him. "When things come easy for you young, the real world can come as a bit of a shock. But when you learn how to weather the storm of human interaction in your youth, you've already learned how to surf some of the tougher waves."

"In other words, not everyone is going to like you and as soon as you figure out that's just life, the better off you'll be."

"Exactly!" I tell him.

Zay laughs out loud before pointing out, "So in your case, the sooner you realize that Ben Williams doesn't need to like you, the better off you'll be?"

I stepped into the trap before I even saw it was there. "Shut up, Zay."

"I'm just saying ..."

"I know what you're saying," I tell him. "Now leave it be, okay?"

In and of itself, I don't care what people think of me. I'm a secure enough person not to let the Tiffany Taylors and Stanford Wellingtons of the world shake my foundation. It's just that for some reason I'm really bothered by the fact that Ben Williams doesn't like me.

FOURTEEN

Ben

"Welcome back to *Wake Up America!* It's going to be a hot one today, isn't it, Hal?" Lacey says with a wide grin.

"*So* hot! It's already run-through-the-sprinkler weather and it's only eight a.m.," Hal says with a chuckle.

"Speaking of things heating up," Lacey says. "We've got our two favorite experts in all things space and astrology-related, Dr. Ben Williams from NASA and Serafina Lopez from *Live for Your Star Sign,* here to duke it out again."

Hal laughs and gives Lacey's shoulder a bit of a shove. "I cannot wait. These two were on last Monday and they're like the original oil and water — you just can't mix 'em!"

Lacey, clearly annoyed at the shove, gives Hal a smile that resembles more of a snarl, then says, "Take it easy on my shoulder there, Hal. I'd hate to have to charge you with assault."

Hal keeps his phony smile in place. "Somebody needs more coffee so she can take a joke!" Before Lacey can respond, he adds, "Let's get our guests out here. Dr. Ben and Serafina!"

I gesture for Serafina to go ahead of me, then follow her out onto the stage. My pulse is racing as I return to the scene of the crime. I'm in the sports jacket and slacks I was supposed to wear last week, so at least I'll be able to maintain a little of my dignity through fashion. Serafina is wearing a turquoise dress that hugs her curves in a way I should *not* be noticing. The crowd cheers as we make our way to the loveseat they have set up for us, and when we sit, we're both pretty much pressed against the arms of the small sofa so we can be as far apart as possible.

"Welcome back, you two. How has life been since your appearance last week?" Lacey asks. Before either of us can answer, she focuses her attention on me. "Dr. Ben, you were quite the hit with the ladies in the audience. Have you had anyone recognize you on the street?"

Is no one else on the planet capable of staying on topic? "A couple people."

"You've been called everything from Dr. Hot Stuff with the Right Stuff to Astro-hotty," Lacey says. "Astro-hotty! Isn't that clever?"

The audience takes this as a sign to start hooting and clapping. This is a clear-cut case of sexual harassment in the workplace, but I think back to what Alec said about getting revenge for my younger self and realize it's not so bad to be adored.

Hal cuts in, "And of course, Dr. Banana Pants is currently the network's most popular hashtag."

On the screen behind us, they put up a picture of me

in the tight yellow pants for the home audience to see. *Perfect*. I nod and offer them a small grin. "Well, that was last week. This week, I'm here to share a little about life on a space shuttle, even though I've never flown on one myself."

On screen, a video of the interior of the space shuttle cockpit appears on screen. "As you can see, a rocket's primary function is to ensure safety during space travel. There's very little need for interior decorating." I hurry to point out, "When an astronaut is piloting a shuttle, they've got dozens of systems to monitor at all times ..."

"Well, it wouldn't hurt them to spruce it up a little. Maybe with some bright colors and some curtains?" Lacey cuts me off mid-sentence. "What would you do to add more beauty to a shuttle, Serafina?"

"First of all, I'd want to know the star signs of the astronauts who will be piloting it. Then I'd add some delightful touches such as soothing colors for the seats and buttons. Things don't have to be ugly to be functional. I'd say they really missed an opportunity to make that cockpit have a homey feel — especially if your pilot is a Pisces. They thrive on serenity."

I scoff loudly and shake my head. "It's a shuttle that will be flown by multiple pilots. Each of those buttons costs thousands of dollars and is designed the way it is for a purpose. There's no room or budget to make it feel like a living room, nor should we. Astronauts must stay alert at all times."

Serafina glares at me, then smiles at Lacey. "In that case, NASA should have chosen a livelier palette that would help keep the pilots awake. Orange or yellow for instance. Dull grey is enough to put you right to sleep."

"You're missing the point," I tell her sharply.

"And you're missing whatever gene it is that allows a person to be open-minded," she retaliates.

"There's no such gene, and if you're referring to the differences between a fixed and growth mindset, that's a learned behavior," I say with a satisfied smile.

"Strange that he can talk about having a growth mindset, but he clearly doesn't possess one," Serafina tells Hal, who laughs.

Hal looks at me and says, "She's got you there, Dr. Ben."

"I disagree," I tell him. "People in my field are absolutely open-minded. We just aren't open to nonsense."

Serafina tilts her head and looks at me for a second. "I think you were lying when you said you are a Gemini. You've got the bite of a Cancer."

"Oh, for..." I roll my eyes, not even caring how rude I'm being on television. "People's personalities are a combination of genetics and environment. Period. There is absolutely no basis for what you're saying. None. That's like believing all blondes are dumb and all redheads have bad tempers. It's simply not true."

"*Are* you a Cancer?" she persists.

"You know perfectly well that I'm a Gemini." Then for good measure, I add, "There is no empirical evidence for anything you believe."

"May I see your driver's license?" she asks, not willing to let it go.

"I don't have to prove to you when I was born."

"So closed-minded," Serafina says, shaking her head. "Sad, really." Then she tells Lacey and Hal, "I bet he won't even sign up for the trial run of my dating app."

"And I suppose you're on it," I scoff.

"I sure am," she says. "In fact, I have my first date coming up this week. It's with a Gemini." She says the last bit while glaring at me.

I take off my glasses and rub the bridge of my nose. "Good luck with that," I tell her somewhat insincerely. Okay, totally insincerely.

"Astrology is real, Ben. It's steeped in thousands of years of exploration — which is far longer than the study of astronomy. It helps people all over the world to grow and learn and understand themselves."

"Desperate people may *think* they derive some benefit from it, but it's all hocus pocus, smoke and mirrors." Then, because I don't know when to leave well enough alone, I add, "It's like believing in some bearded God in a white robe. Just because you want to think he exists doesn't mean he's out there. If you can't see it, taste it, touch it, or hear it, you must question the validity of what you're studying."

Serafina leans toward me, her eyes wild with delight. "Are you saying you don't believe there are an untold number of stars and planets in the universe beyond the ones we can see?"

"Don't be ridiculous. That's totally different."

"Is it?" she asks. "You can't see, taste, touch, or hear them."

"Ooh! She got you again, Dr. Ben!" Lacey says.

"No, she didn't. Thanks to the Hubble telescope, we've been able to run a simulation based on the ingredients that make up the universe. Using the scientifically proven data for the conditions that reflect our reality and the laws of physics, we are able to calculate that there are at least two trillion galaxies in the universe. You don't have to observe all of them with your five senses to know they're real."

"Before Dr. Ben continues to blow our minds with his science, we need to take a commercial break," Hal says. "We'll be back soon with both of our experts. Stay tuned because there are sure to be more fireworks to come!"

FIFTEEN

Serafina

"Pisces do well to decorate with more subtle tones. Sea-foam green, lavender, peach, silvery blues. All of these are reminiscent of the fish's watery home." I'm on fire with this "Decorate for Your Star Sign" segment. So far, Ben has said nothing since the commercial break, which works for me.

"Do me," Lacey gushes. "I'm a Taurus and I've got to tell you, I have not been vibing with my décor at all."

"Taurus is an earth sign," I tell her. "You should focus on creams, browns, and whites as a base, while accenting with the colors of the sunset."

"Wow, it's like you really know me," Lacy gushes. "My decorator said I should go with bold colors to show-case my personality, but I'm just not comfortable with them."

"You don't want your personality to be challenged in your home environment. You need a place to rest and regroup."

"Good God," Ben mutters none too quietly.

"You're not buying this, are you Ben?" Hal asks, as though the pot needs more stirring.

"Of course I'm not buying it. As long as you decorate with things you like, your home will be fine."

"Do you spend a lot of time at home, Dr. Williams?" I ask him.

"I work a lot, so I spend the majority of my time at my office. I sleep at home."

"And how is your office at work decorated?" I want to know.

"I ... it's not. I'm there to *work*, not frolic in sensory fluff." He crosses his arms in front of him like he's in a suit of armor and I'm going to start hurling knives at him or something. *Sooo* tempting.

"I would suggest you bring in some bright colors like yellow, orange, and chartreuse. These hues will resonate with your creative mental frequencies and result in a burst of cognitive acuity. You should also have modern and light furniture," I tell him.

"For the love of ... Are you for real?" he demands. "I spend my days figuring out how humans can inhabit another planet. I don't have time for this nonsense."

I ignore him and turn to Hal and Lacey. "Do you know what would be fun?"

Instead of answering, they appear to be waiting for me to tell them, so I do. "It would be fun if we did a segment at Dr. Williams' work where I redo his office in a way that works for his star sign."

"Absolutely not!" Ben snaps.

"Why not?" Lacey wants to know. "I think it's a great idea."

"I do too," Hal enthuses.

"How can that possibly enhance the lives of your viewers?" Ben demands.

"It'll give you a chance to show the world where you do all of your fabulous hypothesizing," I tell him. "You might even manage to throw in some interesting tidbits about astrophysics."

"If there is such a thing ..." Hal adds. His eyes seem to gloss over every time Ben opens his mouth.

Ben gives him a hard stare. "Astrophysics is extremely interesting for those who can grasp the concepts."

Zing! Now he's turning on the hosts. Perfect. Hopefully, they'll decide they don't need Dr. Grouchy anymore and I'll manage to parlay this into my very own weekly segment. Mine, as in belonging to me, and not him. Now that I'm winning, I decide it won't hurt me to play nice. "Dr. Williams is right," I say. "People *should* start with the works of Carl Sagan and Brian Greene — totally enthralling."

Ben tilts his head and blinks at me. "You've read Brian Greene?"

"Of course. *The Elegant Universe* and *The Fabric of the Cosmos* are two of my favorites."

"Huh, mine too." For the briefest moment, it's like we both forget we're on live TV and we're just two people connecting. But then he opens his mouth again and gets back to being the intellectual snob I know him to be. "The average person wouldn't appreciate those books. The fact that you've read them is surprisingly impressive."

Raising one eyebrow, I say, "I'm not trying to impress you."

The audience makes an *ooohhh* sound and I can almost imagine a scoreboard on which I just got another point.

"I find that hard to believe," Ben says to me with a smug smile. "You've gone pretty far out of your way to mention two of the most famous astronomers in the world."

Nuts. Now he just got a point, didn't he? I quickly shift gears back to my redecorating idea. "Not really, but how about we try to stay on track? We were talking about decor. I'd really love to redo your office. You'll be surprised what a difference it'll make to your productivity, Dr. Williams."

Out of the corner of my eye, I see the producer making a rolling motion with his hands which I've learned means it's time to wrap up our segment. Hal turns to the camera and says, "We'd like to hear from you, America. Would you like Serafina to decorate Dr. Ben's office? Let us know on social media."

Lacey interjects, "We could even have a behind-the-scenes look at what they do down at the Goddard Center at the same time. I vote yes, but as always, we'd love to hear from our fans!" She turns to me and says, "Serafina, we're looking forward to an update on how your date goes." Then, as if a light bulb has just gone off in her head, she says, "Also, viewers, let us know if you think Dr. Ben should sign up for the dating app." She winks at Ben and offers, "I'll do it if you do it."

Hal cuts in. "Coming up we'll be talking with Santana Garcia about how you can spice up your bland dinner fare with a burst of culinary Mexican flare."

"We're in commercial," the director calls out.

Ben stands, says good-bye to Lacey and Hal, then walks out without looking back at me. I give an innocent shrug to the hosts, bid them farewell, then follow him backstage. After the sound tech removes my mic, I hurry to my dressing room in time to see my phone light up.

I grab it off the makeup table and see it's a text from Ben, who is on the other side of the wall.

DrBananaPants: I cannot believe you just did that. We're supposed to come up with potential segments together. Not only did you blindside me, but you practically baited Hal and Lacey into demanding that I join your dating app.

LibraGrl: Would you like to talk about this in person? I'm literally only a few steps away.

DrBananaPants: I have no desire to let the world into my office. Unlike some people, I have real work to do.

LibraGrl: I'm going to ignore your obvious dig and take the high road. I imagine at this point it'll be up to the network and your boss, won't it?

DrBananaPants: I don't want you to set foot into my office and I don't want you to set me up.

LibraGrl: I don't do the setting up. The computer does that according to your star sign.

There's a knock on my open door and I see Waltraut standing there. She reaches over and knocks on Ben's door as well, then waits a second for him to open it. "I just spoke with the powers that be at NASA. The office redo is a go, but instead of live, we'll shoot it ahead of time, then have you both on to watch it together and talk about it. Can you both be available on Wednesday at one?"

I hear a sigh before Ben asks, "Why so soon?"

"We need time to edit the segment," Waltraut says. "So, Wednesday?"

"Sounds great to me," I say.

Ben offers a more sedate, "Fine."

"Oh, and we've decided that having both of you on the air with Hal and Lacey is a lot of energy, so we're going to just have the two of you do your bit from now on."

"Fantastic!" I gush with way more enthusiasm than I'm feeling. I'm preoccupied imagining what a giant pain in the rear Ben is going to be when I redecorate his office.

Ben shuts down the conversation by saying, "I really need to run."

Waltraut says, "Ben, we'd really love it if you'd get on board with Serafina's dating app. Our ratings would go through the roof if you did."

"Your ratings really aren't my top priority." I hear the door click shut and Waltraut turns to me. "He's a total delight, isn't he?"

"Not the description that came to my mind," I tell her.

"Whatever he is, the viewers love him, and you, too," she says. "You're a real natural at this stuff, you know. Keep it up and you could end up with your own show." Before I can thank her, Waltraut grabs a woman passing by. "You were told not to cook with cilantro today, right? Hal is severely allergic to it."

With that, she disappears, leaving me to contemplate the possibilities of my future. I knew when the sun aligned with Neptune, opportunities were going to become abundant, but this is a whole new level of amazing. When my phone pings, I look down to see it's another message from Ben.

> DrBananaPants: I can only spare about 45 minutes on Wednesday. As I've previously mentioned, I have an actual job I'm expected to perform.

> LibraGrl: So you said. If you want this to go fast, make sure to clean up your office so we can do a quick switch.

> Dr.BananaPants: Fine.

> Dr.BananaPants: Oh, and I hate chartreuse so don't bring anything in that color.

> LibraGrl: What was that you said about how open-minded you are?

> Dr.BananaPants: One can be open-minded and aware of his likes and dislikes at the same time.

> LibraGrl: Not if you've never tried something first.

> DrBananaPants: Are you really so incapable of agreeing with a simple request? You got your way. We're doing the silly segment in my office. Just give me this one thing without making a federal case of it.

I don't respond to his text because, first of all, rude!

Second, I have a feeling he'd love chartreuse if he gave it a chance. It's such a happy color and if that man needs anything, it's a lift in his mood.

SIXTEEN

Ben

I arrive at my office at seven this morning to 'clean it up' — as Serafina bossily instructed — before starting my day. I refuse to take a second longer than necessary for such an asinine project.

When I woke up this morning, I remembered I was supposed to have already given Ewan my notes on his article for the Many Worlds space site. It's a piece on the latest determinations about our nearest known Super Earth, Gliese 486. I've totally dropped the ball, which is not like me. Of course, I blame Ms. Lopez. My life has been thrown for a loop ever since she entered it.

Setting down the boxes I brought from home, I look around at all the things I'm going to have to remove. The truth is, I love my space as-is. Not the grey walls and fluorescent lighting, but my personal touches really make it mine. My favorite books are on the shelf as well as my collection of miniature rockets that I build in my free time.

Serafina can't see these after the fuss I made on national television about how I don't care about ambience. She'd know what a big liar I am if she got a look at my rockets. There are thirty-eight of them.

If the rockets don't make me the captain of the nerd squad, my complete collection of *Star Trek* action figures (from the original series obviously, and still in their boxes) would certainly tip her off.

Those are the first to get packed up, followed by my Space Thinking Putty, my astronaut cell phone charger, the mug my mom gave me that says "Warning: May Start Talking about Physics," and my 3D Solar System Crystal Ball (including all eight of our solar system's planets — not Pluto, of course, since it's NOT a planet).

By 7:30, the entire place looks as bare as I claimed it would. All that's left on my desk is my computer and phone. The only things on my bookshelf are books (Carl Sagan's greatest hits included). I quickly boot up my computer and bring up Ewan's article so I can have it done before he gets in.

A sense of dread comes over me as I imagine how starstruck the men on my team are going to be. They talk incessantly about how beautiful Serafina is. Even Carla told me she's "totally been fangirling over her," whatever the hell that means. Although in her case, I don't even mind too much because it's better than hearing her blather on about Chewy's digestive tract (but only by a very slight margin).

At twelve thirty, Serafina texts me.

StarNut: We're here in the lobby. Is there a chance you can help us carry everything up to your office?

ObiWan: Sure. I'll be right down to sign you in.

Dammit. She's early. I quickly toss my coffee cup and sandwich wrapper in the garbage and hurry down the hall to the elevator. When I get off, I see her, looking lovely as usual. (Why does she have to be so darn beautiful? It's horribly inconvenient.)

Her arms are loaded with two boxes and there's a teenage girl with her. The girl is holding one end of a rolled-up area rug as she looks around with wide eyes.

"Ben, this is Charley," Serafina calls out. "She's my neighbor, friend, and one of the best hackers out there."

The girl blushes and offers me a shy smile. "She's exaggerating."

"Am not. She also got accepted to Yale and she's only fifteen."

"Really?" I ask.

Nodding, Charley says, "It's no biggie."

"I beg to differ," I tell her. "That's a very big deal."

Serafina smiles down at her companion, looking like a proud mother. "Charley's a genius. She's behind the algorithm for the dating feature on my app."

"Really? What does a fifteen-year-old girl know about fixing people up?" I can't help but ask.

"Nothing," she says brightly. "The computer will make the choices based on the data the participants give us when they sign up. You should try it."

Like I need more people pressuring me to date a strange Capricorn or something. But an intriguing idea pops into my head. What if I sign up for this stupid dating trial using a fake name? I could go on a couple of dates and then call foul on how poorly it works. Then I could tell the world how dating for your star sign is a load of hooey. Hmm, this is certainly something to consider.

I pick up the other half of the rug Charley is dragging and say, "Shall we?"

Leading them over to the elevators, I press the up button, then do my best not to look at Serafina while we wait. When the doors slide open, Charley says, "This is so cool. I've never been to NASA before."

"Not even space camp?" I ask as we step on.

She shakes her head and I start to wonder if maybe her family can't afford it. Because, honestly, that's the only reason I can think of that someone wouldn't go to space camp. "Everyone should get a chance to go to space camp — it's life-changing. They have scholarships, you know. I can get the forms for you if you'd like."

"That's really nice of you, but it's not necessary."

"I'd be happy to help," I tell her. "We can use all the brilliant minds we can get around here. And I'd like to be part of setting you on the right track."

When the doors open to my floor, Serafina says, "He's trying to get you away from the crazy zodiac woman who's wasting her brain getting rich when she could be doing something useful like contemplating the cosmos."

I glance back at her and see she's got a wry smile on her face. Then, looking at Charley, I say, "She's not wrong."

"Did you just say I was right?" Serafina asks me.

I chuckle, then nod. "Don't get used to it."

When we get to the Exoplanet Research Center, I swipe my key card and the door swings open leading to the large bullpen where most of the team sits. The screens lining the walls are filled with images of faraway solar systems as well as graphs and charts depicting wobbles, temperature changes, shadows, and all sorts of things that bore the heck out of most people, but I find it positively exhilarating.

The entire team is so quiet, you could hear a Post-it note drop. They're all hiding behind their computer screens while simultaneously peering over them to take in the newcomers. We're a roomful of mostly socially awkward intellectuals and I'm their leader. We should just put on our headgear and be done with it. I ignore their gawking and lead Charley and Serafina to my office.

"Wow, you weren't kidding about not caring about decor," Serafina says.

Shrugging, I say, "Did you expect to find a bunch of *Star Trek* figurines or something?" I'm totally pushing it, but there's no way she can really know what my office usually looks like.

She stares at me for a moment before asking, "Are you *not* even a *Star Trek* fan?"

Lifting both hands in the air, I say, "That's like asking a teenage girl if she likes K-Pop."

I give Charley an *am I right* look and she nods while asserting, "Love it."

"I rest my case," I say with a grin. "Listen, I don't want you to go to too much trouble with this. I'm not going to keep whatever it is you do to the office anyway."

"How do you know when you haven't seen what I'm going to do?"

"I need to reduce distractions and maintain a professional decorum at all times," I say. "No offense, but based on what you already told me about adding a bunch of bright colors, I'm kind of expecting it to look like a Ukrainian Easter egg when you're done here."

"Clearly you meant no offense ..." Serafina says, raising one eyebrow.

Urgh. I should not be allowed to talk to women. "That came out wrong. What I meant to say is that I don't want you and Charley to kill yourselves. You don't really know me, so making these types of choices on my behalf means you have an extremely low probability of success."

"Your faith in me is underwhelming," she practically growls.

"I just don't want to set you up for disappointment," I tell her. "Anyway, is there anything else you need to bring up?"

Nodding, Serafina says, "One more trip."

"Let's do this," I say, glancing at my watch.

By the time the film crew shows up, I'm a little sweaty from lugging the world's heaviest boxes up from the lobby. One of the makeup artists comes at me with some powder and I try to avoid her only to end up having her powder my ear. "We can do this the easy way or the hard way," she tells me.

I pause for a second, tempted to ask for her to enumerate the differences, but settle for a nod, before standing still so she can do her worst. One of the crew opens a large box of donuts and sets it on a table that's been set up just outside my office. That ought to draw the team out from behind their computer screens.

Inside my office, Serafina and Waltraut are engaged in a lively conversation, both of them pointing at items in the boxes, and areas in the room. I sigh, wishing we were done already. Charley, who seems to be finished with her duties, stands awkwardly by the donut table, looking very much alone. I walk up to her after the makeup lady is done with me. Folding my arms, I ask, "So, do you think anyone noticed me getting my makeup done?"

She giggles and nods. "Pretty sure a few of your staff were making videos. You might want to check YouTube later."

"Perfect," I mutter. "How do you know Serafina?"

"She lives in my building," Charley says. "She's amazing. I've learned so much from her."

I glance down, feeling slightly concerned about exactly what she's learned from my nemesis. "I was serious before about helping you get a scholarship. When I was growing up, my mom couldn't afford to send me to space camp, but one of my science teachers helped me fill in the forms and I got to go. Greatest experience of my life."

Charley looks at me like I've sprouted extra arms. "Umm, thanks, but really, it's okay."

"Oh, I get it," I tell her. "You're proud. I was the same way, but you shouldn't turn down a great opportunity just because you're embarrassed you can't afford it. If I'd done that, I sure wouldn't be here now."

"What are you two talking about?" Serafina asks, grabbing a donut out of the box.

"Space camp," I say. "I was telling Charley my mother couldn't afford to send me either."

Serafina narrows her eyes, looking utterly confused. "Umm, Charley's dad is a judge and her mom's a heart surgeon."

I freeze for a second, feeling my face heat up one degree at a time. "Oh. And they live in *your* building."

Nodding, Serafina says, "I told you I make bank."

"Right." Turning to Charley, I offer, "I'm sorry for assuming you couldn't afford it. It's just that I can't imagine anyone choosing *not* to go to space camp. It makes absolutely no sense to me at all."

Serafina and Charley both seem to be biting back laughter, while I stand here feeling like a complete idiot. Finally, I clear my throat. "Should we get this over with?"

SEVENTEEN

Serafina

While Waltraut talks to Ben, Charley whispers, "He's adorable. You should totally tap that."

"Charley!" I do my best to sound shocked, but the truth is, even though Ben annoys the snot out of me, I've totally been drooling over him. I like a smart guy who believes in bigger things. The only fly in the ointment is that he doesn't have an open mind as far as my scientific views are concerned, and that's a deal breaker.

"Seriously, Sera, you need a social life," my young friend persists.

"There will be no tapping," I tell her. "Not unless Ben transforms his personality and quits making derogatory comments about how I earn my livelihood. Plus, if you'll remember, I have a blind date this afternoon that your program set up for me."

"I didn't forget, and I'm totally jazzed to see how it goes. I just like Ben. He's super passionate about space. I mean, he seriously thinks the only reason people don't go to space camp is because they can't afford it. How cute is that?"

"You weren't offended that he thought you were poor?" I ask.

"Not in the least. I don't think the guy's a bigot. Well, actually, yes I do. He's bigoted against people who don't love astrophysics, but that's not a skin color issue."

I throw an arm around Charley. "You really are an exceptional human, you know that?"

Waltraut waves in my direction so I give my friend a final squeeze before disengaging. "Wish me luck. It looks like it's go-time."

I approach Waltraut and Ben with a smile. "You ready to rumble?" I ask jokingly.

Ben is standing so stiffly he appears to have been carved out of wood. He gives me a quick nod. "The sooner we start, the sooner it's over."

"Why don't you sit at your desk, Ben, and we'll start filming with Serafina walking in?"

Ben follows orders and I turn around and walk back to the doorway. I wait while Waltraut counts us down, "In five, four, three, two, we're rolling!"

"Hi, Ben! How are you today?" I stride into his office like I haven't been here for the last thirty minutes.

He hurries to stand. He's so tall he makes me feel petite. As I'm five feet nine inches, few men manage that. "I'm well, Serafina, thank you for asking. How are you?"

"I'm super excited to show you what I have in mind for your office. You ready to get started?"

"As ready as I'll ever be, I suppose." He isn't selling it at all.

I call out, "Charley, can you bring in the first set of

items?" Charley drags in a large box before hurrying out of the room.

I open it up and say, "I'm going to need you to keep an open mind, Ben." He looks like he's about to throw up. "Go sit down and close your eyes."

Once he's situated, I turn to the camera and whisper, "Check this out." Then I pull out a wall sticker of an opening into space. Stepping onto a chair, I hurry to unroll it and stick it to the ceiling in the corner of his office.

After several moments, Ben asks, "What exactly are you doing?"

"Open your eyes," I tell him.

As soon as he does, he looks around and says, "It looks like the same old room. What did you do?"

I point at the ceiling and watch as he opens his mouth, closes it, tilts his head back, all before looking back at me.

"Do you like it?" I ask. "It's designed to look like a hole in your ceiling that's showcasing a distant galaxy."

He nods his head once. "Not bad."

"I was worried you'd think it was too 'little boy's room' or something."

"Every astrophysicist was once a young person dreaming of outer space. If I'd had wall art like this as a child, I'm not sure I would have ever wanted to leave my room."

"Ben Williams, are you actually complimenting my design choice?"

"Just because I don't buy your zodiac nonsense doesn't mean I think you lack any talent whatsoever. Of course, this is only one thing. I haven't seen everything you've brought."

I look into the camera. "As far as compliments, he almost gave me one, didn't he? Quick, someone mark this day on the calendar, so we have proof!" Then I turn back to Ben. "I'm delighted you like it, and I can't wait until you see your brand new, fabulous workspace."

Stuffing his hands in the front pockets of his trousers, he shrugs. "To be honest, you could stick my desk next to the garbage bins outside. As long as I have power for my computer, I'll be productive."

Rolling my eyes, I ask, "How can someone so intelligent be so wrong?"

"Are you talking about yourself? Because I'm not wrong. Work is work. You set your mind to whatever task is before you until you complete it. I don't need trinkets or curtains or whatever else you've got in the boxes to make me a good astrophysicist."

"Okay, Dr. Stubborn. Get out of here so I can transform this place." Before he can protest, I add, "Shoo!"

"And cut," the director says. The moment the words leave her mouth, Ben turns to me. "You want me to leave and give you free rein?"

"Thought you didn't care..." I taunt.

Waltraut walks over to Ben and explains that the network decided he should leave me to it because it'll make for better television if there's a big reveal. "Also, it'll give us time to interview you so that you can explain to our audience what you do in a really in-depth way."

He glances back and forth between Waltraut and me, looking pretty rattled for someone who apparently could work between two stinky garbage bins. "Fine," he says before surreptitiously creeping toward the door.

Once Ben is gone, Charley and I hurry to pull in all

the boxes before releasing the blinds on the glass wall. Then we get busy transforming Dr. Ben's inner domain.

Waltraut pops her head back in. "You have two hours, can you do it?"

"I thought we only had forty-five minutes?" That's what Ben said anyway.

She shakes her head. "NASA approved Dr. Williams to tell us about some of the logistics of the Earth Two project. We probably won't be able to air much of it, but we're going to set him loose and let him talk about what he wants. I'll text you when we're about to come back."

Then she's gone; Charley and I get busy. The first thing we do is pull out all of the old furniture, then we assemble a replica of a mid-century modern boomerang desk in blond wood. The only thing we have to do is screw the legs on. Then we bring in a matching chair with a chartreuse seat cushion.

We don't have time to paint or anything, but I've picked out a great quote for the wall opposite Ben's desk. Charley gets busy putting the letter stickers up while I arrange the knickknacks I bought to make this room feel right for the Gemini physicist's psyche.

Nothing is more agitating than fluorescent lighting, so I've brought several lamps along. That way Ben will never need to turn on the overhead. Then I unpack the two posters I had framed for his walls. One of them is of Neil Armstrong standing on the moon with his trademark quote "That's one small step for man, one giant leap for mankind." The other is a picture of the Tardis from *Dr. Who*. The quote on that one is, "It's bigger on the inside ..." I'm gambling with the Tardis, but even if Dr. Pragmatic doesn't think time travel is possible, who doesn't love *Dr. Who*?

After assembling a sleek glass console table, I place two coffee table books about outer space on it, as well as a lamp and a couple *Star Trek* figurines — from the far superior first series. Charley is just finishing the quote on the wall when Waltraut texts that they're on their way back.

I take one last look at Ben's glorious new office, then Charley and I beat it out of there. We close the door for the big reveal.

When Ben approaches, he looks both excited and terrified. "You ready?" I ask him for the benefit of the camera. If it were up to me, I'd run in the other direction while he sees what I've done. If I know Ben like I think I'm starting to, even if he doesn't hate the changes I've made, he's going to pretend to just to get my goat. The key will be to stand by my design and let the American public decide if they like it or not.

Ben doesn't answer my question. Instead, he gestures with his hand for me to open the door. After I do so, he pushes past me — oh, wow, does he smell good — and stands in utter silence while he looks around the room. "It's ... It's ... It's ..."

"It's what?" I fold my arms, preparing myself for whatever insult he's going to sling at me.

"It's ... really nice."

You could knock me over with a feather. "Really?" I demand, not believing my ears. "You actually like it?"

"I do." His smile is so radiant, it totally transforms his face. Look at that face. He is ridiculously handsome, like he-should-be-on-the-cover-of-*GQ* handsome. "It has nothing to do with my date of birth, but you definitely managed to capture my interests and create an enjoyable room, so well done."

"You may think your enjoyment of this space has nothing to do with the fact that you're a Gemini, but I disagree. Everything about my décor choices is astrologically sound," I tell him. "The modern furniture and pops of color are known to keep the Gemini's mind open for enlightenment and creativity."

"I think most people in my field would like this," he says, not willing to throw me a bone.

"Did you see the quote on the wall?" I point to the area Charley worked on.

Ben's eyes practically glaze over as he turns his attention to it. He's quiet for so long, I start to get nervous that he hates it. But then he surprises me again, his voice quiet as he says, "That is my favorite Carl Sagan quote."

I look at the wall and ask, "Really? I picked it because I thought it paid tribute to both of our sciences."

"I can see how you might think so," he says. Then he recites, "Science is not only compatible with spirituality; it is a profound source of spirituality. — Carl Sagan."

I can't seem to leave well enough alone, so I ask, "Are we actually not going to fight about this?"

He shakes his head. "You've done a remarkable job, thank you."

"I've done a remarkable job for an airhead astrologer you mean?" I don't know why I keep poking the bear, but I do.

"You've done a remarkable job for anyone. This is truly a work of art."

Now I'm the one who's slack-jawed. What's happened to the Ben Williams I know and dislike?

EIGHTEEN

Ben

I stare around again, hardly believing how much more at home I feel in my office already. I'll add back my personal items, but now that I've seen it like this, I don't ever want my crappy old desk back. My eyes land on the *Star Trek* figurines and I almost burst out laughing, but I can't because it would mean admitting I do care about any of this.

There's some commotion outside and I see Waltraut talking to my team and gesturing for them to come see my new office. A moment later, they all appear at the doorway, peeking in and making "oohs" and "aahs."

"Come in," Serafina says with a warm smile. She moves closer to me to make room for the team, and I'm surprised when I don't shuffle away from her like I normally would in this type of situation. Instead, I stay put, feeling a warm pull toward her as she stands beside me. Taking a deep breath, I inhale her essence. I don't know if that's just her or if she sprayed something on, but that's a scent I could get used to.

Wait. What? That's not right. I hate her. Don't I?

Carla looks around before announcing, "This is so much better than how you had it, Ben. You should add back your cosmic crystal ball though. It would go really well next to the lamp."

No, no, no, no, no! Do not talk about my crystal ball! I freeze in place, not knowing how to answer that without looking like a fool. Is there a chance Serafina didn't catch that? I don't risk glancing at her in case she did.

Ewan gasps at the *Star Trek* figurines and says, "She took them out of the box?"

"Yup, that's fine," I tell him with a nervous chuckle.

"You said anyone who took your *Star Trek* collector's edition figurines out of their boxes would be fired on the spot."

"No, I didn't," I say, shaking my head. "You're thinking of your last boss maybe?"

"No, it was you, remember?" Alec says. "You said if anyone touches them, they'd be clearing out their desk by the end of the day and you didn't even care what they might be on the cusp of discovering."

Serafina lets out a loud laugh. "You are *so* busted!"

"They're mistaken. I would never have said anything like that because I don't have children's toys. This is a serious place where we do serious work."

She has tears rolling down her cheeks now.

Come on. It's not that funny.

"You *do* care!"

Rolling my eyes, I say, "I may have a few sentimental items, yes, but it's not like I *need* them."

"Really?" Carla asks, wrinkling up her nose. "Because

when you got that astronaut cell phone stand, you were giddy about it for a month."

"Astronaut cell phone stand?" Serafina asks, suddenly straightening up from her position of doubled over laughing.

"Oh, yeah," Carla says. "He's got a ton of nerd stuff. He emptied it all out this morning and shoved it all into a closet."

Clearing my throat, I manage, "Okay, well, thanks everyone for coming in to see the ... new décor, but you really need to get back to work, and so do I."

Their shoulders slump as they walk away, looking like I just canceled Christmas.

I turn to Serafina, feeling like a total ass. "Thanks again for stopping in and doing all of this. I really appreciate your efforts."

"You're welcome," she says, giving me far too wide of a grin for the situation. "Enjoy it."

Just like she's enjoying being right about me ...

"Cut! Great work, everyone," the director says. "Let's get out of here and let the good doctor get back to playing with his space toys."

Perfect. This is exactly how I hoped this day would turn out.

After my office empties out, I'm left with the last person I want to talk to right now. Turning to Serafina, I prepare myself for her to really let me have it about being a hypocrite, but instead she gives me a kind smile. "You know, Ben, I found my life got a whole lot easier when I decided to let people see who I really am."

She couldn't be more wrong about that. I stare at her for a second, memorizing the shape of her beautiful dark brown eyes, then nod. She's handing me an olive branch; I might as well take it. "Possibly less embarrassing too." Letting out a sigh, I add, "You must think I'm a total hypocrite."

She shakes her head. "No, I just think you're a very serious man doing very serious work, who badly needs people to take him seriously."

"You're right about that," I tell her, wishing I was the kind of guy who could just ask a woman like her out on a date.

Waltraut pokes her head back in and says, "Hey, you two, that was wonderful. Really great."

We both thank her, then she looks at me. "Oh, and terrific news! I was just talking with your boss, Dev, and he told me you're going to Florida next week for a conference. Guess who's going with you?"

Holy Captain Kirk. She better not mean who I think she means.

NINETEEN

Serafina

As we walk to the elevator, Waltraut tells me all about how she wants me to accompany Ben to the Kennedy Space Center next week. "While he has his meetings, we thought we'd film you in front of some of the famous rockets they have on display. Then, when he's free, we'll shoot some footage of the two of you together talking shop."

"Wow, okay. I guess that would be fine. How many days will I be gone?" I'm thinking about all the time this side gig is taking away from my real job — my app.

"Three days should do it." Then, like she's reading my mind, she says, "Think of this time as an investment in your future."

"Totally," I tell her. "I'm just about to start trials for the dating portion of my app and I'd like to be around in case there are any problems."

"Have you gone on that date you were talking about

on-air?" she asks as we step into the elevator to head down to the lobby.

"It's today," I tell her excitedly. "His name is Howard."

"How would you feel if we sent a camera along with you?"

A cold shudder washes over me. "Maybe next time. I want to make sure any kinks in the program are ironed out before showing our new feature off to the world."

"Let me know when that is," she tells me. "The network might even want to do a bigger segment on one of the nighttime magazine shows."

Oh. My. God. YES! That would be so amazing, but instead of saying so, I merely utter, "You bet."

I'm actually going straight from the Goddard Institute to a restaurant near the Columbia campus. Oddly, my date is with a Gemini who is a psychology professor there.

After putting Charley into a cab and sending her home, I hoof it the three blocks to Kale Cafe, a vegan restaurant that not surprisingly specializes in kale dishes. This was obviously Howard's choice as I would have suggested we go somewhere that is more comfort-food oriented.

The inside of the café feels like what I think an ashram would look like. The walls are painted with gorgeously bright, intricate patterns. The ceiling is high, giving the space a very open and airy feel, and the seating is actually bean bag-type chairs situated around coffee tables. It's super cool.

I spot a man that I assume is my date, based on the description he gave me online — a lanky intellectual with a ponytail and a goatee. While he's not exactly my physical type, I've vowed to keep an open mind, just as I hope the people who use this portion of my app will.

Veering through the bean bags and tables, I stop in front of him and ask, "Howard?"

He looks up at me and tilts his head. "Sarah?" As the owner of the app, I decided that even though secretiveness is not the best way to start a relationship, I should hide my identity, so my dates feel comfortable telling me what they really think of *Dating for Your Star Sign*.

"Hi," I tell him brightly. Then I plop down on the bean bag opposite him, trying to maintain my dignity while wearing a shorter skirt. "Do you come here often?" I giggle at asking such a cheesy question.

"Yes, I do." He isn't even smiling. "That's why I suggested it."

Oooookay. "So, how did you hear about the star sign app?" This guy is not giving off the warm fuzzies in any way, shape, or form.

"A friend of a friend suggested I give it a try. Being a man of science, I'm not really into the whole astrology thing."

"Oh." Disappointment shoots through me like a wicked case of food poisoning. "But you took the time to fill out the form, so you must not be totally closed down to the idea."

"Yeah, about that." He picks up a lavash cracker from the basket sitting on the table and breaks it in half. "My friend filled it out. I thought the whole 'date for your star sign' thing sounded pretty hokey."

Irritation quickly overtakes my previous optimism. "Are you even a Gemini?" I demand.

"Yeah, for whatever that's worth." He bites into the cracker and crunches it with his mouth open.

"Why exactly did you agree to sign up for this service if you're not into astrology?" I'm suddenly not even hungry and I never turn down the opportunity to eat.

"My friend said that chicks who believe in wacky stuff like the zodiac tend to be pretty easy to get into bed." He doesn't even seem to realize how offensive he's being. Or maybe he does and doesn't care.

"I assure you that it will take more than a bowl of barley and a kale salad to get me into the sack," I practically hiss.

"Really? I thought that was the whole point of this app." Crunch. Crunch. Crunch.

"It's a *dating app*. I'm pretty sure the whole point is finding someone to date." This guy is a total loser, but I'm here on a mission to gain data for my app so I'm not going to storm out like I would normally do.

"Aren't dating and sex the same thing?" He waves over the waiter before I can answer. When the server approaches, Howard says, "I'll have the alfalfa and eggplant falafel, heavy on the cashew butter."

The waiter writes down the order and asks me, "What would you like?"

I'm tempted to say world peace, or equality for all. Barring that, I wouldn't mind a cheeseburger, but none of those things are likely to happen here. "What kind of soup do you have?"

"We've got a chickpea curry or a Thai ginger broth with tofu and kale."

Yeah, no. "What kind of dessert do you have?"

"Our special today is coconut ice-cream served with a flourless dark chocolate cake."

"I'll have that," I tell him while handing over my menu.

For some reason, Howard feels the need to say, "That probably contains all of the calories you need for an entire day and enough fat grams for a week."

"Could be." Gah, I don't even want to talk to this guy. He clearly isn't the consumer I'm interested in.

"So, why are you doing this star sign thing, if not for sex?" he wants to know.

I start to fantasize about grabbing all the crackers out of the basket and crumbling them over Howard's head. "I'm interested in meeting a man that I like well enough to date." Duh.

"You gonna sleep with him?"

"Nope. I'm celibate," I straight out lie. I positively loathe this man and I've barely spent two minutes talking to him.

"Seriously?"

"Yeah, seriously."

"That's false advertising. Why didn't you put that on your profile?"

"Probably for the same reason you didn't write down skeezy sex addict." *Put that in your pipe, Howard.*

At this point, Howard decides to act like I'm not even there and he pulls out his phone and starts typing away. So I do the same. I text Charley.

LibraGrl: Abort! Something is wrong with our app. I'm on a date with the biggest loser in the free world.

BrainyBrain: Howard is a dud?

LibraGrl: Let's just say I'd rather date Homer Simpson.

BrainyBrain: Oh, no.

LibraGrl: He just told me that he's only using our app because he thinks women who are into astrology are easy.

BrainyBrain: Gross. Maybe you should just leave.

LibraGrl: I'm debating that right now. I just ordered dessert though and I'd hate to leave before eating it.

Howard decides to speak. "Just to be clear, we're not going to be having sex today, right?"

"Surely not with each other," I tell him.

He nods his head thoughtfully. "Gotcha. Would you mind leaving then? I mean, not to be rude, but a cute girl from one of my classes just walked in. I thought I'd ask her to join me."

Disgust does not begin to describe the degree of revulsion I feel for this man. Instead of answering him, I stand up, catch sight of the girl he's signaling, and I hurry to her side. When I reach her, I say, "Howard is having a herpes outbreak, so you definitely shouldn't sleep with him today."

Then I walk out of Kale with a sense of dread that the success of my dating app might be in serious jeopardy if fools like Howard sign up for it.

TWENTY

Ben

I stare at the profile I created on Serafina's ridiculous star sign app and take a deep breath. I've put in my real birthdate and information, but changed my last name. Mr. Spock hops up onto the couch next to me and lies down with his side pressed against my leg. "Hey, Spock. I'm about to debunk *Dating for Your Star Sign*. What do you think about that?"

He rubs his head on my pant leg, which I take as his way of telling me to go for it.

"Once I go on a couple of these ridiculous zodiac setups, I'm going to tell everyone on *Wake Up America!* that this star sign crap is a total hoax." I give him a scratch behind his ears. "While Serafina *seems* to be nice enough, she's duping people into paying her to 'live their star life' instead of figuring things out for themselves — which is the best part of living, if you ask me."

Spock closes his eyes and starts purring. "I see you agree with me."

I look back at my phone. My *mom* wants to sign up on this damn app which means she'll be one of the people who gets fooled into giving Serafina her money in exchange for nothing. Well, worse than nothing really, because she could be put in harm's way again if she picks another loser like Phil. He was the guy who took her car and all the money he could find.

I sigh, then hit the create profile button and sit back while the app pretends it's tabulating my answers.

A text comes in from Alec:

Dude, I got my first date on the app. Her name is Candy and we're going bowling on Saturday.

ObiWan: Sounds awful.

Alec: Are you serious? I'll be out on a date with an actual woman.

ObiWan: Just be sure you don't go back to her place and let her roofie you.

Alec: Dare to dream. I was matched with four women already, had conversations with two of them, and I have a date. All in one day. You should really look into this.

ObiWan: I'll take a pass.

Alec: That's such a Gemini thing to say.

ObiWan: ???

Alec: Just messing with you. I have no idea what that even means.

ObiWan: Hilarious. Not signing up for a dating app. Certainly not that one. I have no time for dating and certainly no time for crazies. I need to prepare for Florida.

The thought of going to Florida feels like a gut punch. I'll be meeting with the greatest minds in astronomy, but I have to bring along the very last person who has any business at the mothership — Serafina Lopez.

I open the PowerPoint presentation on Gliese 486 and get back to creating more slides. After about fifteen minutes, my phone pings and I see that I have a match on the *Star Sign* app. "Okay, here we go," I tell Mr. Spock.

The woman's name is Gwen. Apparently, she's thirty, has one rescue cat, and is a dentist. Huh. A dentist? On this stupid app? She's already sent me a message:

Gwen: Hi Ben, I saw your profile. Pretty cool that you work for NASA.

Weird. That's not usually the response women have when they find that out. Maybe she thinks I'm an astronaut. They're the only ones who get all the babes.

ObiWan: I'm not an astronaut.

Gwen: I know. Your profile says you're an astrophysicist.

ObiWan: I just wanted to make sure. A lot of people

are disappointed when they find out I'm not going to pilot a shuttle.

Gwen: Really? That's weird. Astronauts are just glorified pilots. It's the guys like you who really make things happen.

She's not wrong about that.

ObiWan: What type of dentistry do you practice?

Gwen: Pediatric. Most people find that strange because kids don't exactly love the dentist, but I really enjoy it.

Ha! She enjoys torturing children. See? The app *is* a failure. It set me up with a sadist.

ObiWan: Sounds challenging.

Gwen: That's what I love about it. I can usually calm them down and make it fun for them, which is actually very rewarding.

Hmm ... why does that disappoint me so much?

ObiWan: So you have a rescue cat?

Gwen: Yup. Miss Pearl (as in pearly whites. #lamedentistjokes)

ObiWan: I have a rescue cat named Mr. Spock so...

Gwen: Laughing emoji face. Maybe this crazy app works.

ObiWan: You think it's crazy too?

Gwen: Definitely. I'm not at all into astrology. My sister put my profile up and made me promise to go on at least two dates. She's getting married in a few weeks, and she wants to make sure I don't spend my life as a desperate spinster. (TMI? Did I scare you off?)

Okay, hang on. She's obviously intelligent, loves cats, is great with kids, and she's not into astrology. How is this possible? Am I chatting with a bot?

ObiWan: Not at all. I'm relieved actually because I think astrology is a bunch of hooey.

Gwen: Hooey?

ObiWan: You know, crap. Nonsense...

Gwen: Okay, if you use the word hooey, it means we have to meet.

ObiWan: What's the correlation?

Gwen: I've deduced that guys who use the word hooey aren't creepy weirdos.

ObiWan: Why, thank you. That's the nicest thing anyone's ever texted to me.

Gwen: Laughing face emoji. What are you doing tonight?

Am I about to go on a date?

ObiWan: Just getting caught up on some work, but it can wait.

I hit send before I can change my mind, then I watch as she's typing something back.

Gwen: I hope this doesn't sound too forward, but there's this little pub in Hell's Kitchen that I totally love. It's called The Salty Nuts. The owners are from Ireland and they're an absolute riot. You wouldn't want to meet me there for a drink, would you?

Huh. A drink. Much less pressure than an entire meal. Fun pub, so that cuts back on awkward silences because we can people watch. Wait. What am I thinking? I'm trying to prove my hypothesis that the app is garbage, not meet my soulmate.

ObiWan: Sure. Why not? Meet you there in an hour?

Gwen: Perfect! I have long blonde hair and I'll be in a pink sundress.

ObiWan: Okay. Tall, dark hair, and I'll be in a T-shirt and jeans.

Exactly forty-eight minutes later, I step up to the door of the little pub just as a pretty blonde in a pink dress gets out of a cab. I stop and stare at her, then we both do that thing where you point at each other with a questioning look before nodding. Finally, we both laugh and hold our hands out to shake.

"Ben," I offer.

"Gwen," she says with a smile. "Oh, Ben and Gwen. That's kind of cute."

I chuckle, then hold the door open for her. "Nice to meet you."

A tiny woman with shockingly red, spiky hair whizzes past us, saying, "Welcome to The Salty Nuts. I'm nut number one, Mary. Number two is my husband, Joe, behind the bar over there. Have a seat anywhere you like, and I'll be right there to take your order."

Gwen grins at her, then looks up at me. "See? Fun."

"Very." I follow Gwen to a booth near the back and we settle ourselves in while The Dubliners play over the speaker. The crowd joins in every time they get to the part about "the Irish Rover," and I can't help but feel oddly excited.

Mary arrives at our table. "Let me guess, first date?"

Gwen's head snaps back and she grins. "How'd you know?"

"Because he's being all polite-like, letting you pick the booth and go first. That's usually a good sign."

I give her a mock offended look, and say, "That makes it sound like you wouldn't expect me to always be a gentleman."

Mary leans toward me and confides, "You can't keep that up forever, love. Trust me. At some point, you'll need to just treat her like a regular person, or you'll go, dare I say it, nuts."

Her husband hurries by with a tray of beers and cuts in, "It's not the being polite that makes you nuts, it's the wife."

"You old poop!" Mary says, shaking her head. Turning back to us, she says, "White wine for the lady and a pint of ale for Mr. Polite here?"

"He's actually Dr. Polite," Gwen tells her.

Mary gives me an impressed nod. "A doctor, are you? How nice." Turning back to Gwen, she says, "Maybe don't let this one get away. A doctor's wife is a good life."

Gwen chuckles, and I add, "Actually, she's a dentist, so maybe I'd be the one with the good life."

"Oh, he wants to be a kept man," Mary tells Gwen. "Interesting ... I'll go get your drinks while you two plan the wedding."

She zips off, leaving us in an awkward silence. After a minute, I say, "So, your sister is getting married?"

Gwen nods. "Yup. To her high school sweetheart."

"That's nice," I say, wondering if it really is nice.

"It is. He's a great guy, and they really love each other."

"I've heard that helps in marriages."

Gwen laughs and we smile at each other. She is really pretty. And smart. So why don't I feel any spark here? I'd like to say it's because the app is crap, but who would have ever thought it would have set me up with a normal person?

The next hour flies by surprisingly fast. Gwen and I discover we have a lot in common, including the fact that we've both sacrificed love for our careers; we both would like to get married someday; and we both want to eventually end up in Florida (me for my work and her for the weather). I should "like her" like her, but I merely like her.

For some stupid reason, I find myself imagining what Serafina would answer to the questions I'm asking Gwen. How ridiculous is that? I've literally got the perfect woman sitting in front of me, and I can't stop thinking about the woman I love to hate. What is wrong with me?

Maybe I'm putting up a wall because I so badly need the app not to work? That must be it. It's called researcher bias. I believe the app won't work, so I'm creating conditions in which it won't. As a purist, I'm utterly disgusted by myself at the moment. There must be something wrong with Gwen. I just have to find out what it is ...

Two hours later, Mary comes by with the bill and tells us they're closing up for the night. Then she adds, "Being that you're still here, things must be going pretty well."

Gwen blushes and glances at me. Oh, no. She likes me. And I feel ... nothing. I smile back at her, pick my wallet up off the table, and pull my credit card out. "Let me get the drinks."

"I'll buy next time," she says with a shy smile.

"Sounds great." But only because next time I'll find out what's wrong with her so I can prove this app is bogus...

TWENTY-ONE

Serafina

"On paper, Howard looks like the perfect guy for you," Charley tells me while peeling a banana.

"My flesh is still crawling," I tell her as a full body shiver overtakes me. I swear that lunch yesterday — attempted lunch, rather — almost put me off my own app.

"How 'bout this guy?" She sits down on the couch next to me and points to the screen on her laptop. "According to our program, you and Chaz Parker are an ideal match."

I can't bring myself to look. "What does Chaz Parker do?"

"He's a chef. That's perfect for you. You know, because you love to eat and all."

"What kind of chef?" I demand. "With my luck he works at a restaurant that only serves endangered species."

"That's not even a thing," Charley scoffs. "It says he owns an Italian restaurant. Yum."

"What's his sign?"

"Aquarius," she says. "Which, according to you, is the best astrological match for a Libra woman."

I make a grabby motion at her to hand over her computer. Then I check out Chaz's bio. Thirty-three, native New Yorker, loves parties, the Mets, and street tacos. "He does sound pretty perfect."

I pick up my phone and fire off a quick message to Mr. Parker.

LibraGrl: Hi there, my name is Sarah. The Date for Your Star Sign app just pinged me with your info.

Chazzzzz: Cool, they sent me your deets too. I was busy at work when they came in, so I didn't have a chance to check it out. So, you're a Libra, huh?

LibraGrl: I am, and you're an Aquarius.

Chazzzzz: A match made in heaven! I'm not working tonight. Any chance you want to come down to my restaurant in Little Italy? I could make you dinner.

LibraGrl: I'd hate to make you go in on your day off.

Chazzzzz: I love my work, so it's no bother at all. Plus, I'd like to impress you with my culinary talents.

LibraGrl: I love being impressed. What time and where?

Chazzzzz: Noodle on Mulberry Street at six thirty?

LibraGrl: I'll be there. I'll be the tall brunette in the orange sundress. How will I know you?

Chazzzzz: I'll be the chef.

LibraGrl: Lol, good point. Okay, see you tonight, Chaz.

Chazzzzz: Looking forward to it.

"I'm going to let Chaz cook me supper tonight," I tell Charley. "What do you think about that?"

After taking another bite of her banana, she says, "Way to get back on the horse, Ser. I really think this might be your guy."

"Maybe, but I swear Professor Goatee really knocked me off my game." I yawn and tell her, "I think I'll take the rest of the afternoon off and have a nap. I've been burning the candle at both ends with our app work and *Wake Up America!* I'm going to need to clone myself if this keeps up."

"Go catch some zzz's," she tells me. "I'll work for a bit longer and then let myself out. Send me a text tonight and let me know how it's going."

I shoot her a thumbs up and drag myself off to bed. I'm pretty sure I'm unconscious before my head even hits the pillow. I sleep for three solid hours and only wake up because my phone starts pinging like a video game. I look at the screen to find a slew of incoming texts from Ben.

DrBananaPants: Our flight leaves at noon on Sunday. The show booked us at the Radisson at Cape Canaveral.

DrBananaPants: Make sure you bring comfortable shoes.

DrBananaPants: And make sure you bring sunscreen.

DrBananaPants: You might also want to bring a sun hat.

Apparently, my nap is over. I pick up my phone and text back:

LibraGrl: I'm from Florida. I know how to dress for the weather.

DrBananaPants: Oh, okay.

LibraGrl: What time is your first meeting on Monday?

DrBananaPants: Not until noon so I should be able to show you around for a bit first.

LibraGrl: I know my way around.

DrBananaPants: What? How?

LibraGrl: My family and I must have visited NASA at least a half dozen times over the years.

DrBananaPants: Really? You never mentioned that. Did you go to space camp?

LibraGrl: There's a lot you don't know about me, Ben. And no to space camp.

DrBananaPants: Waltraut said the car would pick you up at eight and then you'd pick me up. That ought to give us plenty of time.

LibraGrl: Sounds good. Are you bringing your Star Trek figurines? If so, I'll bring my Harry Potter Lego collection and we can have a battle on the plane.

DrBananaPants: Ha ha.

LibraGrl: Come on. That was funny. Anyway, I gotta book, I have a date tonight.

DrBananaPants: Really, with who?

LibraGrl: I'm pretty sure you don't know him.

DrBananaPants: How do you know if you don't tell me who he is?

LibraGrl: His name is Chaz and he's a chef. Do you know him?

DrBananaPants: No.

LibraGrl: There you go. I'll see you Sunday morning, Ben.

DrBananaPants: May the force be with you tonight.

LibraGrl: Nice Star Wars reference. See, you're not as much of a stick in the mud as you pretend to be.

DrBananaPants: I'm not a stick in the mud.

LibraGrl: Are too Dee too. But seriously, we'll have
plenty of time to fight on the plane. See you Sunday.

Lying in bed texting Ben fills me with a delicious
warmth. I bolt upright as soon as I think that. I chastise
myself, "Serafina Lopez, you cannot develop feelings for
the enemy. Can. Not. No."

I hurry to get up and get ready for my date with Chaz.
After showering and blowing my hair out, I take extra
pains with my makeup. I even use the mascara that makes
my eyes look huge. My orange dress pairs nicely with my
tanned skin, and when I look in the mirror, I give myself a
nod of approval. Eat your heart out, Eva Mendes.

I take a cab to Noodle, even though it's a distance I
would normally walk. After all that work, I don't want to
show up sweaty from my exertions. As good as I look, only
Eva can pull off the sweaty and sexy look. The restaurant
is packed, and I practically have to fight my way to the
hostess stand. "Hi there. I'm meeting Chaz Parker," I tell
the hostess.

"You must be Sarah." She's a busty blonde in a killer
halter dress that bears a remarkable resemblance to the
one Marilyn Monroe was famous for wearing in that
picture where her skirt is blowing up. "Please follow me.
I'll take you to Chaz's table."

We wind through a maze of tables and chairs and
bodies before she stops in front of a half-moon-shaped
booth. A truly gorgeous blond man stands up and asks,
"Sarah?"

"Hi," I practically yell to be heard over all the conversations going on around us.

Chef Hotty says, "Please, have a seat. Angelina here will grab us a bottle of Masciarelli Montepulciano d'Abruzzo. The twenty-sixteen," he tells her.

Once I'm seated across from him, he slides over so we're side-by-side. "It's the only way we're going to be able to hear each other," he tells me.

"You've got a pretty hopping place here."

"It's been like this since we opened five years ago." His smile is truly wondrous to behold with those pillowy soft-looking lips and dazzling white teeth. I might have hit the jackpot with this guy. Charley is a *genius*.

Angelina shows up again with the bottle of wine, but instead of opening it, she drops it in front of Chaz and says, "I'll let you open it." Then she leans in front of him and kisses him. It's not a friendly little peck either. She practically gives the guy a tonsillectomy and he doesn't push her away.

Whaaaa ...?

When she walks away, Chaz opens the wine and pours it for us. I can't just sit here and not say anything. I need to know what that crazy kiss was all about. I take a sip of my wine and blurt out, "Angelina seems nice."

"She's the best," he gushes. "I adore her."

"I got that impression."

Chaz raises his glass and toasts, "To the most beautiful woman here."

I take another sip in deference to my hotness. But even so, I feel super weird after what just went down with the hostess with the mostest. The waitress comes over, Chaz jumps up and says, "Sophia, I'm cooking tonight, so you don't need to take our order." Then, hand to God, he pulls her to his side and practically ravishes her right in front of me.

He knows I'm here, right?

I'm about to ask him what in the hell is going on when he says, "I'll go make our appetizers and be right back." Chaz adds a creepy wink for good measure. I sit back, trying to decide if I should make a run for it now, or get the free meal first. I'm pretty hungry, so I'm thinking free meal. Also, this wine is delicious so I'm going to revenge drink the whole bottle. When my date hasn't come back in twenty minutes, I stand up and search out the ladies' room.

That's when I spot Chaz kissing yet *another* woman. This one appears to be a customer. My date doesn't even see me, and that's when I realize I'm kind of loaded. I don't need to put up with this garbage in order to eat delicious Italian food. There is no way on God's green earth I'm going to stay here and be subjected to the antics of this man-whore. I don't even go back to the table; I just turn around and stagger out of Noodle, but not before saying, "I saw a rat near the ladies' room," to every table as I stride by.

Dear Lord, what exactly has happened to the dating world since I last participated in it?

TWENTY-TWO

Ben

"Mr. Spock hates it if you try to rub under his chin — his reaction is both immediate and severe, so I don't recommend it," I tell Alec, who has arrived in time for me to show him around before the car from *Wake Up America!* picks me up.

I needed someone to watch my beloved tabby, and since Alec has two female roommates that he's become less than enamored with, he happily agreed to stay at my place. The whole roommate thing was an attempt to meet more women but, much to his chagrin, the only members of the opposite sex Cheryl and Laya have introduced him to are their mothers.

I've been going over the rules for not getting clawed by Mr. Spock for the last ten minutes. I'm starting to worry Alec might be having second thoughts about staying here, so I tell him, "Something must have happened to Mr. Spock in his previous life to make him so sensitive."

Alec gives me a concerned look, then glances at Mr. Spock, who is perched on the back of the couch, eyeing him.

"Oh, also, he *really* doesn't like it when people sit on the right side of the couch. That's his spot, so don't forget."

"Got it. So, let me go over this again — no sudden movements, no shuffling my feet, no attempts at picking him up, no chin-scratching, no sitting on the left side of the couch—"

"Right side," I correct him.

"Damn. Okay," he answers. "He eats a can of Fancy Feast every morning and the dry food at night. And he likes his litter box cleaned every day or he'll poop on the rug."

"Exactly. You really can't blame him about that. If someone wanted you to walk around on your old feces, you probably wouldn't like it either."

"Probably not, but I also don't poop in a box so..."

Rolling my eyes, I say, "I get it. He's got very specific needs, but that's what comes with a rescue. The love he gives back is astronomical."

"How will I know he loves me? I'm guessing maybe he won't spit in my cereal?"

"Ha ha." I check my watch and add, "Everything's on the printout in case you forget. I also included the number for my hotel, so if you can't reach me on my cell for some reason, leave a message there."

"You know he's a cat, right?"

Ignoring the dig, I pick up my suitcase and open the front door. "Goodbye, buddy. I'll miss you."

"I'll ... miss you too?" Alec says.

"I was talking to Mr. Spock." I give my cat the *live*

long and prosper signal and he meows back. It's kind of our thing.

As soon as I reach the sidewalk, I find a spot in the shade to stay out of the already-blazing morning sun. July in Manhattan, with all the concrete soaking up the heat is ... well, hot. My phone pings and I assume it's Serafina running late. She probably read that Libras are always running late so she'll use that as an excuse. Oh, it's Gwen.

> Gwen: Have fun in Florida! I'll just be here wearing a clown nose while I scrape tiny teeth.

> ObiWan: Ha! Thanks. I hope you have a great week with the kidlets.

> Gwen: I will. Feel free to say no to what I'm about to ask, but I have to go to my sister's over-the-top engagement party next Saturday. You wouldn't want to be my plus-one, would you? Not in a 'we're getting serious' way, but in a 'I can't stand the thought of showing up alone because my Aunt June is going to try to hook me up with her chiropractor again' way.

> ObiWan: Chiropractor? Yeesh. The pseudo-doctors of the world.

> Gwen: Right?

I re-read her text, wondering if she really does mean it in as casual a way as I hope. She can't think we're a couple. Not after only one date and some flirty texts. But a family function ... hmm.

Wait. Actually, maybe this is the crazy I've been

assuming was coming. Best case scenario, she's made an album of what our children would look like already and she brings it along. I'm so going.

> ObiWan: I'll be there in the name of true medical professionals.

The town car pulls up next to me and I see Serafina in the backseat in a pair of sunglasses. She gives me a small wave as the driver jumps out and takes my bags to the trunk. I jog around to the other side and get in next to Serafina, my heart pounding a little. I hope it's because I'm going to astronomer mecca today, and not because I'm developing a crush on my travel companion.

"All set?" she asks me.

"Yup, you?"

"Hopefully. I didn't start packing until this morning, so I only had a few minutes," she says with a yawn.

I stare in disbelief. I've been packing for three days, complete with itemized lists of everything I'll need for every possible scenario including beachwear and a tuxedo (just in case I'm asked to attend a formal function with the top brass — I'm dreaming a little here, but the Boy Scouts are right about being prepared). "I like to make sure I'll be ready for all contingencies."

"You Geminis are crazy-organized. I figure if I forget something, I can always buy it there. They do have stores in Cape Canaveral." She leans her head back against the seat, looking sleepy. And really pretty. Very natural this morning without a lot of makeup and her hair back in a low ponytail. Not that it matters.

"How was your date?" I ask her, as the car makes a right onto some freeway that leads to an airport.

Serafina rolls her eyes. "Awful. I didn't even make it to the appetizers."

"Really?" I'm extremely pleased by this news, but only because it proves me right. "Something wrong with the app?"

"No, on paper, he was perfect for me. But there's no way the app could know the guy was a predatory narcissist who hits on anything that moves, even when he's on a date with another woman."

"Huh, maybe you should make that one of your questions," I say with a wry grin.

Chuckling, Serafina says, "Definitely." Then, putting on a businessperson voice, she adds, "Are you a creepy sex maniac who kisses and gropes multiple women while on a date?"

I let out a laugh, before remembering I'm not supposed to like her. I clear my throat, then say, "So, when we get to Kennedy, I don't know if it's such a good idea that you mention what you do for a living."

"Why not?"

"Because you probably won't find a very warm welcome there." Also, because I'm totally embarrassed to be arriving with a whackadoo, zodiac-loving ... gorgeous, gorgeous woman. *Stop it, brain! Just stop it already.*

"I'm sure I'm the last person you want to go to Cape Canaveral with," she says.

Is she reading my mind? God, I hope not. Then she'll know how attractive I find her. And how much I hate myself for it. Good thing I don't believe in mind readers either. "While the situation isn't ideal, I'm sure it'll work out."

She nods, looking slightly hurt, which oddly enough feels like a punch to the bean bags. "I actually don't even want to go," she replies. "As much as this is amazing publicity, I'm still ironing out the wrinkles on my dating app. It's a massive amount of work and the timing is way off because every day we stay in beta mode means I'm losing thousands of potential clients."

"What's wrong with the app?" Other than the obvious, of course, which is it's all based on nonsense.

She starts to say something, and I can tell she is about to confide in me, but then a look of realization that I'm the enemy crosses her face. "Just getting the algorithms exactly right. I don't want to launch unless I know it's one hundred percent ready."

"Smart," I tell her, wondering what's really going on. If I were her friend, I'd tell her the app set me up with someone who's pretty much perfect for me. But I'm not her friend. I'm the guy trying to save people from being bilked by her.

"It'll be nice to be in Florida again, though. Sun, fun, and sand in your drawers," she says with a smile.

"I'll do my best to skip the sand part. Do you miss it?"

"I miss my family," Serafina tells me, a wistful look on her face. "My parents, grandparents, and sisters all live in Miami, but I love New York. It's totally me — so much energy and movement."

I nod, thinking of how much I don't like it in the city. You can't see the stars. Not in a meaningful way. "I don't think New York is for me, long term. My dream is to join a team at the Cape someday."

"Really?"

"I'm meant to be in wide open spaces, where I can see the night sky at its finest."

"Sounds lonely." I can't tell if she's pitying me or not.

"Being alone doesn't necessarily mean being lonely," I

tell her. "Extroverts tend to believe we introverts have something wrong with us because we don't want to be the life of the party, or even attend the party. But the truth is, being alone gives me the space to theorize and imagine, which is my favorite way to spend time."

"I guess I never thought of it that way. I love being with people so much, I can't imagine so much solitude."

"A person can be happy on their own."

Serafina gives me a thoughtful look. "You don't want to end up with someone? Like in a romantic way?"

Warmth floods my face, and for some reason, I tell her, "I think I'd enjoy being married, but to someone who has her own life and doesn't mind it if I pack up my telescope and take off upstate for a night of stargazing once in a while."

"What if she wanted to go with you?" she asks.

I pause for a moment, imagining Serafina lying with me on a blanket and sipping hot toddies while we watched the Perseids meteor shower. The pleasantness of the image takes me by surprise. "I guess that wouldn't be so bad. Unless she was a real chatterbug, of course."

Serafina lets out a laugh. "A chatterbug?"

"Yeah, you know, someone who talks too much," I tell her, feeling slightly irritated that she's laughing at me.

"I know what it means. It's just that ... you have a distinct way of describing things."

"You mean the nerd way?"

Shaking her head, she says, "A unique and refreshing way."

Oh, well ... that wasn't the worst thing anyone's ever said to me. Maybe this trip won't be a total disaster after all...

TWENTY-THREE

Serafina

As a rule, I don't sleep well anywhere but in my own bed. The problem is, I barely slept at all last night because my thoughts have been spinning all weekend trying to figure out how to block creepers from using my app for their sleazy intentions. I'm not a prude. In fact, I hope people have *all* the fun when they meet their match, I just don't want anyone who isn't looking for a man-whore to wind up on a date with Howard or Chaz.

As Ben and I walk toward our row, he asks, "Do you want the window or aisle?"

Waltraut told us that she would spring for first class being that we're essentially hosts of the show. Had we only been guests, I'm assuming we would have had to fly economy — which is all I ever flew before my current app started doing so well.

"Window please," I tell him. "I'm going to lean my head against the wall and try to get a power nap in."

"Good for you," he says. "I've never been able to sleep on a plane."

I don't bother telling him that my chances of actual unconsciousness — short of someone hitting me over the head with a frying pan first — are pretty slim. I just throw my carry-on overhead and grab a blanket. Then I scoot into my seat.

Miracle of miracles, I'm sound asleep before the plane even takes off. I'm so comfortable and cozy that I totally forget where I am. In my sleepy haze, the only thing I'm aware of is that I'm in somebody's arms and, whoever he is, he smells positively edible! I love realistic dreams like these. Too bad they're so few and far between.

I float along blissfully in the ether until a truly naughty dream captures my attention. I'm about to let my fingers investigate the man holding me, when I'm rudely jostled awake. I hear someone loudly exclaim, "Whoa!" before the body beneath me goes all rigid.

My eyes open slowly, and I realize I'm not alone in bed having an awesome dream. Reality hits me like a train. I'm on a flight to Orlando. Being that I fell asleep sitting next to Ben, the chances are pretty high that he's the one I'm lying on. Gah! How do I ease away from him and still keep my dignity?

Before I can pretend I'm still sleeping and adjust myself away from him, he says, "I know you're awake."

Drat! I sit up slowly and blink my eyes repeatedly. "Ben? Where are we?" Playing dumb is my only option if I want to maintain decorum. I *was* basically groping the man.

"We're on a plane on our way to Florida. Our density altitude just shifted."

Blink, blink, blink. God, he's cute with that wavy dark

hair and mossy green eyes. When I don't respond, he says, "We hit an air pocket."

"I know what density altitude is," I tell him (which isn't entirely true, but a girl's got to save face, especially when she's feeling extra stupid).

After clearing his throat, Ben shifts away from me. "I wasn't trying to be condescending."

"How long before we get there?" I ask.

He points to the screen on the seat in front of him that shows the plane flying over a map. "We should start our descent at any time."

And then, like magic, the pilot comes over the intercom and says, "Ladies and gentlemen, welcome to Florida. The weather today is a balmy 89 degrees with a light wind. We're about to start our descent into Orlando International Airport, so if you'll please remain seated with your seatbelts fastened, we'll be landing in about ten minutes."

"You had a nice nap," Ben says while avoiding all eye contact. He seems kind of nervous, which is no surprise as I was practically molesting him.

"I didn't think I'd really fall asleep," I tell him while shifting around to make sure my seat is up. "I'm sorry about, well, you know..." I indicate his lap area.

"No problem." He still won't look at me.

Awkward.

The plane starts a righteous rattle on its way down and I notice that Ben is white knuckling it. "You okay?" I ask.

"Yup." He doesn't elaborate.

By the time we land, he looks like he just rode on Space Mountain standing up. "Ben," I reach out and touch his arm which causes him to jump.

"I'm not the world's best flyer," he confesses. "It's why I never tried to become an astronaut myself."

"Good call," I tell him. "You do realize that air travel is safer than driving in a car, though, right?"

"Yeah, and most people don't die when they parachute out of planes either, but I'm not standing in line to do that."

We sit still while the passengers clear out around us. I like knowing that Ben has fears. I don't take pleasure in the fact that he's afraid of something, but he seems somehow more human now that I know he's vulnerable to something.

As soon as we leave the plane, Ben starts to act like himself again. He stands straight and tall and seems to be all business. "I forgot to ask Waltraut if they were sending a car to pick us up," I tell him.

"I assume they will."

Pulling out my phone, I send Waltraut a quick text. Then I follow Ben as he power-walks through the airport. "Let's head to baggage claim. That's usually where the drivers are waiting with their signs."

I'm about to ask him to slow down when we get to the automatic walkway. Once it ends, he's back to sprinting. I don't treat walking like it's an Olympic event, so I'm glad when we arrive at baggage claim. Looking around, we don't see anyone holding signs with our names.

"We can take a cab," I tell Ben.

Before he can answer, I hear someone call out, "Serafina! Over here!!"

No, it can't be ...

I turn around and see my grandmother coming at me as fast as her nearly eighty-year-old legs will carry her.

"Abuela?" I ask in total shock. "What are you doing here?"

Her eyes are sparkling like a kid on Christmas morning. "Your mamá told us when you were landing so Abuelo and I decided to pick you up."

"You live over two hundred miles from here," I say. It's not like I'm not totally thrilled to see her, but she's the last person I expected.

"Don't I know it. Your abuelo almost got us killed four times. The man thinks he doesn't have to signal or wait for an opening when he wants to switch lanes. It's like he's driving us to see Jesus himself."

Dear God. "I hope you're not going home today," I tell her.

I see her eyeing Ben like he's a popsicle and she's been sunbathing on the equator. "Hello, Dr. Banana Pants," she says with a wink. "I love watching you and my granddaughter on television."

"Um, hi there, Mrs. Lopez?" Ben says awkwardly. My abuela seriously looks like she's about to throw all five feet of herself at Ben.

"You can call me Maria," she says, really rolling the 'r' in her name. Then she looks at me and adds, "Abuelo and I thought we'd stay with you while you are here."

"How nice! Were you able to get a room in the same hotel?"

"Of course," she brushes her palms across each other. "Because we're staying in your room with you!"

What?! I force a smile and manage, "I hope I have a room with two beds then."

"We can put Abuelo on a rollaway, if not."

My phone pings before I can say anything else. It's a text from Waltraut.

Waltraut: Hey, sorry, just got your message. Our intern totally messed up on our end. Looks like he didn't order a car to pick you up and he couldn't get two rooms at the hotel, so he booked you and Ben into a suite. There are two bedrooms and two baths though, so that shouldn't be a problem, right?

Oh. My. God. While that would probably be okay if it was just the two of us, I have no idea how it's going to work with my grandparents staying with us. How in the world am I going to break this to Ben?

TWENTY-FOUR

Ben

If I thought space travel sounded daunting, it's got nothing on being in the backseat while Lorenzo Lopez is at the wheel. He swerves wildly and weaves in and out of traffic as though he's Luke Skywalker fighting the Death Star. By the time we get off the freeway, I'm horribly nauseated and my muscles are contracted so tightly, I'm pretty sure I'm moments away from having a seizure of some kind.

I cannot wait to get to my room to lie down for a while so my body can recalibrate back to my normal *not about to die* setting. Serafina, who is sitting next to me, seems to find the whole thing utterly amusing. She didn't even freak out when her abuelo almost side-swiped a semi. She did, however, laugh until tears were sliding down her cheeks because I screamed (in a pitch so high, I had no idea I could reach it), followed by yelling, "We're all going to die!"

Before that little moment, I was actually feeling a bit

sorry for Serafina. Having to share a hotel room with your grandparents sounds like a horror. Not that I didn't love my Grammy and Poppy, because I definitely did. They were wonderful, and if they were still alive, I'd happily share everything I have with them. But still, in my humble opinion, hotel rooms are barely big enough for one.

Maria has been peppering me with questions since we pulled away from the terminal.

"Do you have a girlfriend?"

"No."

"Why not?"

"I'm very busy."

"With what?"

"My job."

"You silly young people, worrying about your careers so much. This one is the same way," she says, pointing to Serafina. "I always tell her, 'Sera, your job won't keep you warm at night or feed you soup when you're sick.'"

Serafina nods as if to mean *yup, she tells me that ALL the time.*

I smile at Maria, who is basically sitting backwards in her seat while her husband accelerates to stop a motor-cycle from cutting into our lane. "But if you make enough money, you can afford to adequately heat your home and you can *order* in soup."

Maria gives me a placating look. She's not buying it.

"Have you ever been married?"

"No."

"Why not?"

"Same answer as before. I'm busy."

More head shaking. "How many siblings do you have?"

"None."

"Why didn't your parents give you any brothers and sisters?"

"My dad ran out on us and my mom had nothing but bad luck with men after that."

"What kind of father runs out on his son?" Maria gasps.

"A bad one."

Serafina interrupts, "Abuela, maybe that's enough questions for now, okay?"

"Why? This is how I get to know people."

"Not everyone feels comfortable sharing details about their personal lives," she says. "Oh, there's our hotel!"

Lorenzo slams on the brakes, not caring one iota that there are dozens of cars behind us.

"Right there," Maria tells him, reaching across his face to point.

He guns it and makes a left into oncoming traffic. I close my eyes and wince, waiting for the impact of the UPS truck that's about to end my life. But then, I feel Serafina patting me on the hand. "It's okay. We made it."

I open one eye just in time to see Lorenzo pull the car into a stall, then he hits the brakes, causing Serafina and me to nearly faceplant into the seat backs. Although tiny and seemingly frail, Maria must have abs of steel because she didn't budge.

Once we're out of the car, I forego kissing the pavement because that would not only be disgusting, but pretty embarrassing. I do thank my lucky stars that I've thus far survived today and promise myself I'll never get into a vehicle with that man again. Ever. After pulling the suitcases out of the trunk, I smile at Serafina's grandparents. "Thank you so much for the ride. It was lovely meeting you both."

"You're welcome," Lorenzo says.

I smile down at Serafina, and continue, "Let's text each other later to set up a time to leave for Kennedy. Have a wonderful night getting caught up."

Nuts. I forgot they have to check in, too. As they all trail behind me to the entrance, I realize I shouldn't have made such a deal about saying goodbye to them in the parking lot.

Serafina tells her grandparents to go have a seat on one of the palm tree print couches while she checks them in. Then she hurries to stand next to me in line.

"I hope you're not a line cutter," I tease. "Because I got here first."

"Ha! Hardly," she tells me. "So, here's the thing..."

She pauses long enough for me to get a little nervous which is not what I need after the day I've had. Instead of saying anything, she hands me her phone, then waits while I read. "No ... nononononononono. This is completely unacceptable. I don't have roommates. Ever. No. Not happening."

I hand her back her phone and see she's wearing an apologetic expression. "I had no idea they were coming."

"I gathered that." I rub the bridge of my nose under my glasses. "No matter. I'll just sort it out at the desk. There's no way the hotel is sold out. And even if they are, I'm sure I can find a room somewhere."

"Right," Serafina says. "That would be great, actually, because then I can have my own bedroom and bathroom and so can my grandparents."

"Next," the woman behind the desk barks. She's got the darkest tan I've ever seen which is quite shocking against her bleached hair.

I have to force myself not to look surprised as I step

up. I smile and glance down at her name tag. "Hello, Bonnie. I'm Ben Williams and this is Serafina Lopez. We're work colleagues, sort of, and I'm afraid there's been a mix-up. We've been put into the same suite."

"I'm afraid there's nothing I can do about that. We're completely booked through the week."

I pause and blink a couple of times, then smile. "No problem. Can you find me a room at a hotel nearby?"

Shaking her head, Bonnie says, "There's a huge cosmetic surgery convention happening through Friday. They've booked every room in the city." Glancing at Serafina, she lowers her voice, "I gave one of the docs a free upgrade. In exchange, he's gonna pump my face so full of fillers, I won't be able to move it for months." She sounds positively giddy.

I stare at her in disbelief, trying to figure out what the hell to do now. I decide to turn on the charm, not that I'm all that practiced in such a maneuver. Leaning one elbow on the counter, I smile. "Bonnie, I know you have to tell *most* people there's no room at the inn, but between you and me, there's got to be something." I pull a twenty out of my pocket and slide it across the counter. "How about if you just check again?"

"Are you trying to bribe me?" Bonnie asks.

"Not at all," I tell her. "I found that on the floor."

Bonnie grabs the money and puts it in her bra before saying, "It's like I told you before — we don't have any rooms. Do you want the one you're already booked into or not? Because if not, I bet I could barter the one you had for a nice mole removal. I've got something growing on my shoulder that does not look healthy."

She's actually taking the money and saying no? I thought New Yorkers were tough.

Sera takes over with, "We definitely need the suite we have."

Turning around, I see Maria and Lorenzo grinning at us. They wave excitedly at me and I offer them a weak smile in return. So to recount what's happening, I'm about to go to one of the most important conferences of my life with an astrologer and now will be bunking with her and her grandparents for two nights. At least it can't get any worse. Right?

TWENTY-FIVE

Serafina

"A suite!" Abuela gushes as we walk into our airy ocean-view room on the third floor. "How exciting!"

Scooting her out of the way, my grandfather hurries past in the direction of the bedrooms mumbling, "I shouldn't have had that pizza at lunch."

"Told you." Abuela starts to follow him. "We'll take this room and you kids can have the other one." She opens her mouth and gives us an exaggerated wink, before adding, "It's a good thing Renzo and I are hard of hearing, huh?"

Oh no, she didn't. "Abuela, Ben and I are work colleagues. We aren't a couple."

"No time like the present." She winks again. This is so embarrassing.

"I think we should call down to the front desk for that rollaway. That way you can sleep with me and Abuelo can sleep on a rollaway." I hurry to pick up the phone and punch in zero for the operator. After chatting with Bonnie again, I discover that all the cots have already been claimed. "No beds," I tell Abuelo and Ben who are both staring at me expectantly as I hang up the phone.

Abuela waves her hand in front of her face. "We don't need one. Renzo can sleep with Ben and I'll sleep with you."

Ben bolts toward the love seat and lifts the cushions. Why didn't I think of that? I bet it's a sleeper. The look of disappointment on his face disabuses me of that notion.

"How about if Abuelo sleeps on the loveseat?" I ask, already knowing the answer is going to be a no. He's short, but he's also in his eighties so...

My grandmother shakes her head like she's trying to dislodge an earwig. "His back would go out. The man needs a bed." I should take one for the team and say that I'll take the love seat, but there's no way I'd ever sleep. I'm a sprawler as my little nap on the airplane so clearly indicated. I'd fall off in no time.

Ben finally grumbles, "He can sleep with me." Then he takes off for the room my grandfather walked into. I hear him exclaim, "Urgh! What's that smell?"

Abuela looks sheepish when she tells me, "Abuelo has been suffering from some digestive issues. We're pretty sure he's lactose intolerant, but he loves his dairy so much he refuses to go to the doctor and have my diagnosis confirmed."

Ben immediately comes out of his room and stares at me with a murderous glare. I shoot him an apologetic expression then tell my grandmother to go into our room and get settled.

She looks between the two of us and makes a *tsk*ing sound. "If the two of you would just accept that you want to do the horizontal cha cha, there wouldn't be a problem."

"Abuela!" I practically shout at her.

"What? The whole world sees how the two of you go at it on television. Passion like that would burn up the sheets." She walks into the other bedroom leaving me and Ben to deal with the fallout of such a statement.

"I'm so sorry," I tell Ben. "I'll make it up to you, somehow."

"How do you suggest doing that?" I can't tell if his tone is flirtatious or angry. Maybe both?

"Well, I'd normally offer to give you a free natal chart, but I don't think that would be your thing."

"No, it wouldn't." That's all he says but he's glaring at me so intensely I take an involuntary step backwards.

"I'll pay for all your meals while we're here," I suggest.

"We have a per diem for that."

"Okay, fine," I concede. "I'll owe you one. Whatever you want, you have a chit to call in at any time."

He glances up at the ceiling as though considering it, then looks back at me with a half-smile that makes me nervous. "As long as that ticket comes with no restrictions..."

I don't know whether to be scared or excited by the expression on his face. Scared, right? Like he'll probably say I have to renounce my beliefs on live TV. I should say no. But I *am* about to make the man sleep with my intestinally-challenged grandfather for the next couple of nights.

I nod my head. "Fine. What do you say we unpack and then go downstairs for supper? It must be six o'clock and I'm getting hungry."

Ben turns and walks away from me, which I take to mean that we have a bargain. I hurry after my grandmother with thoughts of begging her to please quit being so salacious with her suggestions, but when I open the door to our bedroom, I discover her sound asleep on the bed.

After splashing some cold water on my face, I go back out to the living room to wait for Ben, but he's already sitting on one of the armchairs. "That was fast," I tell him.

He looks up at me with a haunted if not horrified expression. "Your grandfather is taking a nap and he's practically naked."

"What?" *Dear God.*

"He has his underwear on, but that's all. Also, the room is so odiferous, I'm pretty sure the oxygen level is depleted beyond safe levels."

"I'm going to give my parents an earful about this," I tell him. Then, hoping to find the silver lining, I add, "At least they didn't come, too."

The look of terror on Ben's face has me laughing out loud. "Perish the thought!"

"Are you close with your grandparents?" I ask.

He shakes his head. "I don't know my dad's parents and my mom's both died when I was in college. You're lucky yours are still around."

"I am. I just wish I saw them more often."

"Why don't you move back to Florida?" he asks while opening the door leading to the hallway.

"I love New York," I tell him while following behind. "Plus, I figure I'll probably move back to Miami when I have kids. I want my children to grow up around lots of family."

"That's a nice thought." He sounds pensive.

We remain quiet, both of us ostensibly lost in our own thoughts until we are back on the first floor. We follow signs for the restaurant and a hostess leads us out onto a patio that looks out onto a tropical courtyard. She sets our menus down at a table for two in the corner, then lights the candle on the table, and tells us our server will be right with us. I stare around at the palm trees swaying against the darkening sky and breathe in the scent of tropical air. This would be really romantic if I weren't here with a man who can't stand the sight of me.

The waiter shows up as the hostess leaves. "Good evening. Can I get you a drink to start off with?"

Ben nods. "Yes, please. I'm thinking of getting a Corona." Glancing at me, he adds, "Unless you want to split a bottle of wine."

"You have beer. I'm all about the piña coladas when I'm in Florida," I tell him.

The waiter, whose name tag says Ricardo, tells us he'll be right back with our drinks, then leaves us alone again.

Ben gives me a little grin. "Piña colada? Is that a Libra thing or a girl missing her home state thing?"

I stare at him for a second, wondering if he's making fun of me, but the look on his face is relaxed and ... well, almost teasing, so I decide he's being sincere. "What if I said both?"

"I'd say that makes sense."

"You're a nice man, Ben," I tell him before I can think better of it.

He looks up from his menu with a look of total surprise. "That's a first."

"I know it might seem that I love arguing with you, and while you definitely do make me crazy with your rigid views of science, you're also a really good guy. I first suspected it when I saw you with Charley, but today confirmed it. I don't think most men would have agreed to sleep with my grandfather."

He shrugs. "What other choice did I have?"

"You could have sent them back to Miami," I tell him.

"I'd have to be pretty heartless to do that. Especially after they drove all this way to see you."

"But still. It's not your problem and you're here for work, so it would have been understandable."

"If there's one thing life has taught me, it's to roll with the punches," he says, sitting back in his chair.

"Is that because of your father taking off?"

"Among other things," he says with a sigh. "My father wasn't the last loser my mom fell in love with, to be honest. And each one left her worse off than she was before. It didn't make for the most stable of childhoods."

"I'm sorry," I tell him, imagining him as a much smaller version of himself — still with glasses, maybe in *Star Wars* jammies that are a little too short for his long legs. Suddenly, I have a clear view of why he has such a crusty exterior. "That must have been a rough way to grow up."

He waves off my pity. "It was a long time ago and I'm a better man for having gone through it."

"How so?"

"Because I've learned to read people, which has been exceedingly valuable in life," Ben says with a firm nod. "Also, I do my best to protect my mom from similar situations, even though it's difficult now that I live so far away."

"Where is she?" I ask, realizing I don't know anything about the man who's about to spend the night with my abuelo.

"Astoria, Oregon. Where I grew up."

The waiter comes by with our drinks. "Are you ready to order?"

Ben looks slightly surprised at the question. "We completely forgot to open our menus."

"No worries," Ricardo says. "I'll come back in a few."

The entire time we study our menus, my body is feeling all sorts of light, airy, wonderfully happy feelings. I have to fight the urge to lean across the table and slip my fingers through Ben's. Those are some manly hands. The kind I wouldn't mind feeling on my skin. Actually, I wouldn't mind sliding in next to him and crawling onto his lap.

Ben snaps me out of my reveries by closing his menu and saying, "I'm going for the cheeseburger and fries. I figure after surviving the ride from the airport, I should let myself indulge."

I wince a little, then chuckle. "Abuelo's friends call him Mario Andretti Lopez."

"About that. I don't think your grandfather should be allowed to drive anymore. Not just for his sake, but for the welfare of everyone else on the road."

"To be fair, he's driven like that ever since I was a kid and he's never been in an accident."

"That's astonishing. But maybe your grandmother should take over."

"I don't think so," I tell him. "Abuela has been the cause of three accidents. When she went to have her license renewed, they made her take a driving test and they refused to pass her."

The look on his face is one of concern. "Let's make sure we do all the driving while we're here. Maybe we should rent a car."

A wave of admiration washes over me. "That's really kind of you, Ben."

"It's nothing anyone who doesn't want to die wouldn't do," he answers with a wry smile. Then, he lifts his beer and says, "A toast — may you live as long as you want, and never want as long as you live." We each have a sip of our drinks and then Ben says, "I heard that the other night at a crazy little Irish pub."

"Sounds like a fun place."

"It was. We should go sometime." He looks slightly panicked, then says, "I mean ... if we needed to have another work meeting or something."

"Right. I knew what you meant," I say, feeling totally disappointed he didn't mean it as a date.

A crazy thought pops into my head that shakes me to the core. Ben Williams is a super sweet Gemini man which, astrologically speaking, is a really good match for me. The truth is that I find him enormously attractive, and now that I see how nice he is with my grandparents, I'm even more sold on him. Could something happen between me and Ben? Is it possible that he might be interested in me too?

TWENTY-SIX

Ben

I stand in the doorway of my bedroom, listening to the jackhammer-like snoring coming from my bedmate. I don't think he's gotten up since we left for dinner because he's still in his underwear, out cold on top of the covers. It's late and I should be tired after such a long day and three beers over a lingering dinner with Serafina, but I'm not. I'm absolutely wired right now.

Between the stench and the snoring, there's no way I can sleep in the same room as Serafina's grandfather. I grab my overnight bag and take it into the bathroom, then I have a quick shower and brush my teeth, doing my best to be as quiet as possible. (Although Lorenzo probably can't hear anything over the sound emanating from his throat.)

Sneaking over to the bed, I get my pillow. In the hall, I see a small closet, which has blankets and extra pillows in it. I grab a couple of blankets to make myself a bed on the living room floor. I'm pretty sure I haven't slept on the ground since I was a kid, and while it won't be comfortable, at least it'll be quiet.

As soon as I stretch out, my mind starts to swirl with thoughts of Serafina. I hate to admit it, but I was thoroughly enjoying her nap on the airplane. The warmth and the smell of her was absolutely mesmerizing. The day's events click through my brain like photos on a slideshow and each one is of her smiling or laughing.

Nuts. I have feelings for her. Real ones. Which is *not at all* convenient because not only are we work colleagues, we're also polar opposites when it comes to our very core beliefs. I cannot let myself entertain the thought of anything happening between us. Even if she is one of the loveliest women I've ever met. It's just that our verbal sparring is ... well ... it's like foreplay. Maria wasn't wrong about the spark between us. We're like gasoline and a match.

I grab my phone off the coffee table to distract myself and see I have a few messages waiting.

Mom: Hi, Peanut, how was your flight? Are you checked into your hotel? Love you!

Alec: So? How's it going in mecca? Did you go straight to Kennedy or are you waiting for tomorrow? Also, anything happening with you and Serafina? Sometimes those tropical locations can really get women in the mood, if you know what I mean...

Gwen: Hi Ben, I hope you're having a great trip. I just wanted to thank you for agreeing to come with me to the party. My aunt has already sent me a photo of her

chiropractor and ... yikes. Top knot and scraggly
beard. You're totally my hero.

I'm about to answer when I notice some movement
down the hall. I lift my head up and see Serafina coming
toward me with a pillow. She's dressed in a nightgown
that cuts off just above her knees and she's got a sleeping
mask resting on her forehead. She stops short when she
sees me. "Oh, darn. You beat me to it."

"Does Maria snore too?"

"It's like someone's sawing down a redwood in there."
She shifts awkwardly before saying, "I'll see if I can get
her to turn over. I don't want to crowd you."

"No, that's okay," I tell her. "You can share the floor if
you like. I emptied out the closet to build my little nest
here." Suddenly I realize I'm basically asking her to sleep
with me. "Or you can take the love seat? Or take some of
the blankets and make your own bed somewhere ... or you
can have this one and I can go somewhere else?" I'm
rambling, but I can't seem to help myself.

Tucking her bottom lip between her teeth, Serafina
holds back a laugh. "It's okay, Ben. I'm not going to think
you're some sort of player who's trying to get me into
bed."

"Good because I'm not in any way a player," I tell her.
"Also, I have no interest in sleeping with you. None at
all."

Liar, liar, pants on fire.

"Glad we got that cleared up," she says, walking over
and dropping her pillow next to mine.

"Good, yes, me too," I tell her, trying not to watch her
as she lowers herself onto the floor and tucks herself in.

Holy protons, for all practical purposes, Serafina and

I are in bed together, and I'm in nothing more than my boxers. I should have at least worn a T-shirt, but I can't stand to sleep in one. Also, I wasn't expecting company. But I definitely have company now. I'm in bed with a beautiful, highly intelligent woman, and my whole body responds to the thought.

I risk a glance and see that Serafina's curled up with her back to me, creating a rather alluring outline in the moonlight. A wave of longing, so strong it rivals the kind you feel as a teenager, comes over me. What was I doing before she got here? Oh, yeah, I was about to text that dentist person back. What's her name again?

Oh, God, it doesn't matter, does it? Because I clearly can't string her along when I'm having feelings for another woman. I lie on my back, staring at the ceiling fan as it slowly spins above my head, telling myself to just go to sleep. Nothing is going to happen, nor should it for many good reasons. Albeit none of which I can think of at the moment.

I should make a list of all the reasons we shouldn't pursue a relationship with one another. That should help focus my attention on something other than how good she smells.

Number one: Her grandparents went to sleep at six p.m., which means they'll likely be up for breakfast in about, what? An hour? What if one of them catches us and has a heart attack and dies?

Good, Ben. Thinking about old people having heart attacks is not sexy. Keep that up.

Number two: The whole colleague thing. Our situation is complicated enough. I don't need to add to it.

Number three: She believes in astrology. That should

probably have been number one, really, now that I think about it ...

Two hours later, I'm still wide awake, listening to the calming rhythm of Serafina's breathing. It's so hypnotic it should have lulled me right to sleep, but after thinking of twenty-nine reasons we shouldn't date (to be honest, twenty-four of them were pretty lame, like "she may not even like cats"), she rolled over and slung her leg over my midsection and her arm over my chest. She's been snuggled against me for a long time, while I lie here facing the awful truth. I'm quite possibly in love with this woman. Deeply, ridiculously, horribly, wonderfully, nonsensically in love with her. And I can't think of anything worse.

TWENTY-SEVEN

Serafina

I'm having the most arousing dream I've ever had in my life. Like, I can totally feel the guy next to me and smell the lingering scent of his aftershave. In my fantasy, my arms and legs are wrapped around him like he's a tree and I'm a bear trying to climb him. I'm fully invested in this amazing sensation, when I hear, "Um, Serafina ..."

Oh my, the guy I'm trying to climb is Ben! If I were conscious, I totally wouldn't let myself go there, but because this is a dream, all reticence is off the table. Even though I've got the hots for my co-host but would never come on to him in real life, he never has to know what I dream about. "Ben ..." I purr in response. Then I find his earlobe with my teeth and give it a playful tug.

His neck smells warm and spicy. I feel my body move, so I'm straddling him, giving me better access. The groan beneath me affirms that Dream Ben is just as into this as I am. Suddenly, I'm so hot it feels like flames are licking at me. Reaching down, I grab the hem of my nightgown and pull it over my head. Woohoo, I am about to have the most realistic sex dream ever!

That is until somewhere in the deep recesses of my brain, I hear, "Ride that bull!"

Is that my abuela? Gah, the craziness of dreams never ceases to amaze me. As I try to ignore the cheers from the peanut gallery, I hear my grandfather scream, "Dios mio! I'm blind!"

The body I'm pinning to the ground jolts upright and I'm thrown to the side with a sharp thud. Ow, I don't like this dream anymore. I force my eyes open, hoping the pain in my elbow will stop once I'm awake.

I am a person of many words. I'm a talker, an engager of people. As a rule, I love to be the center of attention. That all changes as soon as I see Ben and both of my grandparents staring at me. Holy hell, I wasn't dreaming, I was in fact in the process of "tapping that" with an audience. There are no words. None.

Yet, when no one says anything, I feel the need to explain, "I was dreaming."

Abuela is nodding her head, shrugging her eyebrows, and winking all at the same time. If I didn't know her better, I would guess she was having a stroke. "I'll move in with your abuelo tonight and you two can have a real bed."

"Abuela, I was dreaming."

My grandfather makes the sign of the cross and mutters, "Jesus, Maria, and José! What is this world coming to?"

Ben is oddly quiet next to me. I turn to him as the heat of extreme embarrassment consumes me. "I'm sorry,

I was dreaming," I repeat again like this will somehow magically make the whole scene less embarrassing.

It doesn't.

With a blanket clutched to my chest, I turn to my grandparents and suggest, "If you could leave for a minute, I'll put myself together here."

"We'll go down for breakfast," Abuela says. Then she grabs my grandfather's hand and drags him away.

Once they're gone, I repeat, "I am so sorry."

Instead of accepting my apology, and pretending this horrible thing never happened, Ben merely says, "I'm not."

Wait, what?

"In fact," he continues, "Now that your grandparents are gone, I'd be happy to let you go back to sleep and continue your fantasy."

Is Ben Williams flirting with me? "I, um, well ..."

He takes me off the hook. "I'm just kidding. Why don't we get up and grab breakfast ourselves? I'd love to have some time at the Space Center before my first meeting starts."

With the blanket still wrapped around me, I answer, "Oh, yeah, sure ..." It's like the articulation police have come and revoked my use of the English language.

"Go on," he says.

"You go first," I tell him. "I'm a little, you know, naked."

"I'm not really in any shape to be walking around myself." His eyes roam to his lower half.

"Oh!" This could not be any more awkward. "Close your eyes," I tell him, "and I'll make a run for it."

"You don't have to run." Is he being funny or flirty?

"Close your eyes," I repeat. Then I jump up and dash down the hall to the room I was supposed to be sharing with my grandmother. Once I'm safely inside with the door closed, I let myself relive what almost took place. While horribly embarrassed that my grandparents walked in on us, I'm not in the least bit upset by what almost happened.

While taking a shower, I let myself peruse the idea of me and Ben as a couple. Clearly, we like each other and are attracted to each other. The only problem on my end is that he thinks astrology is a complete hoax. And being that astrology is what I do, can I really be with someone who thinks I'm a charlatan?

My grandparents come back to the room before Ben and I are ready to leave. I'm in the kitchen drinking a cup of coffee when they walk in. I offer, "Again, I'm so sorry about this morning," I start to say when my grandmother waves me off.

"Please. I'm sorry we disturbed you."

"Do you guys want to go to NASA with us today?" I ask, thinking that the best way to move on from this is to pretend it never happened.

"Not even a little bit," Abuela says. "Renzo and I will just stay here at the hotel and wait for you kids to come back."

"I don't know when that will be," I tell her. "Are you sure?"

"As long as they have cable, I'll watch my telenovelas while Abuelo watches midget tag team wrestling or whatever nonsense he's into these days."

My grandfather grumbles, "I need a nap first."

"Do you mind if we take your car?" I ask my grandmother after he leaves. "Ben and I were thinking of renting one, but if you're not using yours, we might as well use that."

Grabbing the keys out of her purse, Abuela hands them to me with a wink. "You know your grandfather and I had sex before we were married."

I have no words.

"It's a natural part of life, *nieta*. There's nothing to be embarrassed about."

Ben walks in at that moment, so Abuela turns her attention to him. "I was just telling Sera that I support the two of you having relations before you're married."

His gaze shifts nervously between her and me before saying, "Uh ... thank you?"

Abuela walks up to him, stands on her tippy toes and kisses him on the cheek before adding, "Welcome to the family, Ben." Then she walks down the hall to join Abuelo.

I have no idea in this world how to make things normal between me and Ben again. Not only did I literally jump the man's bones, but my grandmother has pretty much insinuated that we'll be announcing our engagement soon.

Ben says, "I suppose after we leave the Space Center today, we should go pick out rings."

What?!?

His eyes twinkle with merriment as he adds, "I assume the scene this morning was your way of proposing?" He stares at me in earnest for a moment, then finally lets me off the hook by laughing.

"Oh, ha ha!" I grab a handful of napkins from the counter and throw them at him. "This morning was the singular most embarrassing moment of my entire life."

He forces his features into an exaggerated frown.

"That's too bad. I was going to say it was a highpoint in mine." He picks the napkins up off the floor. "You ready to go?"

I dangle the car keys in front of him. "I figured we'd take my grandparents' car. That way they won't be driving around today."

"Do you mind grabbing breakfast there? I want to spend as much time as I can at the mothership."

Smiling at him, I say, "You're like a little boy in a candy shop there, huh?"

"It's pretty much my everything," he says, sounding like a starstruck teenage girl talking about her favorite rock star.

We don't say much on the drive to Cape Canaveral, but it's not a weird silence like you might expect after I threw myself at him this morning. Instead, it's a pleasant quiet, like we're simply enjoying being together.

After parking, we walk toward the main entrance. I get the same thrilling rush I always got as a kid coming here. Walking under the giant letters that spell "Explore," with an array of past rocket ships displayed in the rocket garden just beyond fills my being with such hope and excitement about the stars, I can barely stand it.

When Ben gives our names to a woman behind the counter, she types away at her computer before saying, "Ah, yes, Dr. Williams, someone will be arriving in a few minutes to greet you."

I nudge him in the arm and say, "You're a VIP here, huh? How cool is that?"

"I'm pretty sure it has more to do with *Wake Up America!* than with me."

Then we both hear a voice call out, "Benjamin Williams, as I live and breathe!"

A nice-looking man approaches us with a big smile on his face. I'm about to offer him a wave when Ben mutters beneath his breath, "Anyone but him..."

"Friend of yours?" I ask.

"Not even close."

TWENTY-EIGHT

Ben

Well, this is just perfect. Patrick Ennis, the Darth Maul to my Obi Wan, is here. He and I went to MIT together and we always battled for the top spot in every class. I have such a strong hatred for this man, that I paid the MIT yearbook editor a hundred dollars to put only Patrick's first initial under his picture, so it ended up spelling "P. Ennis." Immature I know, but he had just told a girl I was trying to date that I only had one testicle and it kept me from performing like a man, so...

Anyway, three years ago, we were both up for a lead researcher position here at Kennedy, and sadly, evil won that day. I was *really* hoping to avoid him while I was here because I can't stand another "friendly" conversation about how much better his life is than mine. He's all over the astrophysics forums going on and on about his "Star Life in Florida."

"Patrick," I say with a quick nod. "Good to see you." FYI, that's said in the same tone that I'd use to declare,

"Yay, liver and onion on my hot fudge sundae." I'm not asking him how he is because I don't really care, and I also don't want to give him an opportunity to gloat.

"You too," he answers. "I see they've got you doing a dog and pony show on morning television." He bursts out laughing like it's the best joke he's heard in his life. But I suppose in a way, it is. My face heats up as I realize he's seen me in my banana pants. *God, strike me dead right now. I mean it. Right. Now.*

"Just doing my part to further NASA's public profile."

"You sure about that, Dr. Banana Pants?" he asks, then slaps me on the arm as if to mean he's just goofing around.

If I'm near this man for another second, I may snap and karate chop him right in the neck. "Anyway, we've got to run, but you are ... exactly as I remember you," I tell him with a deadpan expression.

Ignoring my attempt at brushing him off, he says, "I never thought I'd see your ugly mug here at Kennedy. What, are you on vacation so you thought you'd come for a tour?" He laughs at his own joke while I contemplate his slow and painful dismemberment.

"I'm here for the TRAPPIST-1 Conference."

He's already so bored, he's not even looking at me. Instead, he's eying Serafina like she's a freeze-dried salmon treat and he's Mr. Spock (my cat, not the television character). "Nice," he answers, even though he clearly couldn't care less. "This must be your lovely co-host, Serafina Lopez."

He picks up her hand and brushes a kiss on her knuckles like he's Rico Suave. Serafina yanks it away with a look of total disgust. He tells her, "Oh, you're as feisty in person as you are on TV. I like that."

Before I can put him in a full nelson and bang his head into a wall, Serafina loops her arm through mine and says, "So does my Benny."

His face falls and he points back and forth between us. "You expect me to believe *you're* with *him?*"

"I don't care what you believe," she says. "As long as I wake up every morning next to this stud muffin, that's really all that matters." She glances up at me and bats her eyes before turning back to him. "I can't get enough of him. In fact, we didn't even make it into the bedroom last night, did we, sugar lips?"

I could kiss her for this. Instead, I smile at her before turning my attention to Patrick. "It's true. We spent the night on the living room floor in our suite."

"Gross," he says, but I can tell by his expression, he's filled with envy.

Serafina says, "When I want him, I have to have him right that second. Doesn't matter where we are."

Patrick looks decidedly nauseous and it's all I can do not to laugh out loud when Serafina adds, "I don't suppose you'd mind if we used your office today? You know, in case Ben gets a break from the conference?"

"I'm not ... no ... ew ... you can't ... I don't allow that kind of thing in my office." Patrick adds, "There is no sex in my office. I mean, I'm the only one who can have sex in my office. Me, alone." He says that just as two women with NASA lanyards around their neck walk by. They both start to giggle, and Patrick turns bright red.

"It's a lot more fun with a partner," I tell him.

"*So* much more fun," Serafina says, resting her head

on my shoulder. "Anyway, I'm starving, babe, and you promised me breakfast before you have to get to work."

"Right," I tell her. "She needs to replenish her energy for later. See you, Pat. Have a good one."

With that, I take Serafina's hand and we start in the direction of the cafeteria, both of us trying desperately not to laugh until we're out of earshot. Holding her hand gives me such a warm feeling, like hot cocoa on a cold winter day. Oh boy, I'm in trouble here.

When we round the corner, I don't let go of her, even though I should. "Thank you for that," I tell her in a quiet voice.

Serafina grins up at me. "You're very welcome. That guy needed to be brought down a peg or six."

"You accomplished that swiftly and effectively."

"It's the Libra way." She takes a step toward me and for a split second I think we might be about to kiss right there in front of the Orbit Café, but a family walks out and nearly runs us over. Talk about a buzzkill.

With my hand on Serafina's back, I lead her into the restaurant. We enjoy a quick breakfast of scrambled eggs, bacon, and toast, while we rehash the fun we had sticking it to Patrick.

"How long do you suppose it'll be before everyone in the building knows he has sex with himself in his office?" she asks as she slathers some strawberry jelly onto her toast.

"Hopefully, by lunch time," I tell her with a grin.

"Fingers crossed." She takes a bite of her toast.

"What are you going to do around here all day?" I ask her.

"I'm going to walk around with the film crew and talk

about the early connections between astronomy and astrology," she says, her face morphing into trepidation.

I'm pretty sure she's expecting a snide comment from me, but at the moment, I have no desire to try to persuade her away from the dark side. "That'll be really fascinating for the viewers."

"You mean the wackadoodle ones, right?"

"No, everyone. I'm sure you know far more than I do about astrological connections," I tell her. "I kind of wish I could skip my thing and go around with you." Huh, oddly enough, that's true.

"Really?" Serafina asks, giving me a skeptical look.

"Really." Yup, I've got it bad because that's the least logical thing I've ever said.

"Does that have anything to do with our early morning wake-up call?"

"While that *was* very nice, I'm actually interested in what you have to say." Grinning, I add, "But ... this morning's ... activities didn't hurt matters."

Serafina smiles at me and blushes a little, then she shakes her head a little as if trying to get back her focus. "Okay, the film crew should be showing up any minute, so I better go out front to meet them."

"Right, yeah," I tell her, unable to look away. "I should also go to that thing I'm here for..." What again? I've gone totally blank.

"The TRAPPIST-1 Conference?"

"That's the one."

We both stand and I take our trays to the garbage. After unloading everything, we walk out and turn to each other. I completely forget where I am and who we really are to each other, and almost give her a quick peck on the lips before catching myself.

Sera bites her bottom lip. "Text me when you're done, and we can figure out where to meet."

I nod my head mutely. I want to kiss her. Badly. But this is not the time or the place. "Have a great day," I tell her as I watch her walk away.

Suddenly I know without a shadow of a doubt that I will kiss this woman properly before we leave Florida.

TWENTY-NINE

Serafina

I spend the morning and the first part of the afternoon with a producer and cameraman who are on loan from a local affiliate. I talk about the planets that govern the different star signs and how their position in the heavens affects the personality traits of the people who were born under them. I share how amazing it is when you connect with the zodiac because it not only helps you understand yourself, it helps you to grow as a person. There's no word from Ben until two in the afternoon.

> DrBananaPants: Hey, just finishing up. How about if you meet me by the Saturn V rocket and I can tell our viewers the details of how we can launch such a massive rocket into space.

> LibraGrl: Sounds great, we'll meet you there.

I tell Drake, the producer with board shorts and a

ponytail, what the plan is, but instead of looking enthused, he says, "Yawn. No one tunes into morning television to hear a lecture."

He looks around for a second, his eyes landing on the area where families are dressing up in space suits and having their pictures taken against a green screen. "That!" he says, "That'll be fun for the audience."

He's not wrong. I've done this before and it's a real hoot. The green screen image is transcribed onto outer space backdrops. In one scene they'll show you in the shuttle; in another you'll be standing on the moon with an American flag, and they've even added one where you're floating in space.

But poor Ben is going to be disappointed. "Drake, what if you just film the segment about jet propulsion and let Waltraut decide what to use?"

"Kind of a waste of film."

"How can you know unless you give it a try?"

That seems to have worked because he gives me a shrug that I take as a yes. Ben shows up moments later looking positively delectable. His eyes are burning so bright you'd think he was at Disneyland, not NASA. Although, I suppose for him, this is better than any amusement park. "Hey," he says, extending his hand toward the producer and camera guy. "I'm Ben."

"Drake," the producer says before motioning toward the cameraman. "He's Tizz, but you don't need to know that. Just look at the camera and talk to it like it's your mom."

"Okay then," Ben says while positioning himself underneath the Saturn V rocket. "I'll just talk a little bit about action force versus reaction force and then maybe get into ballistic curves."

"Can you do it in under thirty seconds?" Drake asks. "Because I can guarantee you people will be changing the channel if it goes longer."

"No, it's a complex topic and, to properly lay it out for people, you need at least a couple of minutes."

"Then let's move on, okay, Beck?"

"It's Ben, and I thought the whole point of my being on *Wake Up America!* was to excite the American people about space travel."

Urgh. Poor Ben sounds so disappointed.

"You know what will excite them about space travel?" Drake asks.

Ben's eyes light up. "Newton's three laws of motion?"

"No," Drake says, wrinkling up his nose like he just walked in the bathroom after Abuelo was in there. "Seeing you and Serafina dressed up like astronauts. If they can imagine the two of you in space, then they might start imagining themselves. *That's* the way to cultivate interest in NASA."

"You want us to play dress up?"

"A hundo p, man. That's the way to go."

Ben looks at me and whispers, "What does that mean?"

"A hundred percent," I whisper back.

"Playing dress up though? That's for kids."

I take his hand and pull him toward the other side of the massive building. "Come on, we'll have fun, I promise!"

Drake says, "Wait up. Tizz, roll film while they walk over there. Let's get a real feel for how much fun it is to be at NASA."

"People come here to learn," Ben tells him in a schoolmaster tone.

"Wrong," Drake says. "People come here to imagine. You gotta feed that sense of wonder, man."

Before Ben can contradict him, because believe me, the look on his face says he's ready to rumble, I give his hand a little tug and start toward the photo area. "Come on, Dr. Banana Pants," I tease him. "Let's show the American people what a good sport you are." Even though he seems reticent, he lets me lead the way.

When we get to our destination, Drake talks to the people running it and gets us bumped up to the front of the line. We're led to a staging area where there's a rack of costume space suits for us to pick from. Ben looks totally aghast. "We can't put these on. Do you know how many people wear these things?" Then he looks at the helper and asks, "How often do you clean these?"

The kid shrugs his shoulders. "Got me. But it's not like they ever really get dirty. People are only in them for a couple of minutes."

I've already picked a jumpsuit out and am putting it over my clothes. "Come on, Ben; it'll be fun."

"But I'm wearing loafers. No astronaut would ever wear loafers."

"I'm wearing sandals," I tell him. "If you're worried about looking authentic, you'll be light-years ahead of me."

"You can't wear sandals in space," he practically shouts. Meanwhile, I look at the camera and see that Tizz is filming all of this. I nudge Ben and point to the camera and wave. "Do it for the fans, Ben."

I hear him curse under his breath before he forces a smile and says, "Okay ... Fun times ahead." He looks like he's in actual pain while he puts on his white space suit. The helper leads us to the green screen and says, "In the first shot, we'll want you to lie down and hold hands with each other. That'll be your jumping out of the shuttle picture."

"No one actually jumps out of a space shuttle," Ben tells the kid. "First, you're harnessed to a tether that's connected to the ship and then you gingerly step out into space. There is no jumping."

"Dude, whatever." The kid is obviously not impressed by this knowledge.

Ben and I assume the position we've been ordered to take, the whole while my co-host complaining, "We don't even have space helmets on. We'd die within seconds of being exposed to deep space."

"One, two, three..." the kid yells before our picture is taken. For the next shot, we're given sunglasses and are told to stand arm in arm. "This is your moon shot."

Drake calls out, "Hold up! Wouldn't it be fun if we had a picture of you carrying Serafina across the moon?"

"Why would that be fun?" Ben asks.

"Let's just try it."

Ben picks me up and holds me like I'm a plutonium bomb or something. I know Drake is trying to get Ben to loosen up, so we actually look like we're enjoying ourselves and aren't, in fact, hosts of a germaphobe convention.

"Ben," I lean over and whisper in his ear.

"Yes ..." he looks paralyzed by fear.

"Remember this morning in our hotel room?"

His eyes sort of glaze over and he nods imperceptibly.

"Remember how I nibbled on your neck?"

I hear him gulp.

"I want to do that right now. In fact, you're so damn

sexy in that space suit, I want to rip it right off of you and pick up where we left off."

Somewhere along the line, I'm no longer trying to relax him by taking his mind off of what we're doing. I really mean it.

"Serafina …" Ben growls as he brings his face down to mine.

"Yes?"

He doesn't answer with words. Instead, he kisses me like he's attaching himself to the only source of oxygen in deep space. We are fused, body and soul, and it is the most amazingly wonderful feeling ever. Ben kisses like he was meant for me. When I feel the tip of his tongue part my lips, I open to him fully. I have no idea how long we make out. A minute? Five? Three hours?

All I know is I have never been more turned on kissing a man as I am at this moment. I'm so focused on Ben that I lose all track of what it is that we're supposed to be doing. It isn't until I hear Drake call out, "That's a wrap!" that I realize our first kiss has just been filmed for national television.

Ben sets me down, looking as shell-shocked as I feel. That kiss had enough force to throw the entire planet off its axis. And that's when I notice them. The families patiently waiting in line, the moms and dads covering their young children's eyes while they themselves glare and shake their heads.

"Oh, dear," Ben mutters. "Sorry about that, folks. It's for a space movie. You can uncover your children's eyes now."

"Yup," I tell the crowd in a high-pitched voice. "All done."

"For now," Ben says, giving me a sexy grin.

THIRTY

Ben

It's five p.m. and we're currently at The Fondue Factory with Maria and Lorenzo for a painfully early dinner. As soon as we got back to the hotel, they hopped in the back-seat of the car and gave me the address. I tried to get out of it — in the name of allowing Serafina time alone with her grandparents. But here I sit, having the sweltering first course of cheese fondue. Seriously, who eats fondue when it's ninety-five degrees out? Also, am I the only one worried about the repercussions here?

Serafina and her abuela are engrossed in a long conversation about her brother, Zay, who I gather has some sort of pituitary issue based on what they're saying. Apparently, he has his first girlfriend at the age of thirty-two? And they're both thrilled for him. *But there are more pressing matters at hand here, ladies.* We have an old man who's in serious lactose-intolerance denial eating hot cheese by the spoonful. He just keeps going back for more. Cheese-dipped bacon, apples slices, bread cubes, cherry tomatoes. Lorenzo is sucking them down like an anteater who just found the world's last termite colony.

Serafina and I are going to have to sleep in the car tonight. In fact, I'd venture to guess that most of the guests in the hotel are going to have to clear out after this meal hits his intestines.

"You didn't try the bacon yet, Ben," Maria says, forking a piece of it onto my plate. "It's so good."

"Thanks," I manage with a nod. I stab it and dip it in the communal pot, then scald my lips before saying, "Mmm ... delicious."

She gives me a satisfied nod. "So, you two have a problem. You want to express your love, but you can't while sleeping on the living room floor. I mean, what's that gonna do to your backs?"

"That was just a dream, Abuela," Serafina says in a warning tone.

"But dreams can come true. That's why I'm going to help you by sharing the secret to Renzo's and my happy marriage. We've been together for sixty-one years already," she tells me.

"Sixty-one?" Just how old are these people?

Maria must be a mind-reader because she says, "We're not *that* old. We started dating when we were fifteen and got married at seventeen." She puts a couple more pieces of bacon and some bread on my plate and gestures for me to get eating. "Now, marriage isn't easy, especially at the beginning. Sometimes, when Renzo would leave the house, I used to hope for him to get hit by a bus and SMACK! Over."

Lorenzo says, "That's true. She used to tell me that on my way out the door in the morning. She'd yell, 'I hope you get hit by a bus.'"

The two of them stare into each other's eyes and laugh like the crazy people I'm starting to suspect they are. But then Renzo reaches over and places his hand on top of Maria's and gives it a squeeze. "Dios mio, I love you. We had the best time making up, didn't we?"

Maria chuckles. "Remember how I used to tell you that I hoped a piano would fall on you?"

They laugh like lunatics while Serafina and I look on. When they're done sharing the delightful memory of Maria's bloodlust, she turns back to us with a serious expression. "We learned to talk openly about our feelings. I accepted his faults, and I stopped wishing he would die," Maria says wisely. "Couples are never going to agree on everything. From watching you two on TV, I've learned how Ben here is very narrow-minded when it comes to astrology, and I'm guessing ghosts, and religion too."

Serafina nods, confirming her abuela's suspicions. Well, thanks for that. Even though she's right. "I prefer the term logical to narrow-minded," I tell her.

"Different word, same thing," Maria tells me. "You need to open your mind up to my granddaughter's beliefs. That doesn't mean you have to agree with her; you just have to be willing to listen to her without shutting her down. You both want to help people — you, Ben, with the space stuff, and my Serafina wants to help people live a better life here on this planet. Focus on that part of her work and you'll be fine. Her heart is in the right place, even if her ideas are a little out there."

Serafina pulls a face while I grin. "Hey, Abuela, astrology isn't out there, it's been studied—"

Holding up her hand, Maria silences her granddaughter's impending lecture. "You already told me, corazoncita. And that's part of the problem with you. You think you have to convince the world you're right about everything, but you're not. You don't know everything. No one does."

Tell her, Maria.

"And neither do you, Ben. Nobody has all the answers, so instead of focusing on facts and fighting over things you can never prove to each other, focus on *intentions*. You both want to help people, but you do it in different ways. Respect each other's *reasons*, and if you can't agree on the 'how,' just leave it alone."

It's like we're in pre-dating fondue counseling or something.

Lorenzo lets out a burp and rubs his belly. "I might have overdone it."

If only someone could have predicted that...

It's late in the evening, but instead of going to bed, Serafina and I are lying on two pushed-together lounge chairs on the balcony with blankets and pillows. We decided it would be safer out here because Lorenzo's cheese addiction hit him hard when we got back. The lights are off inside, so I'm sure Serafina's grandparents have gone to bed already. My feisty Libra suggested we sleep out here tonight. I love that she's so spontaneous. Not to mention sexy as anything and an amazing kisser. I really want to pick up where we left off in the photo shoot, or early this morning, but after Maria's lecture about love, this all feels very serious, and all our differences are cemented in the front of my mind.

A warm breeze blows off the ocean and even though there are lots of lights from the hotel grounds, we can still make out some of the stars over the water. "Why didn't we do this last night?" I ask her.

"I guess we just didn't think of it. Now that we're out here, though, it seems painfully obvious, doesn't it?"

"Sometimes the most obvious things are easiest to miss," I tell her.

"Why is that?" Serafina asks, tilting her head to face me.

"Humans are weird. We don't make much sense most of the time," I say. "But your grandparents seem to have it all figured out. They don't take themselves too seriously and they can laugh about ... things that would likely end most relationships."

Serafina chuckles. "That they can. I come from a long line of happily married people and now I'm wondering if that speech is one Abuela got from *her* abuela."

"Could be," I say, reflecting on how I come from a completely opposite family. "I wish someone had shown my parents how to be happy," I say without really thinking about it. "Although, I don't think any amount of advice would have helped as far as my father was concerned."

"Do you remember him?"

"A little. I remember playing catch with him once in the backyard."

"That sounds nice."

I sigh and stare out at the night sky to avoid eye contact while I unburden my soul. "Not really. I wasn't good at it and he wasn't exactly patient."

Serafina reaches over and slips her fingers through mine. "I'm sorry you had such a bad father."

"Me too. But my mom's amazing and she more than made up for his absence." I offer Serafina a small smile.

"I'd do anything for my mom," I tell her, thinking about how my mom wants to try her dating app when it's live, and how badly I don't want her to with her rocky history with men. But if I tell Serafina that, she'll hate me. Which means I can't tell her how I signed up for the app just to prove that it's a dud.

I chew on my bottom lip for a second while I contemplate my options. Gwen pops into my mind and a pang of guilt comes over me. I have the perfect woman back in Manhattan who thinks we're dating. And here I am, falling for the last person I should be. But it's happening, whether I like it or not.

As soon as we get back to New York, I'm going to have to cancel my account and tell Gwen I'm not able to go with her to the engagement party. It wouldn't be fair to her or to Serafina.

"You seem far away," Serafina says in a gentle tone. She leans over to me, then turns my face to hers with one hand and gives me a soft, slow kiss. Suddenly I forget all about my plans and my concerns and let myself disappear into this moment, right now with her.

THIRTY-ONE

Serafina

My grandmother's advice to me and Ben about keeping an open mind seems to have been very well received on his part. Ever since Abuela's talk, he hasn't disparaged my app once. He's even asked me some questions and listened to the answers without a pained expression on his face.

We stayed up almost all night on the balcony, snogging each other senseless and talking about everything from our childhoods to our dreams to what our favorite cereals are. I'm obviously a Fruit Loops girl, and Ben eats steel cut oats every morning but wishes it was a bowl of Frosted Flakes because *they're ggrrrrreeeattt*. He's got a playful side. He hides it well, but it's there.

Our flight back to New York was delightful. We held hands and kissed and just kept right on talking. I feel like he knows me better than my best friends do. Big things, little things, we shared it all. For instance, he told me all about his cat Mr. Spock (how adorably nerdy is that?) and

I told him all about my love of circus peanuts — not actual peanuts, but the rubbery, orange candy version. SO good.

We skipped our morning segment this week on *Wake Up America!* because we were in Florida, so we have a reprieve before the whole country witnesses our lip-lock. I texted Waltraut to see if she could not show that part, but her response was evasive. I totally get it. I mean, what we gave the network was ratings gold, especially since so far Ben and I have done little more than fight when we're on the air. It's just that, with our relationship so new, I don't want to come out to the whole country before we know if we have staying power.

Ben is coming over tonight, which gives me an entire day to visualize my apartment through his eyes. I'm more than a little nervous. It's not that my overstuffed furniture and eclectic knickknacks aren't perfect; they are. It's just I imagine Ben's apartment is sterile and totally lacking in imagination. Which leads me to believe he won't appreciate my extensive assortment of Native American dream catchers or my decorative hookah collection. I even briefly consider taking down the beaded crystal curtain I use in lieu of a bathroom door.

My front door bursts open with a crash and Charley charges at me like I'm a bullfighter and she's ready to do battle. "You're home! Tell me everything!"

"What would you like to know? NASA was really cool, and I even got to go into a retired space shuttle."

"Who cares? How did it go with you and Ben?"

While advanced beyond her years, my young friend is still only fifteen, so I'm not going to go into great detail. I answer, "He kissed me on national television. It'll probably air on Monday."

"What!?" She flops down on the couch next to me. "Did he *kiss you* kiss you or just kiss you?"

"What's the difference?" I'm pretty sure I know the difference, but like I said, I'm not going to volunteer anything.

Charley kicks her feet up on my coffee table and scoffs. "Did he kiss your hand or your mouth?"

I point to my mouth and laugh when she jumps up and starts to dance around. "OMG, are you dating? Are you in love? What?"

"I think we're dating," I tell her. "Obviously, we aren't in love, as we just started dating..."

She holds her hand up. "Stop. I'm a firm believer in love at first sight. Rom-Coms are my life. I will not have you disparage the voodoo of insta-love before I even go out on my first date."

I can't contain my laughter. "The voodoo of insta-love?"

She nods her head forcefully. "Having an IQ of one seventy-five doesn't deter me from romantic notions. In fact, I would argue that I need *more* magic to balance out all the real data. As a Libra, I'm sure you get that."

"Kid," I tell her. "Believe in *all* the magic you want. I'm a total fan."

"You're never going to guess what I did yesterday," Charley says.

"You went to Coney Island and overdosed on footlong hot dogs."

"I wish. Try again," she orders.

"You walked to Brooklyn all by yourself to check out the Bushwick Street art."

She releases a long sound like a buzzer going off to

indicate I'm wrong again. "I was interviewed by *The Post!*"

"What? Zay never told me. How did it go? When is it going to run? Tell me everything."

Charley grabs a donut hole off the plate in front of me before saying, "It was great. Shelby's mom is so cool. She'd already interviewed people from my school and they may have mentioned how amazing they all thought I was."

Raising my eyebrows in question, I say, "Nice. What kind of things did they say?"

"She wouldn't tell me that. She just said they really seemed to love me." Charley releases an involuntary shiver of joy. "If it's true, I might go back and take some classes even though I've already graduated. You know, I could do theater or pottery or maybe even learn another language."

"What a terrific idea," I tell her. "It might help you acclimate to Yale better to be as social as you can before you go."

"I have a confession," she says quietly.

"What's that?"

"Sometimes I wish that I were a normal kid with a normal IQ so I could have had a normal educational experience. A lot of times I really hate being different."

"I get it," I tell her. "But being different is what makes you special. Would you rather peak in high school or peak when you're an adult?"

"That's an unfair question. Obviously, I want success for as long as I can have it which would mean waiting. But I also want to have normal high school experiences too. I want a first kiss, I want to go to prom, I want to belong." She sounds so defeated.

I pull Charley close to my side and tell her, "Whatever your experience, there will always be things you wished were different. That's just life. The only thing you can control is your attitude. With a good attitude, you increase your resilience and change your perspective."

She tilts her head back and forth while rolling her eyes. "Okay, *Mom*."

We spend the rest of the day researching why our app isn't proving effective for me. According to Charley, it's tweaked to the point of perfection. Yet, since my last failed blind date, I've received messages from three other men, all of whom come across as total losers. One of them has been unemployed, by choice, for four years and claims that, while he can't afford to take me to dinner, he'd be happy to go out and let me pay.

The next one was a high school biology teacher who shared that he has a soap allergy. It's been twenty years since he's used an actual cleaning agent on his body. When he confessed to really enjoying the organic smell of the human body, I was out. I *really* love the smell of clean.

The third guy was a stockbroker and claimed that the stock market is his life so I should expect a crash course in the best yielding hedge funds. Yawn and pass.

It's not that I'm actually looking to date anyone now that things have changed between me and Ben, but I still need to figure out why my app isn't working. I can't go public with it until I know I can stand behind the matches it makes, and the only way to do that is to pretend that I'm looking.

When Charley leaves for the day, I hurry to take a quick shower and then I pore over takeout menus. Ben and I are eating in tonight, which means romance is definitely a possibility. Therefore I want to make sure my food selection is a romantic one. I settle on sushi from a

Japanese restaurant down the street with appetizers from an Italian restaurant. Then I order dessert from the Sunshine Bakery.

Twenty minutes before Ben is due to arrive, I slip into a pair of super soft capri pants and a sleeveless cotton blouse that ties in the front. Then I put on some big silver hoop earrings, a delicate bracelet, and my mood ring.

When I look myself over in the mirror, my stomach starts to jump around like it's hosting a Mexican jumping bean tournament. I make a kissy face just for practice, then go into the living room to light some candles.

I'm full of excitement and trepidation. I really, really want tonight to go well. It's one thing to connect with someone while you're away — I mean, that saying "What happens in Vegas, stays in Vegas" is a saying for a reason. Getting back to your own space is the true test, though.

Having said that, I already knew Ben was an exceptional man before we went to Florida (even though I did find him inordinately irritating). But all that head butting is behind us. From here on out, our path should be smooth sailing.

THIRTY-TWO

Ben

"Hi! How was the big trip?" Gwen asks.

My stomach tightens as I think about all the things I'm not going to tell her. Not because I was cheating on her or anything. We've only had one date, but I still need to let her know we aren't going to have anymore. "Good, yeah. How've you been?"

"A bit stressed, to be honest," she says. "I had to pull five teeth from a nine-year-old sugar-addict. Five. Can you imagine? Poor little guy has a condition that makes him high risk for anesthetic, so he had to be awake for it. It was *not* fun. Also, two of my sister's bridesmaids got into a huge fight yesterday when we were at my parents' house working on guest favors."

"Really?" I ask, my heart sinking a little. How am I going to tell her I'm not able to make it on Saturday?

"Oh, yes, it was delightful. There were even some clumps of hair on the kitchen floor by the time we got them separated. And I ended up with a black eye out of it, so that's lovely."

"That's terrible. Are you okay?"

"I'm fine. Honestly, the only thought that's kept me going is that I'll have you with me at the party. Thanks for that, by the way. You're my knight in a shining space suit."

I rub the bridge of my nose as the pressure in my head builds. Glancing at my watch, I see I should be on my way to Serafina's already. I have to just say it. "So, Gwen, there is something I need to tell you ..."

I'm currently in a cab heading to Serafina's place in SoHo. I've already texted her that I'm running seven minutes late (which is actually nineteen minutes late in my books, but since she doesn't share the same sense of time as me, I'm calling it seven). My conversation with Gwen went so much better than I thought it would. She took the news like an absolute champ. She actually said she wasn't feeling the whole romantic vibe with me either, but that she'd love to add me to her friend group, which is a massive relief. She even admitted she'd been wondering if Serafina and I had something going on between us based on all the bantering we do.

I decide that maybe I'll have Serafina come with me to The Salty Nuts one evening to meet Gwen (and maybe see if we can bring a fourth for my new buddy). The only fly in the ointment is that I'm still going with Gwen to the engagement party, but as a friend only. Well, she may let her busybody aunt think we're an item, but other than that, no strings attached. Except, of course, finding a way to tell Serafina, which I am not looking forward to.

When we pull up in front of her building, I step out and take a good look at it. It's a ten-story modern structure with huge windows and I'm sure a price tag to match. She really must make twelve times as much as me to afford this place.

Serafina buzzes me up and I step into a freight elevator, then I'm whisked upstairs to the third floor. She's standing in the doorway when the elevator door opens. "Hey, handsome," she says with a grin that any man would be honored to be on the receiving end of.

"Hey yourself," I tell her. See? I can do the flirting. I hand her the bottle of Sancerre I brought from home, and we give each other an I've-missed-you-so-much-even-though-it's-only-been-a-few-hours kiss before she pulls me into her apartment and slams the door with her foot. We stay right in the entry and make out like I imagine a couple would after one of them has spent several months in space.

"Wow, that was quite the hello," I tell her. "I hope you don't greet all your dinner guests that way."

"Only the hot ones," she says, holding her free hand on my chest. "Supper will be here any minute."

"Fondue, I hope," I tell her with a mock-hopeful expression.

She laughs, then pulls a face. "Never again." Holding up the bottle of wine, she asks, "Should we crack open this baby while we wait?"

"Sounds good." I get my first real look at her apartment — it's a veritable colorfest in here, filled with paintings and bean bag chairs and the most comfy-looking sofa I've ever seen. Everywhere I look is bright and happy, just like Serafina.

"What do you think?" she asks as she glances around her own home. "Is it too much for you?"

"I love it. It reminds me of you," I say before I think through my words. My cheeks heat up and I feel a slight panic. *Abort! Abort! It's too early for this. You're going to freak her out.* "I mean, it's bright and happy, like you ... which is ... very welcoming."

Serafina laughs while she pulls the cork out of the bottle. "Relax. I don't think you just said you love me."

Letting out a breath, I tell her, "Thank God, because I was nervous I may have scared you off there."

She pours us each a glass, then walks over to me and hands me one. "You can't scare me. I'm a Libra. We're very resilient creatures."

I chuckle. "I'm starting to see that."

"Really?" she asks, raising her eyebrow excitedly.

"Really," I tell her, pulling her to me and brushing my lips along her neck. "If you're a typical Libra woman, then I'm totally sold on that star sign." Then I put my finger to my mouth in an exaggerated Dr. Evil manner, and add, "Although, I have seen you let two tiny octogenarians boss you around."

"That doesn't count. They're my grandparents," she tells me, putting her arms around my neck and pulling me toward her. "I have to let them boss me around. But I'm afraid *you* won't have those same privileges."

"I'd never dream of telling you what to do." We kiss again, and I have a very good feeling tonight is going to be one of the best of my entire life.

"Glad we got that straight," she says. We're just about to do some more delicious smooching when the buzzer goes off. "Dinner's here."

Serafina starts for the door, but I pull her back and give her one more quick kiss. "I'm actually more excited about dessert."

"Oh, there's going to be some dessert. Believe me."

THIRTY-THREE

Serafina

I'm not a kiss and tell kind of girl, but suffice it to say, if I were, I could write a really steamy romance novel based on Ben's and my recent activities. He stayed over at my house and we barely slept. In fact, he called in sick to work, claiming that he must have caught a bug on the plane. The entire next day was spent napping and relishing in the new sensations we've unlocked in each other. While I would never say this to Ben, I'm starting to believe in Charley's insta-love voodoo. Not that we just met, but it has been less than a month and most of that time has been spent sparring.

When Ben got up and went to work this morning, I promised to go over to his place tonight to meet Mr. Spock. I've been warned there are about seven hundred behaviors his tabby will perceive as an act of war, so I'm a little nervous. Which is why I plan on having a little baggie of lunch meat in my pocket. I need this cat to love me.

Charley and I spend the day poring over the feedback that our test-daters are emailing to us about our app. Most of them are glowingly positive. Meanwhile, I get another email from a potential suitor. Bob is a proctologist who felt it necessary to tell me that the human rectum is the most under-appreciated part of the human body. While this may be true, it's also not the most romantic lead-in. I messaged him back that I'm a nostril girl, so I don't think it'll work out.

Lying prone on the floor in front of one of the eight-foot windows in my apartment, I bemoan, "How can everyone else seem to love our dating app, but I've attracted every weirdo in the metro area?"

Charley laughs, "Maybe it's you and not the app." She clicks away on her computer before saying, "It says here that you are open-minded. That could be part of the problem."

"Being open-minded in no way suggests I'm easy, into orgies, happy to pay all the bills, or that I encourage butt-hole fixations. Open-minded is good. It means I'm tolerant, and caring of my fellow man…"

Before I can finish my thought, Charley interrupts, "Oh, look. You just got another message." Click, click. "It's from a woman who read your profile. That's weird." Then my young friend starts laughing. "She thinks you might be her soulmate."

"I'm not gay!" Not that there's anything wrong with that. I'm just not looking for women.

"You want me to remove 'open-minded' now?"

"Please," I tell her, wondering if people really think open-minded is an invitation to, well, everything.

After Charley leaves, I make myself pretty for my date with Ben. I curl my hair in beach waves which causes me to fantasize about how much fun we'd have on a tropical vacation. Then I put on my best red lipstick, Russian Red, and dream about all the places I can leave my mark on him.

By the time I get into a cab and head uptown, I'm not sure I want to bother with dinner. I'd much rather take a tour of my new boyfriend's bedroom, living room, kitchen counter ...

It isn't until I get to Ben's building near the Columbia campus that I realize I forgot Mr. Spock's treats. I hurry to a deli a few buildings away hoping to find something suitable. On the advice of the woman behind the counter, I buy a can of Cheez Whiz. According to her, cats can't get enough of the stuff. It isn't until I'm back on the street that I wonder how I'm going to surreptitiously pull out a can of processed cheese and offer it to Mr. Spock without Ben noticing.

Ben is standing in front of his building when I get there, looking around. "Lose something?" I call out when I'm about ten feet away.

He runs toward me. "I saw you get out of the cab and walk down the street. I was afraid you were lost."

"You were looking out the window for me? That's pretty cute." I take a step toward him. Then I reach up and leave the first of what I'm sure will be many lipstick prints on his person.

When we pull apart, he says, "I missed you."

"I missed you too," I practically purr. "Now let's go inside so we don't get arrested for indecent exposure." His look of confusion prompts me to add, "I want to see you in less clothing."

Grabbing my hand, Ben practically pulls me into his building. It's not quite as impressive as my loft, but it has some solid pre-war charm. By the time we get off the elevator, I'm already working on the buttons of his shirt. I'm in such a fog of need that I don't even look at his apartment until a ball of fur launches itself across the room and lands on Ben's head.

"Hey there, Mr. Spock," he greets the orange and brown cannonball. "I want you to meet Serafina."

Mr. Spock eyes me with what I can only interpret as scorn. I don't make any false moves, and instead I whisper, "Mr. Spock, it's a pleasure." I heard somewhere that you shouldn't talk loudly when you first meet an animal. That could be utter nonsense, but so far Mr. Spock hasn't hissed at me, so...

"Why don't you go sit on the couch and hang with Spock while I open a bottle of wine," Ben suggests.

I reach into my purse to assure myself that the Cheez Whiz is still there. Then I walk across the small living space with a tabby on my heels. These pre-WWII buildings are not open concept, so I can't see Ben in the kitchen. This allows me to pop the top off Mr. Spock's treat and spray a small amount on my finger. He attacks it like I go at a hot fudge sundae. Nice.

I spray several more dollops until he's perched on my lap and purring like I'm his favorite person in this world. Ben walks in and whistles, "Wow, look at you two. Fast friends already."

"Cats appreciate my innate balance," I tell him. *Liar, liar, pants on fire.*

Ben sits down next to me and hands me a glass of wine. He raises it in the air and toasts, "To the perfection of the Libra woman." My insides turn into molten lava. While I know he doesn't believe in the zodiac, I still find it endearing that he no longer seems antagonized by it.

After we toast and sip, he leans over to kiss me. Just as our lips touch, we're enveloped by a stench so intense I immediately start to gag. Ben leans back and looks at me with an alarmed expression. "Are you okay?"

He thinks I did this? "Are you?" I counter.

We both look down at Mr. Spock. "Spock, was that you?" Ben demands. The cat lies down on my lap and rolls over before releasing more noxious fumes.

"Does he do that often?" I ask in total horror.

"Only when he has milk products. Much like your grandfather, he's lactose intolerant."

Holy. Crap. I've just fed this little feline a good half-cup of Cheez Whiz and he's lactose intolerant? This cannot end well.

As I'm about to confess my crime, Mr. Spock jumps off my lap and makes a run for what I'm assuming is the bathroom (or wherever people have their litter boxes set up). Ben says, "I better go check on him." I know he doesn't make it when Ben yells out, "No, Spock, not on the rug."

"Do you need some help?" I call, hoping against hope Ben turns down my offer.

"No! I mean, no, thank you, this is not how I want you to see my little guy here." If he only knew I was the responsible party...

I reach over and grab my wine glass when Ben's phone starts pinging away. Just to be clear, I'm not a snoop. I firmly believe that all people have a right to privacy, but on the sixth ping, I start to think there might be an emergency, so I pick up the phone and take a peek.

Gwen: Hey, Ben, I just got off the phone with my aunt and she can't wait to meet you.

Gwen: She says that it's about time I found myself a good man. -smiley face-

Gwen: We're going to have so much fun at the engagement party this weekend.

Gwen: Be warned though, my family is going to want to know when our big day is. -laughing face- What do you think, would a winter wedding work for you?

Gwen: ...

What in the fresh hell is going on here? Is Ben seeing someone else? What kind of question is that? Of course, he's seeing someone, and apparently her name is Gwen and she's planning their wedding.

Oh. My. God. Ben is a cheater. And he's cheating *with me*! Which makes me the *other woman*. No way am I on board for that. This upsets my delicate balance to the point where I want to scream. But instead of alerting him, I simply pick up my purse and storm to the front door.

Before I can leave, I walk back to the coffee table, pull out the Cheez Whiz and spray it all over. That'll show him not to mess with me. I really want to slam the door as I leave but I don't want Ben running after me. I don't need a major scene at the moment. I just need to go home and have a great big, fat cry.

THIRTY-FOUR

Ben

"Poor Mr. Spock. What happened to you, buddy?" I ask, as my cat arches his back to do his business while maintaining eye contact. I glance up at the ceiling, wondering if this is as awkward for him as it is for me. The timing literally could not be worse. Well, I suppose that's not true. It would be worse if it happened about two hours from now.

"Sorry, Serafina!" I call down the hall, while opening the bathroom window to let the smell out. "I'm afraid he's really not feeling well."

Hurrying to the medicine cabinet, I get out my bottle of emergency kaolin-pectin for just such an occasion. I pour some onto a small plastic plate and set it down for him to lap up when he's done in the litter box. Then I get on my rubber gloves and get ready to change out his litter. It's got to be done immediately to stop the smell from lingering. I've probably been in the bathroom for a good ten minutes.

I yell out an apology to Serafina and tell her I'll be there as soon as possible. "I don't think we should go out for dinner though!" I say. "Just in case Mr. Spock needs me."

Serafina doesn't answer, which I find a little odd. She's not exactly what you'd call a quiet person, so I'm not sure what's going on. Could she be mad that we're not going out to eat?

Finally, Spock seems to be okay. He lies down on the cool tile floor and rests his face on my bathmat. I crouch and give him a few scratches. Then, after refreshing his litter box, I tie up the garbage bag, wash my hands, and hurry down the hall with the bag held as far from my person as possible. "I'm just going to run this to the trash chute and be right back."

When I get back, I go straight to the living room, only to find it empty. "Serafina?" I call, walking over to the kitchen. "Where'd you go?"

No answer.

After a quick check around the apartment, I realize her purse is gone and so is she. I call her number and wait, tapping my foot on the hardwood floor while it rings and goes to voicemail. I hang up and text her.

> ObiWan: Hey, where are you? I hope you didn't go out to pick up supper for us. I really wanted to treat you tonight.

I stare at my phone like a I'm waiting for water to boil, but there are no bubbles coming and I have no clue as to why. That's when I see some kind of odd orange stuff all over my coffee table. Gross, what is that and how did it get there?

It smells like some sort of cheese product. I wipe it up while I wait. Then I text Serafina again.

> ObiWan: Are you at a takeout place? If so, I could meet you there so we can walk back together. Mr. Spock took his medicine and he seems okay for now.

Fifteen minutes later ...

> ObiWan: Are you okay? Did an emergency come up? Because I can't think of any other reason you'd leave without saying anything. Text me back, so I know you're all right.

Two hours and three unanswered calls later ...

> ObiWan: I hope you're all right. Please get a hold of me as soon as you can, even if it's the middle of the night. I'm really worried about you and I'm about to call the police.

———

The next day...

Turns out the police don't go on red alert when your girlfriend walks out before supper. Once they got done laughing over poor Mr. Spock's stomach ailment, Officer James said, "Maybe your girlfriend doesn't like cats." *As if.*

> ObiWan: I see that you've posted on your app about

today's moon position and the weather, so I'm
guessing you're fine but aren't talking to me for some
inexplicable reason. Please call me so we can talk
about whatever the hell happened. We still have to
see each other every Monday.

I set my phone on the coffee table and start scrolling
through Netflix for something to distract myself. It's a
rainy Thursday and I'm sticking around in case Mr.
Spock has another flare up today. My phone rings and I
grab for it, but instead of Serafina, it's my mom calling.
"Hey, Mom."

"Hi, sweetie! How's it going with Serafina?"

I made the mistake of telling her we were seeing each
other and now I really wish I hadn't. "Umm ... I'm not
sure that's going to work out, to be honest."

"Is it because she can't get past how closed-minded
you are?" she asks.

"No, actually, but what an impressive leap for you to
reach that conclusion," I say, sounding snarkier than I
intend.

"Are you all right? Did she dump you already?"

"Already?" I ask, irritation rising in my chest.

"Oh, no, I didn't mean *already* already, like I assumed
she would be the one to dump *you*. I just meant ... is it
already over as in..." She rambles and scrambles to repair
things, but let's face it, she meant already. "Relationships
rarely work out for me, not that I've been in that many."

When I don't answer, my mom continues, this time
with some trepidation in her voice. "So you've been
dumped?"

I let out a sigh and mutter, "Looks like it."

"Oh, my sweet boy. Come home for a visit. I'll make

you sloppy joes like I used to when you had a hard day at school and I'll even let you have as many potato chips as you want."

I kind of do want sloppy joes now that she mentions it. Unfortunately I have a job. "I can't, Mom, work is so busy right now. But I promise, I'm still coming home for Thanksgiving. Can you make me some sloppy joes then?"

"Of course. I hate being so far away from you," she says with a deep sigh. "Listen, you forget all about that woman. And I'm going to tell Lita and Lynda to get off her silly *Live for Your Star Sign* app."

"They're on her app?"

"We all are. It's really great, but we could never support someone who wasn't nice to you. Even though Lita has already used it to redecorate her living room and she says it feels like an extension of her soul." She adds, "But, for you, we'll boycott it and even leave her bad reviews. She's clearly got something wrong with her if she can't see what a catch you are."

"Clearly," I tell her, wishing I knew what was going on. Needing to change the subject to something that doesn't feel like shards of glass to my heart, I ask, "How's your garden doing these days?"

"My garden is of no consequence, dear. You are all that matters."

"Thanks, Mom," I tell her, wondering what I can say to make this conversation end. If I know my mom, and I do, she's not going to rest until she pries every ugly detail out of me. The problem is, I have no idea what happened because Serafina won't return my texts.

THIRTY-FIVE

Serafina

Ben sends me forty-seven texts before telling me that he's not going to contact me again. *The ball is in your court,* he said in the last text. Whatever. Who in the world would have ever expected a nerdy astrophysicist from NASA to be a cheater? Are there no professions safe from philandering pigs?

Charley was really mad when I told her Ben was seeing someone else. So much so that she asked if she could use my credit card to send him a glitter bomb. I was so down with that idea, I had her send the biggest one the website offered. Apparently, they put a spring mechanism in a box with a shallow cup full of glitter setting on it. When the box is opened, the cup flings out and sprays glitter everywhere. Can you imagine, the herpes of the craft world shooting all over the apartment of your worst enemy? Such a brilliant concept.

Although glitter isn't even enough to take away the pain of discovering that Ben is a cheating cad. Normally,

I'd just chalk the disappointment up to life experience, but that's not going to work in this situation. I really liked Ben. Really. A lot. Also, I have to see him every week at *Wake Up America!*, so I won't just be able to walk away and forget he's alive. Then a terrible thought hits me. Our kiss is probably going to air on Monday when we're on TV again. Under no circumstances can I allow that to happen.

I pick up my phone and fire off a text to Waltraut.

LibraGrl: Hey, listen, um … well, it's like this. Things are not going well between me and Ben and I would really appreciate it if you didn't air our kiss.

Waltraut: What happened? I thought you guys had such a great time in Florida.

LibraGrl: We did, but things turned south after we got back to New York. I know how excited you were about the kiss, but really, you can't air it, okay?

Waltraut: It's already gone to the producers, so I'll have to talk to them. I'm not sure they'll pull it though. They were really excited when they saw it.

Damn. Damn. Damndamndamndamndamn.

LibraGrl: See what you can do, okay?

Waltraut: Of course. It'll be fun to have you back on Monday. We got a ton of emails and calls from disappointed fans when you weren't on this week.

I do my best to focus on work for the next few days, but I do a miserable job of it. It's like I just don't care anymore.

On Saturday, I fixate on how Ben is going to an engagement party with Gwen this weekend. Are they spending the night? Are they going to get engaged themselves like it sounded like Gwen is expecting? By the late afternoon, I'm so upset I'm ready to rip my hair out or start breaking dishes. I settle for trying to invent the perfect break-up cocktail.

I start with a vodka base, a vodka middle, and a vodka topper. Then I shake it all together. In an attempt at feeling less like a boozy alcoholic, I add a dash of orange juice and turn it into a Screwdriver. Although, I decide to change its name and call it a Screwed-Over-Driver. I drink three of them before the first starts to kick in.

As I'm a total lightweight in the alcohol department, I don't have a lot of experience with being sloppy drunk. Turns out I don't like to be drunk alone so I start texting people.

I start with my brother Zay.

LibraGrl: Hey Zay! Ha, get it? HeyZay rhymes! So does, say, Zay wanna play? Hurray!

Zay: Sera, are you okay?

LibraGrl: Totes and way!

Zay: What going on?

LibraGrl: I'm in the fray of today mon cher-ray!

Zay: Seriously, I'm going to call the paramedics if you don't say something that makes sense.

LibraGrl: …

LibraGrl: …

LibraGrl: Men are pigs, eh?

Zay: Uh-oh. Did something happen with Ben?

LibraGrl: Dunno. Would you think he's a cheater if he's about to marry someone else after sexing me up?

Zay: Ew.

LibraGrl: He's the north end of a southbound donkey all right.

Zay: Agreed. But never use the words "sex me up" in reference to yourself. Better yet, never use those words.

LibraGrl: He done me wrong. That low down, good-for-nothing son of a female dog in heat. I hate him. I super double-dog hate him. And I hate his cat, too!

Zay: Should I come over? You're making me nervous.

LibraGrl: I'm not going to stick my head in the microwave if that's what's worrying you.

Zay: I wasn't until you said that. I'm on my way. Stop texting people, okay? There are some things you can never recover from and drunk texting is one of them.

LibraGrl: K. Off to text Ben. Gonna give that snake in the grass a piece of my mind!

Zay: Sera, don't …

LibraGrl: BYEEEEEEEEEEEEEEEEEEEEEEEEEEEEE!!!

I feel great. Great like I'm eight out of state carrying freight by the weight. It's rhyme time, friends of mine. I wander around my apartment when a sudden urge to eat chocolate hits me. I tear through my kitchen cabinets like finding it holds the key to world peace, but the only thing I come up with is unsweetened cocoa.

What kind of Libra doesn't have a solid chocolate stash? A bad Libra, that's who. Although, I've eaten a ton of chocolate during my mourning period this week which makes me a good Libra again.

I plant myself on a bar stool at the kitchen counter and pour some sugar from the sugar bowl right into the cocoa. Then I stir it before putting a big spoonful into my mouth. It's dry, very dry, but once I mix it with enough spit it gets better.

I pick up my phone and text Ben.

LibraGrl: You suck eggs, Banana Pants!

When he doesn't respond, I remember he's at an engagement party.

LibraGrl: Screw you, you phoney baloney. I hope your boss sends you to Mars and leaves you there.

LibraGrl: I hope you go on Survivor and they don't give you any rice and you have to eat rats.

LibraGrl: I hope when you fall asleep tonight someone sneaks into your apartment and gives you a perm.

LibraGrl: I hope your toenails fall off…

I'm really warming up here, but I'm also starting to get seriously nauseated. Oh God, vodka, orange juice, and cocoa are not the best combination on an empty stomach. I stagger to the kitchen and open a bag of bread. After pulling out a handful, I shove it into my mouth. I need something to sop up the booze, but I think I'm too late.

On my wild sprint to the bathroom, I trip over an area rug and fall flat on my face. The pressure of hitting the floor is all it takes to trigger the release of my stomach's contents. I don't have the strength to pull myself up, yet alone clean up the mess. In fact, I don't have the strength to do more than lie there and cry.

Luckily, unconsciousness claims me like the Grim Reaper trying to hit his monthly quota. As I pass out, my last thought is that I hope Ben breaks up with Gwen and comes crawling back to me. Damn it, I think I went and fell in love with the guy.

THIRTY-SIX

Ben

"... as much as I hate to admit it, your rocket scientist here is so much more handsome than Dr. Kwak," Gwen's aunt says, grinning back and forth between us.

We're sitting at a table together, having endured the speeches, and a lengthy dinner interrupted by a tinkling of champagne flutes every thirty seconds for the newly engaged couple to kiss. I thought that was just a wedding tradition, but this family apparently uses it for the engagement too. It's seriously over the top.

Having been inexplicably dumped exactly thirty-eight hours ago, I'm a little irritated by the sight of happy people right now. I have a long sip of my white wine while Gwen's aunt drones on about how adorable we are together.

"You're going to have *the cutest babies!*"

No. No, we're not.

"Well, Auntie June, it's a little early for that kind of talk," Gwen says with an uncomfortable smile.

June shakes her head vigorously, causing the fake flower clipped into her far-too-dark-for-her-age hair to flop back and forth. "I can tell. You two have a connection, everyone's talking about it."

She's the seventh person to say something similar. What is it with this family? They really want to marry Gwen off. Is it so they can see more PDA-on-demand? Not happening, weirdos.

My phone buzzes in my pocket, and I pull it out as discreetly as I can to check it, my heart pounding. June's now picking out our best features for our babies, as though it's possible to put in an order or something. *Her eye color, but his eye shape, his chin, her nose ...* I hate people.

Rapid-fire texts are coming in from Serafina,. My first thought is I'm so relieved she's okay, and then I see what she wrote. Phoney baloney? She hopes someone gives me *a perm*? What in the hell is she talking about?

"How come you two aren't out on the dance floor?" Aunt June asks.

"Good question. Let's go," I say, standing quickly and pulling Gwen with me.

The band is playing "The Chicken Dance" (of course), which is my least favorite of all barnyard dances, but in the name of getting away from June, I'm willing to humiliate myself. Gwen and I stand next to each other and flap our arms like birds.

"Great escape plan," she says.

"Thanks," I yell over the music. "I thought she'd never stop talking."

"Oh, she wouldn't have," Gwen yells back as we clap our hands four times fast with the rest of the other chickens. After we spin around, Gwen says, "Are you all right? You seem a little quiet today."

"I'm fine," I lie. There's no way I'm going to talk about what happened with her. Even though we've agreed to just be friends, it feels wrong. "I'm just not that great with crowds."

"Are you sure? Because as I might have mentioned before, when I was watching some of your TV appearances, you and that Serafina woman seem to have a real chemistry between you." We wiggle our way down to a low crouch, then back up. "Did something happen between you two on your trip?"

"Unfortunately, yes." *I fell in love with her.*

"Why unfortunately?"

"She's ... not exactly a stable Mable." As soon as I say it, I feel a smack of guilt for being so unkind. But, it's true, so...

"That's too bad," Gwen says with a look of understanding.

Flapping my arms some more, I reply, "Better to find out early though."

"Good point."

I should change the subject. Forget all about *her.* Maybe get drunk and do something I might regret. I glance at Gwen, then realize I'd have to be a completely horrible person to do that. Also, Gwen doesn't like me that way either.

I blurt out, "Everything was going so well, or so I thought, then she just left without an explanation."

And suddenly, I find myself telling poor Gwen everything...

I'm angry before my alarm goes off at four a.m. I've been in the worst mood of my entire life since Wednesday night. I talked poor Gwen's ear off on Saturday night about Ms. Takes-Off-On-You-Then-Wishes-You'd-Eat-Rats-for-NO-Good-Reason. I've also taken to grumbling about Libras (of all the inane things to even *think* about, let alone talk about) and muttering curse words when I'm alone at my apartment, my office, and once at the grocery store. Mr. Spock must be able to tell I'm on edge because he hasn't attempted to scratch the side of my couch even once since Wednesday, which is kind of nice actually. But this feeling? Decidedly not nice.

I have no idea how today's segment is going to go, but to be honest, I'm kind of looking forward to facing off with Serafina. I'm in exactly the right mood to shut her and her stupid ideas down. Which is what I'm going to do when we get on air.

When I arrive at the studio, I go directly to my dressing room, then shut the door. I have no desire to see the breaker of my heart before I absolutely must. Justin comes to get me for my hair and makeup, and I sit the entire time while Tony is brushing bronzer on me without saying two words. Luckily, I make it back to the safety of my dressing room without bumping into She-Who-Shall-Not-Be-Named. Although my phone buzzes and it's her.

> Sera: In the name of professionalism, we need to set our personal issues aside on air. Agreed?

> ObiWan: What personal issues? You're the only one with personal issues. I'm normal.

> Sera: You know what I'm talking about.

ObiWan: I don't think I've ever known what you're talking about because it's all a bunch of nonsense and lies.

Sera: That. What you just wrote. That stays off air.

ObiWan: Fine. I'm a professional (unlike some people). Just know I'm bringing the force of *all* the science to go after you.

Sera: Oooh, I'm so scared.
ObiWan: You.

ObiWan: Should.

ObiWan: Be.

Sera: Bring it, nerd.

Oh, I'll bring it all right. I'll bring it big time.

THIRTY-SEVEN

Serafina

Standing in the wings of the *Wake Up America!* set, I listen while Hal says, "When we come back from commercial break, Serafina and Ben will tell us all about their trip to the Kennedy Space Center!" The live audience claps like they've just been promised a brand-new Buick, Oprah-style.

As soon as I hear, "We're in commercial." I hurry out on set and sit down. There are four chairs instead of two, which is the tip-off that Hal and Lacey are going to be sitting in.

As Ben takes the seat opposite mine, I whisper to Lacey, "I didn't think you guys were going to be sitting in on our segments anymore."

"Just this once. The producer said something about having concerns about you and Ben?"

"What concerns?" I demand. So help me, if Ben ruins this publicity opportunity for me, I'm going to send daily glitter bombs. Speaking of which, I can't help but smile when I see some shiny flecks coming from his hairline. Looks like my first offering has already arrived.

"We're back in five, four, three..." someone off set counts.

"Welcome back to *Wake Up America!*" Lacey practically shouts. "Serafina and Ben are back from their trip to Cape Canaveral, and they have a lot to tell us. Isn't that right, Ben?"

"Sure," Ben says but doesn't offer anything more.

"Tell us about it," Hal encourages.

"It was hot." Ben looks beyond annoyed.

I decide to do my part to keep the conversation rolling. "As you know, Hal and Lacey, Florida is a steamer this time of year, but the Space Center didn't fail to deliver its one-of-a-kind, out-of-this-world excitement."

They both turn to me while Ben stares daggers at me. I continue, "I, for one, have been there no fewer than a half a dozen times and I can't get enough."

"What do you like about it most?" Hal asks.

"When you see all of those rockets and shuttles and realize they've all been to outer space, it's, well, it's just awe-inspiring." I'm playing my part of the happiest woman on the planet. My face is so frozen into place, my cheeks are starting to cramp.

"I think something else happened in Florida too, am I right?" Lacey asks with a secretive smile on her face.

Damn, I thought Waltraut was going to tell the producers the kiss tape was off limits. I decide to play dumb on the off chance she's talking about something else. "What are you referring to, Lacey?" Then I shoot her a panicky look that doubles as a plea not to do her job and show the tape of our kissing.

Ben seems to finally clue into what's about to go

down, because he jumps to his feet and starts to babble, "I'd like to take a moment and tell our viewers about the fantastic opportunity to send their kids to space camp. The program includes a full week of space activities, like the anti-gravity simulator. All meals and snacks, and even a graduation ceremony and certificate, are provided at no additional cost!" He sounds like he's trying to sell blenders on late night television.

Hal interrupts him, "I hear you two got to actually suit up and visit the moon. That had to be fun."

Rats, here we go. We watch the television monitor off-set, the same one I know they've cut to on camera. Ben and I are hand-in-hand, walking toward the photo op. Video Ben says, "I can't wear *that*. How long has it been since it's been cleaned?" The audience laughs. When he says "You can't wear loafers in space," they're in near-hysterics.

Then, as expected, they've spliced the tape together to show us against the green screen, followed by the photographs we were given at the end — us in the space shuttle, floating in space, and on the moon. As I watch, I feel like a defendant in a courtroom waiting for the jury to come back with a death sentence.

Lacey looks into the camera and announces, "Just when you think Ben and Serafina will never like each other..." We all turn to look at the screen as our first kiss is unveiled right there on national television. Words escape me. That is one hot kiss and even though I'm annoyed it ever happened, my skin still heats up like I'm a pig on a spit.

The audience oohs and ahs, whistles and claps. Hal interrupts them by asking, "Is there something you two kids want to tell us?"

I merely look down and stare at my hands while shaking my head.

Ben, on the other hand, announces, "I'll tell you what happened. Serafina here laid on the charm super thick during our trip and I momentarily lost my mind."

"Are you saying that what we just saw was a one-off?" Lacey asks.

I say, "Yes," at the same time Ben gives a firm, "NO!"

It's no wonder they turn away from me and give Dr. Banana Pants all the attention. Ben says, "I thought Serafina and I were actually a couple. But then she came over to my apartment and poisoned my cat."

What? "I did not poison your cat! I wanted him to like me and the lady at the deli suggested Cheez Whiz."

"Mr. Spock is lactose intolerant and he nearly exploded as a result of all the cheese you gave him."

"How was I supposed to know that?" I demand. "Of course, it should have occurred to me that your cat would be just as persnickety as you are."

He glares at me for a long second. "You really are evil, aren't you? Making fun of an innocent cat with a medical condition?"

"I was making fun of you, bonehead."

Nostrils flaring, Ben snaps, "*I'm* not persnickety."

Mimicking him, I say, "I can't wear a space suit if anyone else has ever been in it. How often do you clean these things?" I thought the audience would laugh along with me, but they're so quiet you could hear a pin drop.

"*I'm* not the one who walked out for no reason." He's jabbing his finger in my direction like it's a weapon.

"No reason, you say?" I turn to the camera and continue, "Oh, I had a reason." Then I announce, "I was sitting on Ben's couch minding my own business when his phone started pinging like someone was sending Morse code. I picked it up to make sure there wasn't an emergency and that's when I discovered that Dr. Banana Pants here is seeing another woman."

The audience releases a collective gasp that I find quite satisfying.

"You looked at my messages?" Ben asks incredulously. "That's a violation of my privacy."

"You slept with me, all the while knowing you were going to get engaged at Gwen's sister's engagement party," I spit. "That's a violation of decency!"

His head snaps back and he sputters a bit before he manages to say, "Get engaged? What are you talking about?"

Folding my arms across my chest, I level him with a death glare. "Read her texts again."

"Oh, my God, she was kidding. Gwen is just a friend. She had a family function, and she couldn't bear to go alone because her family is full of meddling busybodies, one of whom wants to set her up with *a chiropractor*." He says chiropractor like it's a dirty word. That's *so* Ben.

I roll my eyes in disbelief. "So, you thought you'd be her knight in shining banana pants and save her from the awful fate of possibly meeting a medical professional?" I slap the back of my hand on my forehead dramatically. "Oh, the horror!"

"Medical professional," Ben scoffs. "Would you let some guy named Dr. Kwak crack your neck?"

I pause for a second trying to formulate the right response, but he doesn't let me answer. He mistakes my hesitancy as agreeing with him, and yells, "Exactly!"

"You don't believe in chiropractors either?"

"Believe it. Don't believe it. It's irrelevant to me at this point," he says. "You proved who you are when you walked out the door while I was tending to my gravely ill cat."

"Gravely ill?!" I roll my eyes again. "He had the runs, Ben. Big deal."

Ben narrows his eyes at me. "Are Libras known for having no empathy or is that just sociopaths?"

"Speaking of sociopaths, *you're* the one who was going on a big date with a 'friend' you neglected to mention."

Hal and Lacey are turning back and forth between us so quickly they look like their in jeopardy of giving themselves whiplash.

Ben's nostrils flare. "I was going to tell you, but you took off before I got a chance, and then you refused to answer any of my phone calls or texts. I was also going to invite you to meet Gwen because I thought — however erroneously — that you two would hit it off since I believed you to be something you are not."

"And what exactly is that?" I ask, even though my brain is screaming at me not to go there.

"Sane."

That's it. I don't care if I die in prison. I'm going to take off my heel and stab him clean through the temple with it. "I don't believe for one minute you were going to tell me about Gwen. Your manipulation won't work on me."

"I am not manipulating you!"

"Kind of sounds like you are," Lacey says. When I glance at her, she gives me a nod that says *I'm on your side, sister.*

Emboldened by her support, I lean toward Ben and hiss, "You're the two-timing liar. How dare you question my sanity just because I won't put up with your nonsense."

"I am neither a liar nor a two-timer. Your sanity however?" Ben shrugs. "Not so sure about that, *cat poisoner*."

Hal lets out a nervous chuckle. "Okay, things are getting a little awkward here on *Wake Up America!*"

"I was trying to be nice to Mr. Spock, you idiot. How could I know he can't handle dairy?" Turning to Lacey, I say, "What kind of cat can't have dairy?"

She shrugs. "I've never heard of it myself."

Hal cuts in with, "I think we should move on from this, don't you, Lacey?"

Lacey turns on Hal. "Do you believe this Gwen person is some old friend who he was just helping out?"

Hal clearly doesn't want to get into it, so he just lets his mouth open and close like a middle-aged goldfish in a toupée.

Ben clears his throat. "We're actually new friends."

"That's even worse," Lacey says.

"Definitely worse. Where'd you meet her?" I demand, knowing how jealous I sound but not caring.

"For your information, we met through *your* dating app." If looks could kill, I'd need last rights.

"What are you doing on my dating app? You don't even believe in astrology."

Ben shrugs his shoulders. "To be honest, I joined your trial to prove to America that dating for your star sign is a load of crap. I was hoping to debunk your nonsense."

I can't help it; I feel like my heart has been ripped out. "You were *trying* to hurt me?"

"No, I was trying to keep a lot of *other people* from

being hurt by you. Astrology doesn't have magic answers for people to find the perfect partner."

I'm so mad I can't even think straight. The worst part is that Ben might be right because I have had zero luck finding a compatible match for myself. "And you met Gwen on my app?"

He nods his head, so I continue, "And you like her?"

"We decided we weren't a love connection, but we were definitely a good friend connection."

Nodding my head, I turn to Lacey and say, "That sounds like success to me. How about you?"

"It sure does," she enthuses.

I turn to Ben, who's looking at me with what appears to be true regret. I simply shake my head and ask, "How could you do that to me? All the things you said and all the things you did, and the whole time you were purposefully setting out to *harm* my business? It's bad enough that you don't believe in it, but you want to ruin me too?" My voice breaks with emotion.

Lacey cuts in with, "That's pretty awful, Ben."

My eyes fill with tears and I realize I can't sit here anymore and pretend not to be wounded to my core. I thought I knew who Ben Williams was. In fact, I thought I loved him, but the truth is, I could never be with someone who would do something so awful to another human being.

I stand up and tell Hal and Lacey, "I would love to come back another time and talk to you and your audience about the zodiac, but I can no longer be here with Dr. Williams. He is not a good person." Then I walk off the set, not caring one whit what this will do to my career. My heart is too broken to care.

THIRTY-EIGHT

Ben

My team is deadly silent when I walk into work. No one looks up from their computers and no one says a word, for which I'm glad. I storm past them straight into my office, then close the door and let out a long sigh. I can't even begin to process what happened today. That was the most embarrassingly asinine argument I've ever allowed myself to engage in — on *live television*, no less. I close my eyes and lean back against the door as every crappy thing Serafina and I said to each other swirls around in my mind like a cyclone of rage. It's one thing to have a fight and break up with someone, but a whole other level of humiliation to have everyone you've ever met watch the entire ugly scene unfold before their eyes.

All over some stupid misunderstanding that could have been resolved in a two-minute conversation, until she had to go and *do that*. Sociopath? I'm not the sociopath in this relationship.

When I finally open my eyes again, I stare at the office

Serafina created for me. Dammit. I came here to work and forget all about her, but every inch of this place is her doing. I head straight for the storage closet and get out two empty boxes, then hurry back to my office and immediately start dismantling my cool Gemini decor. Lamps go. Inspirational posters — you're out of here. I climb onto my desk and peel the black hole sticker off the ceiling, then roll it up and toss it into the box. Next are the *Star Trek* figurines. Who takes them out of the box? A crazy person, that's who. The resale value is almost nothing on these things now. My heart squeezes in my chest as I force myself to rid the room of every sign of Serafina Lopez.

Even though I wouldn't admit it in a Neptune year (which is the equivalent of 164.8 years on Earth), I'm going to miss my office this way. It was really, really nice. Incomprehensibly, it actually *did* stimulate my creativity, but that isn't worth a nanogram of space dust because I'm driven to rid myself of every memory of that woman. Memories cause feelings and I *do not* need to be reminded about my feelings for her.

I spend thirty minutes trying to dismantle the desk and console table. I'm standing up, stretching out my back when there's a light knock at the door. "Come in," I bark.

Alec pokes his head in. "Hey, Ben, I've got my computer running a sequence that'll take about an hour, so I thought I'd check to see if you needed some help with anything."

"No, thanks. I'm okay."

He slides in and shuts the door behind him, completely ignoring my words. "You sure? There's been an awful lot of banging and clanging coming from in here."

Throwing my hands in the air, I say, "You'd think this

desk was created by the inventor of the Rubik's Cube. It looks like you're just supposed to unscrew the legs, but I think you must have to turn some damn security latch first, and I can't find one."

"Uh, I don't think Ernő Rubik made desks, actually," he says in a quiet voice.

"I know that. I was being sarcastic." Rolling my eyes, I add, "It's a very complicated design and, of course, *she* didn't leave the instruction manual, so I have no idea how to take the damn thing apart."

I start to mutter under my breath while I continue my search for a button or screw to remove the legs. "Who doesn't leave the instruction manual for the user? A sociopath, that's who."

Alec shakes his head, a wary expression filling his face. "A sociopath?"

"Exactly," I say, with a frustrated laugh. "You stayed with Mr. Spock for three days and didn't poison him once. She was in my apartment for all of one minute and my poor kitty almost exploded." Throwing my hands in the air, I add, "And she sent me a glitter bomb! Do you know how hard it is to rid your entire home of glitter? It's worse than having bed bugs. We might as well just burn down the building." I'm ranting now, really loud too so I'm sure the whole team is hearing every word. "Then she called me a two-timer and a liar on national television? That's going to do wonders for my career."

"Not to mention your dating life," he says with a look of trepidation.

"Crap, I didn't even think about that, but you're right. Who's going to date me now? No nice, normal, intelligent woman is going to have anything to do with me after all the abuse Serafina hurled at me. She made me sound like a real loser."

While I continue complaining, Alec steps forward, takes one of the legs in one hand and starts to unscrew it.

My shoulders drop. "Are you serious? It just unscrews without a safety latch?"

"Apparently."

I collapse into my chair and look up at Alec. "What a mess," I groan.

"It's not that bad," Alec says. He's already taking off the last leg. "We can have your old office setup by muffin time."

"No, I meant my life. This is why they say don't fish off the company pier."

"Who says that?" Alec asks, narrowing his eyes.

"I don't know. People, I guess."

"You went fishing at Cape Canaveral?"

"It's an expression about not engaging in workplace romances ..."

"Gotcha. Yeah, that didn't exactly work out for you," he tells me.

Thanks for your support, Alec.

My phone rings and I pluck it off the coffee table. My heart is pounding at the thought that it's Serafina. But it's not. It's Gwen. Suddenly I remember what I said about her family on TV. "Crap. I'm afraid my ugly scenes aren't over for the day."

"I'll leave you to it," Alec says, hightailing it out of my office and closing the door.

"Gwen, I'm so, so sorry," I say in place of hello.

"I cannot believe you threw me under the bus like that, on live television, no less! What is wrong with you?"

Crap. Angry Gwen is a force to be reckoned with. "Honestly, I completely forgot the cameras were there."

"How in the hell would someone forget they're on a stage in front of a *live studio audience* and that they're being broadcast across America?!" she yells.

"There's no excuse, I was just extremely ang—"

"The bit about Dr. Kwak? Are you kidding me? You called my entire family meddling busybodies? And you made me look like a complete liar to all of them. Did you forget we were pretending to be a couple?" She's full-on raging now and I'm going to do exactly what one should do when they've been a total idiot. I'm going to sit here and take it. "And that kiss? Well, my goodness, no wonder I never had a shot because you were already clearly very in love with someone else."

"To be fair, I wasn't in love with her when we first met."

She pauses for a breath, then really lets me have it. "You're an idiot. Of course you were in love with her. Why else would you sign up for her dating app just to prove her wrong?"

"I know it sounds bad, but—"

"It *is bad*," Gwen shouts. "You're a sicko, you know that? A total sicko. You *used me* to ruin another woman's career. Not only that, but my whole family thinks I'm pathetic now."

"I wasn't trying to ruin her career; I was trying to save other people a lot of heartache. And when I met you, I really liked you. I honestly *do* want to have you in my life as a friend."

"That rocket has already blasted off, buddy," she growls. "And it's never coming back to Earth. NEVER.

Delete my number because I don't ever want to hear from you again, you ... you sick pig."

She hangs up on me, leaving me to think about what she said.

I am a sicko.

A sick, science-loving, bad man. No wonder Mr. Spock is the only long-term relationship I've ever had. Well, him and my mom, Lita, and Lynda. They'll always be there for me. I stare around at the chaos that used to be a very nice office, realizing nothing will ever be the same again. I was in love, *really in love,* for the first time in my pathetic life, but I've gone and screwed it up so badly, it's over forever.

While I want to think I was justified in what I did, that conversation with Gwen really brought the truth home. I did what I did because I wanted to be right. My stupid intellectual pride has really screwed me over this time.

My phone buzzes and I see an incoming text from my mom. Oh, nice. This should make me feel better.

Mom: I thought you should know, Lita, Lynda, and I are all VERY disappointed in you, Ben. We still love you, of course, but we cannot condone or respect what you've done. Maybe it's time you moved home where you'll have better influences in your life. It seems like those space people are leading you to forget humans have hearts that can be broken.

Et tu, L-Triad?

THIRTY-NINE

Serafina

My brain hurts, my heart is broken, and my pride is positively shattered. It's bad enough that Ben is a two-timing man-whore, but he also set out to ruin me at the same time he was wooing me? How could I have fallen for that?

I slam into my apartment like I'm Dwayne "The Rock" Johnson, late for my mid-morning grilled chicken feast. Charley is sitting on the couch staring at me, but she wisely sits back and watches me before saying anything.

"Did you see it?" I demand.

She nods her head tentatively, so I ask, "Can you believe it?"

Shoulder shrug.

"I swear to God, first my dating app doesn't work for crap and then this? This is a debacle of *Titanic* proportions." I fall onto the sofa as though my bones have melted. "I'm sunk. My career is over, and my love life remains a non-existent wasteland of sadness."

"Uh-oh," Charley mutters.

"What do you mean by that?" I demand harshly.

"I mean that when you allow drama to get the better of you, we're in for a wild ride."

"Drama?" I yell. Then repeat, "Drama?! You think I'm being dramatic? You don't think my reaction is justified?"

She rolls her eyes.

"Charlotte Francesca Jenkins, don't you dare call me dramatic. I have been run through the wringer of life. I have been treated more harshly than I've ever been. My life is a tornado of grief." Then, as if on cue, sobs erupt from my soul. I cry and snuffle and weep until I've exhausted myself. Charley remains silent.

When the buzzer rings announcing a guest, I cover my head with a pillow and declare, "I'm not receiving visitors right now."

"Oh. My. God," Charley mutters as she walks to the intercom. "Who is it?" I hear her ask.

"Hey, Charley, it's Zay."

She buzzes him up before saying, "I know Your Highness said she wasn't receiving, but it's your brother."

"You're making fun of me," I pout.

"Glad you noticed. I feel for you, Sera, I do. You're just being so melodramatic about this. It's not like you guys were in love or anything."

I don't answer her or make eye contact, which has her asking, "Were you?"

I remain silent.

Charley demands, "Was it rom-com insta-love? Oh, Sera, that's the best! I've got to tell you that if that's what it is, then you and Ben are *still* going to wind up together. How exciting!"

"As if. There's no way on earth I can ever forgive that

man for what he's done to me. He ... he ... he ran a harpoon straight into my heart!" I release another anguished sob.

Charley jumps up when the doorbell rings and lets in Zay, who walks straight toward me carrying a bakery box and a grocery bag. "We'd best commence phase one," he declares.

"Phase one?" Charley asks.

Nodding his head, my brother tells her, "When Sera has a broken heart, she requires copious amounts of sweets and comfort items."

"Too much will knock her off balance," Charley warns.

"It's how she rolls. First, she'll overindulge to the point of making herself sick. Then she'll go so far in the opposite direction that she'll eschew all things she loves as punishment, and finally the scales will balance out and she'll be back to normal." He feels the need to add, "You know, as normal as she can be."

"Wow," Charley says. "Does this happen often?"

"This will only be the fifth time since she's graduated from college."

"Stop talking about me like I'm not even here!" I yell. Then I open the box full of donuts and take one in each hand.

Charley looks at me with surprise registered on her face. "You're going to double-fist it?"

With my mouth full, I tell her, "Yup, not only that, I'm not going to stop until I've consumed six donuts." Then I ask Zay, "Did you bring a can of whipped cream?" When he nods his head, I tell him, "Grab it and spray some on my donuts, will you?"

"I've never seen you like this," Charley says. "I feel like I should help you somehow."

"If you want to help, make me a cup of hot chocolate and call down to the Surrey Diner and order two family-size french fries with extra ranch."

She shakes her head. "I'm not going to enable you."

"What are you, forty?" I practically snarl. "I'm going to get what I want whether you help me or not, so you'd better just earn your pay and do what I tell you to do."

Charley stands as still as a statue. Before she can click into gear, my brother says, "Aside from aiding you in your grief process, Ser, I've brought news for Charley." Then he reaches into his backpack and pulls out a newspaper and hands it to her. "Your article came out today."

Charley grabs it so fast I barely see her hands move. "I didn't think it was coming out until next week."

"It wasn't supposed to, but *The Post* had to pull another article and they put yours in its place. You even got a better slot. They put you on the first page of the People section right next to Kim Kardashian."

"What?" Charley rips the paper open before falling into a bean bag chair. She reads quietly for a minute before reciting, "According to fellow Mathlete Jacob Fein, Charley Jenkins is one cool chick." Charley drops the paper in her lap before flailing her arms and screaming like she's being attacked by a swarm of bees.

"Isn't Jacob Fein 'Hunky Pants McHottiestein'?" I ask her. At my brother's questioning look, I explain, "Just the most studly math nerd at Eleanor Falls Academy."

"He's a senior," Charley interjects. "We had the same advanced calculus class, but he never even looked at me, let alone spoke to me. I can't believe he said I was cool."

She picks the paper up again and reads while giving us the highlights. The principal said she was a tribute to private school education, and Tiffany Connor — head cheerleader and mean girl extraordinaire — said that she always thought Charley should be a model, and that some girls felt threatened by her because she's so smart and beautiful, but not Tiffany (who apparently was one of her BFFs and really wishes she were back in the halls of Eleanor Falls).

"Sera, thank you, thank you, *thank you* for letting me be on *Wake Up America!* with you and for suggesting this article." Then she turns to Zay and adds, "Please thank Shelby for me for passing the idea on to her mom."

I stare at my brother and young employee, who have completely forgotten that my life is falling apart at this very moment. They continue to chatter excitedly about the newspaper article, leaving me to fend for myself.

"Fine," I mutter, even though they clearly aren't listening. "I'll just get my own whipped cream." I grab the can and spray it over all the donuts that are left in the box. Then I turn my attention to eating as many of them as I can, hating myself for not being mature enough to let Charley have her moment in the sun.

I am actually thrilled for her to have such epic revenge on her horror show of a high school career. I'm just having a hard time showing it at the moment. Finally, when there are only five donuts left in the box and my stomach is stretched out to maximum capacity, I smile at my young friend and say, "I'm really happy for you."

Zay and Charley both stop talking and turn to me with matching expressions of horror.

"What?"

"How did you manage to get sprinkles on your forehead?" Zay asks.

"I don't have sprinkles on my forehead."

"Yeah, you do," Charley says, pointing and making a wide circle to indicate the spread of tiny hard candy bits that I can't feel for some reason. "And you're literally covered in icing sugar."

I glance down at my dress and see she's right. I don't care, but she is right. "Forget about that. I said I'm happy for you. You did what few people manage, which is to get sweet, sweet revenge on the jerks in your high school."

Charley grins while Zay narrows his eyes at me. "Nope. Do not even think about it."

"What?" I ask innocently, even though I know he knows exactly what I'm thinking.

"You're wondering how you can get your revenge on Dr. Banana Pants."

"I am not!" I spit out, even though I *totally* am.

"You want me to order another glitter bomb?" Charley asks.

"You sent him a glitter bomb?" Zay asks, rubbing his temples with both hands. "What are you, twelve?"

I shrug as if to say *pretty much*. The donuts expand a little more, making me feel very much like I imagine a beached whale would feel. "Quick, get me some black olives. I need to balance out the sugar."

FORTY

Ben

Dev emailed me at the very end of the day yesterday and told me to report to him first thing this morning, which can't be good. After a night of tossing and turning under the weight of regret, I'm still exhausted, even after four cups of high-test coffee. The only plus of being up all night is that I managed to write and memorize an apology speech to end all apology speeches that I'm about to use right about ... now.

I knock lightly, even though Dev's door is open. Without looking up, he says, "Come in and shut the door."

Nuts. I do as he says, then sit down on the chair across from his desk and just wait while he taps away at his computer. After a good long minute, he lets out a sigh, then sits back and folds his arms. "Well? What do you have to say for yourself?"

"There's no way I can begin to express the depth of regret I feel about how I've conducted myself. I lost sight of our mission and I've humiliated not only myself, but NASA, and my friend Gwen as well as her family." I sigh before continuing, "I never should have allowed my personal feelings to come into play while acting as a representative of the team, and if you want to let me go, I completely understand."

He stares at me, his brown eyes boring into mine like he's trying to see into my soul to determine if I'm really sorry or if I'm just saying what I think he wants to hear. "Have I ever mentioned my oldest son is currently employed as a male stripper?"

What? I shake my head.

"There's a reason for that. He got a full academic ride to Harvard and pissed it away to strip for horny old women. He's been the single largest disappointment in my life."

Okay, so maybe it's not as bad as I thought. It's not like I've taken my intellectual abilities for granted or something...

"Until now..."

Damn. It's much worse.

"Do you know what you were supposed to do on *Wake Up America!*?"

I start to answer but he holds up one finger to stop me. "You were supposed to make astronomy more accessible, more fun, more exciting. You were supposed to make us heroes again. Do you think you did that, Ben?"

Shaking my head, I open my mouth, but he says, "Ah-a-a," which must mean it's still not my turn to talk. If he doesn't want me to say anything, he should really stop asking me questions. "You confirmed for the American people that we're narrow-minded intellectual snobs who are also, ironically, too stupid to remember we're on national television. Are we too stupid to behave in a manner befitting of the greatest space agency on the planet, Ben?"

I stare, waiting for him to go on, which apparently is the wrong choice, because he barks, "Answer me!"

Crap. Now I've completely forgotten the question. Oh, right. Are we stupid? "Yes. No, I mean *we're* not, I am."

"Do you know what I spent my day doing yesterday?"

"No, I—"

"Be quiet. I'm the one who's talking here," Dev says.

"I spent the day taking calls from reporters who wanted the inside scoop, a four-star general who was mad as hell about your conduct and wants you court-martialled—"

"Court-martialed? That's not a thing at NASA." *Is it?*

"If he has his way, it will be."

"You know who else called me? Some woman named June Devereaux, who you called" — he glances down to consult his notes — "a meddling busybody. Looks like we're going to hear from her lawyer for a defamation suit."

I snort at that, even though I really shouldn't. "Good luck with that, June." Dev's nostrils flare and I mutter, "Sorry."

"If all of that wasn't enough, your mother called."

My shoulders slump. Seriously, my mom?

"We wound up having quite the long chat about you. Apparently, Lydia thinks I should force you to go home for a few months to get your head on straight. I'm not sure she's wrong about that."

"You can't actually send me home," I tell him. "You can fire me, but you can't physically put me on a plane to Oregon."

"I know that, but believe me, your mom and I racked our brains to come up with ways to make that happen."

"Am I being fired?" I ask, my palms feeling suddenly as clammy as a pot of hot chowder.

"I thought about it. In fact, last night when I got home, I was positive I was going to end your chances of ever working at NASA again." He lets me stew on that for a minute before adding, "But then I talked it over with Dina at supper and she said, 'Dev, you're going to do with Ben what I did with Errol.'"

"Your son, the..." *Don't say stripper. Don't say stripper.* "...stripper?"

Nuts. Well, at least I whispered it.

He nods, a pained expression passing over his face. "Dina and Errol still have a wonderful relationship, whereas he and I haven't spoken in over a year. She told me that you made a mistake, but that one thing doesn't define who you are, and you still have a lot of value to bring to the team."

Thank you, Dina!

"So I called your mom and told her I wasn't sending you home, but instead, I'm stripping you of your spokesperson duties and handing them over to Carla."

Phew! I hated that bit anyway.

"But, that's not all. Because as Lita pointed out—"

"Lita was there?" I have my PhD in astrophysics, for crying out loud. How are my mom and her best friend both involved?

"And Lynda," he adds. "Anyway, Lita reminded us all that you hate doing the public appearances, so I'd actually be rewarding you for your..." — he glances down at his notes again — "...hurtful and humiliating actions. So, you're going to get a pay cut, which will be diverted to Carla, since she's taking over that part of your job."

Oh, well, thank you, Auntie Lita. "A pay cut? How much?"

"I haven't figured that out yet. I have someone in HR helping to determine the value of that job function, but I expect it will be somewhere around ten to twenty thousand a year," he tells me. "I'm also going to take you under my wing and keep a careful eye on you until I can trust you again. The L-Triad seemed satisfied with that arrangement and so am I."

Well, that's ... just great. I'm so glad my mom and her besties are pleased.

"Expect me to come by your office randomly throughout each day to see what you're doing."

I nod and say nothing. After all, I did the dance and now it's time to pay the band.

"You can go," he says. "But I want you to spend the rest of the morning thinking about how you can make things up to everyone you hurt."

"Wouldn't you rather I spend the morning analyzing the atmospheric pressure on Gamma-Four Eighty-One?"

"Gamma-Four Eighty-One has been there for billions of years. It can wait."

Sitting at my boring metal desk with a pad of paper in front of me, I've written: *How to Fix Things*, and under that title are several columns: *Gwen/her family, the NASA team*, and, finally, *Serafina*.

The rest of the page is blank because I have no clue what to do to make things better. I've even Googled how to repair a relationship you've ruined. I'm simmering with anger, to be honest, which isn't exactly conducive to high-level problem solving. The focus of my ire is aimed at the three women who are probably lying out in the sun in my mom's yard cackling away about their call with my boss.

After picking up my phone, I dial my mom's number. She crossed the line and she's going to hear about it.

When she picks up, she says, "If you're calling to yell at me about my intervention with Mr. Grover, don't bother. I'm not sorry and I'd do it again."

Lovely. "Yeah, not cool, Mom. Not cool," I say. "You know, *you're* the reason I wound up in this situation in the first place."

"What? Me?"

"Yes, *you*. You and your ridiculous psychics and your ... healing crystals that you spend a fortune on and your ... inability to make your own decisions without shelling out your hard-earned cash to some charlatan instead of using your own perfectly-functional brain!"

"Okay, I see what's happening here," she says. "You're transferring your anger onto me because you can't face the fact that you screwed up royally."

"No, that's not it at all. You had no right to phone my boss and suggest he send me home for a morality update."

"Well, clearly you need one. What you were trying to do to that poor Serafina was unforgivable. And that Gwen girl? You've humiliated both of them and that is not the man I raised you to be."

I let out a long sigh of frustration. "The man you raised me to be is one who is absolutely terrified you're one email from a Nigerian prince away from losing everything!"

"You're making me sound stupid, Ben. I am not stupid."

"But you're ridiculously naïve!"

"Watch yourself, young man," she says in a clipped tone. "Maybe I am a little too trusting at times, but that doesn't give you the right to project your fear of being hurt onto other people. Onto Serafina."

"I didn't—" I start to say, then I slam my mouth shut because my mom is right.

"Just realized it?"

"Yup," I say, completely deflated. "And you're right. That's exactly what I did. But as far as calling my boss? Way out of line, Mother. Way out. You do know I'm a *grown man*, don't you?"

"That's a bit of an oxymoron, dear," she answers. "But, I get your point. The thing is, I'm really worried about you and I'm too far away to help."

"I don't *need* you to help. I'm an adult — and a highly intelligent one at that."

"Fine, then why'd you call?"

"Because I need your help," I answer, palming my forehead.

FORTY-ONE

Serafina

"Have you become bulimic or something?" Charley demands while standing over me and the remains of my Chinese food feast from last night.

"Bulimics throw their food up," I inform her.

"Are you saying that you're somehow keeping all of this down?"

"Yes." Barely. *Man, does my stomach hurt.*

"Serafina, you are not well. You need to pull yourself together and recalibrate or something."

"You make it sound like I can just snap my fingers and be fine. You, of all people, know that romance doesn't work like that."

"It's true that romantic comedies don't work like that, but as you've told me so many times, rom-coms aren't real life."

"Why are you here?" I glare up at her.

"Because it's Tuesday and, according to our calendar,

you've scheduled calls with our test subjects to find out how they're doing with our app."

Crap on a crouton, I don't want to work today. I'm not even sure my stomach will bend enough for me to get off the couch. "Please get me some coffee," I say while I roll onto the floor in hopes of positioning myself onto my knees enough to enable a standing position next.

I hear Charley clanging away in the kitchen while I use my arms and push myself onto my feet. Then I shuffle to the bathroom like a ninety-year-old woman with only two toes to help keep my balance. How in the world do I recover from what happened on television yesterday? Was that only yesterday? It feels like I've been on the couch eating for months. I have no idea what kind of fallout Ben's tirade will have on my professional life. I imagine it will be huge though. He essentially called me a fake and a liar.

Standing under the spray of hot water I let my brain go *there* ... What would have happened if I'd stayed at Ben's apartment and let him explain about Gwen? What if he decided my app wasn't a hoax and that, even though he originally intended to out me as a fraud, he'd changed his mind? What if we spent the night affirming our feelings for each other instead of starting World War III?

Damn. There's a slight possibility I may have blown it. In my heart of hearts, I can't accept that Ben was really planning to hurt me or my business. Not after what transpired between us. It's just that sometimes I leap to conclusions which is *not* the Libra way. It's the Serafina Lopez way. Dear Hera, goddess of women, I may be astrologically challenged.

Squeezing the shampoo out of the bottle, I'm suddenly overcome by the urge to shut the water off, throw on a towel, and run to Ben's to tell him I messed up. Make that get dressed and take a cab because running is not possible with as much food as I've recently consumed.

After yesterday's scene, there's no way I can even call him. He is never going to talk to me again. Plus, I'm not sure if I should want to make up. Even though I instigated everything by reading his texts from Gwen, what he set out to do is so much worse. My heart may be whispering for me to believe him, but my logical side is shouting at the top of her lungs not to be stupid.

By the time I get out of the shower, I feel semi-human again. I put on a clean nightgown and a robe before walking out into the kitchen. "Yum, I smell bacon."

Charley announces, "I made you a healthy breakfast of scrambled eggs, toast, and two strips of bacon."

"I just want bacon. Twelve or fourteen strips should do it."

"No." Charley stands with her hands on her hips. "If you don't have the strength to use self-control, I will be here to force you."

Jabbing my pointer finger in her direction, I say, "You seem to be forgetting who works for whom."

"Whatever. Sit down and I'll serve you up." Clearly Charley isn't intimidated by me. Rats.

"You know, Charley, grown-up love is very complicated. You don't just bounce back because someone tells you to."

"Love? Are you and Ben in love?" she asks, her eyes filled with hope.

I nod my head slightly. "I think we were. But I ruined it by reading his text messages and blowing things out of proportion."

"No, no, no, no ..." She's waving her hands in front of

her. "This is perfect. You and Ben just need to come together and have your big rom-com moment."

I visualize a vintage Ben standing under my window in a long brown trench coat with a boombox, but the image is absurd. Besides, I'm not sure a Peter Gabriel song is going to work here. "I'm going to tell your parents they need to institute a ban on romantic movies."

She waves off my threat. "You both have to mope for a little bit, but something big has to bring you together. Then the camera will zoom in on you as you catch sight of each other." Now she's making a square with her pointer fingers and thumbs and she's walking around me like she's the lens of the camera.

She continues, "Maybe your eyes meet across a crowded restaurant, or you run into each other on the street ... whatever it is, it has to be epic. The audience has to feel the tug of emotion and the back and forth of your thoughts as you decide what to do."

She runs across the room to the far end of the living room and starts to act out her vision of Ben's role. "Serafina ..." she declares with her hand jutted out in front of her.

What in the heck is she doing?

"Now you say 'Ben,'" she instructs.

I put my fork down and pick up my bacon. "Ben." I mimic her, wondering where this is all going.

She takes a step toward me. "I haven't been able to eat or sleep ..."

Clearly, I haven't suffered the same dilemma, so I say, "I wish things had worked out differently."

Charley prompts me with her hands to keep talking, so I add, "I shouldn't have read your text messages." Prompt, prompt, prompt ... "I'm sorry about Mr. Spock."

"And ..." God, this girl is annoying me.

"And I miss you." *Are you happy now, Charley?*

Charley runs across the room and gets down on one knee. "I miss you too. So much. I would never hurt you, Sera. You are my one true love. The sun and the moon are nothing compared to the love I feel for you."

"I think that's a bit much, don't you?" I ask her.

"Shut up," she says. "Rom-com love is big and over the top and requires a speech of impressive proportions." She contorts her face back into her Ben character. "I love you, Serafina, and if you don't say you love me back, I'll throw myself out the window! Death would be far preferable than living in a world where you don't love me back."

"I feel like we've skewed a little Romeo and Juliet here. Can we pull it back to maybe Hugh Grant and Julia Roberts?"

Charley throws her hands up in the air like she's giving up. "We could, but to do that, you would have to see the guy or at least talk to him on the phone. Are you willing to call him?"

I shake my head. "I'm too mortified."

"That's okay," she says. "Classic rom-coms always have friends and family getting involved to bring a couple together — I'm referencing *Sleepless in Seattle* here. Usually it's done on the down low so the couple is utterly surprised, but since you're my boss and I don't want you to fire my behind, I'm asking. Do you give me permission to orchestrate a truly grand rom-com scene with you and Ben?"

I should be terrified. I should say no. But the truth is, I *want* Ben to be a part of my life. I really do love him, even though he's a high-handed intellectual snob. At the heart of it, I know he's also a really good person, full of curiosity and compassion. And, on top of that, the man is one heck of an amazing kisser and he's insanely hot for a nerd.

"Fine," I tell her. "I give you permission to butt into my love life and help me and Ben find our way back to each other."

Charley screams like she's just been stabbed in a dark alley. "YES!!! You won't be sorry! I promise I will not rest until your love story is declared rom-com of the year by the masses."

"You do know this isn't a movie, right?" I ask, concerned that she's lost track of reality.

"It kind of is," she says. "I mean you're pretty much going to re-enact the whole thing on television."

"You're not suggesting we make up on television, are you? Because I'm putting my foot down at that."

Charley waves me off. "Too late, you gave permission and now it's up to me."

"You have to tell me what you're going to do," I order.

"No, I don't. All the best rom-coms have that surprise element. If you know what's coming, you won't be able to play your part convincingly."

"Charley ..." I say in my most stern motherly tone.

"Sorry, gotta go. You're going to have to make your calls alone because I have a movie to write."

"Charley," I yell after her to no avail as she hurries out my front door without a backward glance.

What have I just agreed to? A shiver runs through me right before a wall of panic hits. Charley is capable of really messing things up. Although, I'm not sure how much worse things could possibly get.

FORTY-TWO

Ben

It's been eight days since I ruined my life, but honestly, it feels more like eight days on Venus, which is the equivalent of 1944 days on Earth (or 5.32603 Earth years). I've spent the entire time in a state of *how can I make this up to the world?* and so far, in spite of my best efforts, I've fallen short.

I've sent flowers (along with heartfelt handwritten notes) to Serafina, Gwen, Gwen's aunt June, Waltraut, even Hal and Lacey. I enrolled Dev and Dina in a wine-of-the-month club (along with another heartfelt apology note). I arranged (and footed the bill) for a catered team lunch by a couple of women who call themselves Nibbles and Noshes. Delicious, by the way. Best roasted chicken and goat cheese sandwich on the planet, and the gingersnaps... Wow.

So far though, Carla and Alec are the only ones treating me like my normal self. The rest of the team is pretty much giving me the silent treatment. Well, Dina did write a little note back to thank me for the wine and tell me that "failure is not fatal," so that was nice.

No one has responded to my flowers, which I guess is understandable. I suppose it was an uninspired, if not obvious choice. Waltraut sent me a text that said:

> Thanks, but you're not coming back on the show. Not my choice, your bosses. Good luck.

In the last two days, I've switched gears and, instead of using my wallet to solve the problem, I'm trying to expand my mind. I spent the entire evening yesterday browsing at a weird little shop called Namaste Friends in an attempt to open my mind to the whole metaphysical world. I wound up having a surprisingly deep conversation with Astrid, the woman who runs the place. I even teared up at one point and somehow left with a singing chakra bowl, a pillow to sit on while I use it, and some anointing roll-on oil called Connect. She even threw in a baseball shirt with the moon phases on it. Astrid's good people.

Today, instead of hurrying into my office, I walked directly over to Carla and asked her how Chewy's been doing since she added pumpkin to his diet. Then, I sat on the corner of her desk for a full twenty minutes, doing my best not to make faces or gag while she told me all about it. As always, there was way too much detail in her reply — we're talking texture, size, shape — but I didn't hurry away. Because that's what people who care about other people do. They ask questions, they respect other people's opinions and beliefs, and they're willing to listen.

My mom was right. In my quest for astronomy great-ness, I lost sight of what's important — human connection. I'm determined to get that back, even if it doesn't result in finding my way back to Serafina. When I get to the other side of this, I will be a better Ben. Having said that, I really want to figure out how to get Serafina to forgive me.

I'm currently Googling creative ways to apologize. Blech ... some are truly horrid, like offering to clean the person's house for a year or telling them you'll be their slave. Who thinks of this stuff?

Then I hit on one that says to send them a can of air freshener with a note, "Let's clear the air between us." That one isn't too bad, but I'm afraid I've muddied things beyond the abilities of mere Lysol.

Oh, here's one — show up at their door and sing your apology. It's not that I'm not willing to be humiliated for love. I am. I'm just worried that the sound of my singing might be the final nail in my coffin.

I look up local singing telegram sites and come across one called Drag-o-Grams, that is run and operated by a local drag performer. That's just out-of-the-box enough to work. After a quick search of apology songs, I land on just the right thing to show that I'm truly sorry for being such a schmuck. Then I call Drag-o-Grams to see if this song is one that they can perform.

The man on the other end of the line answers, "Drag-o-Grams, where we have a song for every occasion. This is Madonna, how can I help you?"

"Um, hi Madonna, my name is Ben Williams ..."

He doesn't let me finish before he interrupts, "Not THE Ben Williams from *Wake Up America!*?"

"I'm afraid so," I tell him. "I need to hire your company to make an apology to someone I really care about."

"No kidding. Listen, Ben, may I be frank?" He doesn't let me answer, he just continues, "You have more than one person to apologize to."

"You mean other than Serafina?"

"What about poor Gwen? Watching that segment was like witnessing a car wreck. I couldn't turn away."

I cringe at the thought that even Madonna from Drag-o-Grams saw me make a total ass out of myself.

"I already sent Gwen some flowers."

"Not enough," he says with force. "Flowers are nice for your garden-variety minor infraction, but when you screw up as monumentally as you did, they're just the jumping off point."

"Um, okay. I guess I could send a singing telegram to Gwen, too. I was thinking about the song 'I'm Sorry' by Brenda Lee, or 'Bye, Bye, Love' by the Everly Brothers ..."

"Are you eighty? Don't answer, I know you're not." Then Madonna instructs, "You need a song that they've already heard and sung in the shower."

"What, like 'All Apologies' by Nirvana?"

"We at Drag-o-Gram don't sing songs by men, but at least you're entering the right decade. Listen, Ben, I know the exact tune that will yield the best result. Do you trust me?"

"Uh, well, Madonna ..." This is such a crazy conversation. "I trust you as much as I should, being that you're a total stranger."

"Good, then leave it up to me. I'll take care of you and if all isn't forgiven and forgotten, I'll give you fifty percent off your next order. All I need is your credit card number..."

FORTY-THREE

Serafina

"Now that Dr. Williams won't be returning to *Wake Up America!*, we need you to be able to carry the whole segment on Monday. Do you think you can do that?" Waltraut asks while I sneak bites of my everything bagel with extra cream cheese. Charley rolls her eyes at my continued feasting.

"Of course, I can," I tell the producer enthusiastically. "Since it's summer, how about if I talk about the best vacations for your star sign?" I know I could use a week or two in Florence, Italy. There's no better place for us Libras to tap into our massive creativity than the birthplace of the Renaissance. I wonder if I could talk my way into an on-location shoot?

"Great idea. Just make sure that everything fits into a ten-minute time slot."

I hang up just as the buzzer rings. "That'll be the UPS guy who should have been here yesterday," I tell Charley who is prematurely putting the bagels away.

I push the intercom button and bark out a hello.

"Delivery for the fabulous Ms. Serafina Lopez!" a deep voice calls.

Is UPS getting a lot friendlier? Charley and I glance at each other with confused grins. "Come on up."

I hear loud footsteps coming down the hall, so I swing the door open to accept delivery of my peony candles, only to come face-to-face with Cher. Not Cher from today, but a slightly-off version of her from the late 1980s. Same big hair, make-up totally on point, but this version must be almost seven-feet tall with her staggering heels.

"Wow. You all are really stepping up your game," I say, feeling like I've fallen through a portal into an alternate universe.

In a surprisingly masculine voice, Cher says, "I'm Madonna from Drag-o-Grams with an apology from Ben."

Madonna? "You mean Cher..."

"My name is Madonna, but I'll be singing Cher."

"So you're *not* from UPS."

"Not in a million years."

I stare at her and am flabbergasted by the idea of this being a man. Madonna's Cher costume appears to be authentic from the time — the tiniest black sheer teddy that's so high cut, there isn't more than a landing strip around the girly bits, or, in this case, boy bits.

I'm obviously staring because Madonna explains, "Fitting into this costume requires a strap and wrap." What is he talking about? Before I can ask, he explains, "I need to strap it down and then wrap it tightly in plastic wrap. It's hotter than hell, but it hides the goods."

"Oh." I mean, really, what else is there to say? I call out, "Charley, you might want to come over here for this."

She trots out of the bathroom, takes one look at Cher, then at me, before telling our guest, "So, no UPS?"

"Nope," Madonna exclaims in a very deep voice. Then she bends over and turns on a boom box. When the intro for "If I Could Turn Back Time" starts to play, I can barely grasp what's happening.

While Cher (or Madonna) sings about how if she could reach the stars, she'd give them all to me, I stare in awe.

Then, like someone flipped a switch, I burst into an ugly cry. No delicate sobbing for this Libra. I sound like I'm being drawn and quartered in some kind of medieval torture ceremony. I'm so loud that Madonna stops singing half-way through the song and throws her brawny arms around me.

"There, there, Serafina," she says. "I know Ben was horrible to you. I watched the whole thing live. But you've got to know that he feels awful about how everything went down."

"Then why doesn't he tell me that himself?" I demand before blowing my nose on a tissue that Charley hands me.

"He said you won't take his calls or texts."

"He should have come here himself," I say.

"Would you have let him in?" Madonna asks, sounding so sure of herself.

"Whose side are you on?" I demand while pushing her away and putting my hands on my hips.

"I'm on the side of love, honey. Ben asked me to call him before I performed, and I've never heard such a sorry sack. That man is full of regret and would do anything to make up his past misdeeds to you."

"Anything?" Charley asks.

"I'm pretty sure," Madonna tells her. "That man sounded lower than an earthworm in hell. So much so, I decided to do this job myself." She confides, "I'm the owner of the company and hardly ever go out on calls anymore, but this was a special case. Now, can I finish singing my song?"

"From the top," Charley tells her with a giant smile on her face. Something is going on in that girl's mind and it's making me nervous.

After Madonna is through, I hand her a twenty-dollar tip and thank her for such an amazing performance. Only in New York City can you get such a high-quality sing-o-gram.

"Do you have a business card, Madonna?" Charley asks.

"Who are you planning on sending a singing telegram to?" I demand.

"What? You don't think my parents would totally jam to some vintage Alanis Morissette?"

"Oh, honey, we don't do her. At Drag-o-Gram we stay away from the angsty stuff. How about some Aretha or Beyonce? Bert sings the hell out of both those ladies."

"I think my parents could both do with giving me a little respect," she says. "I'll be in touch."

Madonna offers a weird curtsy that doesn't quite fit the look as she adds some parting advice. "Being that no one can actually turn back time, Serafina, sometimes you just have to forgive and forget. Take it from me, you don't want to miss out on life with your soul mate just because you're too proud to take him back. Pride won't warm your bed at night."

"Thanks for that, Madonna. I'll definitely think about

it." Yet even as I shut the door, I don't know if I have the courage to pick up the phone and call Ben. After all, he isn't the only one who needs to ask for forgiveness.

FORTY-FOUR

Ben

Email from Dev.Grover@GoddardInstitute.com
To: Ben.Williams@GoddardInstitute.com

Subject: Wake Up America! Appearance

Ben,

*Top brass has decided you need to go on the show
one more time to undo some of the damage. The
masses seem fixated on seeing you apologize to Ms.
Lopez and that Gwen woman so I'm sending you
to do that. Once you've accomplished your
mission, Carla will take over for you.*

Be at the studio Monday at the usual time.
Dev

I never thought I'd say this, but thank the Lord for morning television viewers across America. Their interest in my sorry life might just be what gets me Serafina back. Lord knows chocolate, flowers, and a singing telegram didn't do the trick.

I'm so determined not to blow it, I took a trip back to Namaste Friends and got myself the most Gemini of all the Gemini outfits they had. I'm currently waiting backstage in something called a super-soft and breathable Thai yoga shirt with a Nehru collar and long sleeves. It's bright yellow (and, true to its advertising, is super-soft). Astrid paired it with some loose yoga pants in a dark grey and added a hemp necklace that has rose quartz beads sewn into it to "reset my heart chakra" (whatever that means). I'm hoping when Serafina sees my outfit, she'll realize how much I'm trying to change. If this were *Grease*, I'd be Olivia Newton John to Sera's John Travolta.

Justin walks into the dressing room and stops in his tracks when he sees me. "Whoa. That's ... a new look."

"Too much?" I ask, feeling silly all of a sudden.

"Ah ... hmm ... I guess just not what I was expecting."

"Maybe I should change." The way he hesitates makes me nervous that maybe this isn't the right look for me after all.

He shakes his head. "No time. We've got to get your mic on."

I follow him backstage, my heart pounding as I wait for my one shot at winning back the woman I love. I can hear Serafina out there chatting with Hal and Lacey, and I'm sure she looks as gorgeous as ever. My pulse is racing so fast, I feel like it's taken on the cadence of the *William Tell Overture*.

I feel decidedly dizzy while I listen to their conversation. "We've got a special surprise for you, Serafina," Hal says. "Courtesy of your assistant, Charley."

I can see them from where I'm standing and Serafina raises one eyebrow while she shifts uncomfortably in her chair.

"You look worried," Lacey says. "Are you worried?"

"A little..."

"Well, don't be. As you know, Charley is a delightful young woman. She told us she'd do almost anything to see you happy. We're going to talk to her later, but first, we want to welcome back astronerd, Dr. Banana Pants himself, Ben Williams, to the *Wake Up America!* stage!"

My legs feel like I just got back from ten months on the International Space Station as I walk out. Serafina's eyes light up, then she looks me up and down and her expression immediately hardens. I give her a sad smile, then take my seat on the empty armchair next to hers.

"Dr. Williams," Lacey says. "You're quite a sight for sore eyes."

Hal actually rubs his eyes before adding, "Yes, welcome back. That's quite the shirt you're wearing." Hal laughs like crazy while Lacey rolls her eyes at him.

"Thanks for having me," I tell them both. Glancing at Serafina, I add, "I have some apologizing to do."

Serafina snorts. "Do you mean you have some more people to make fun of?"

"No ... not at all." Damn, this isn't starting out well.

"What's with the outfit then?" she demands angrily.

"I picked this up at Namaste Friends in the Village. I've been trying to immerse myself in the metaphysical world to better understand it."

Raising one eyebrow, Serafina says, "You've been to Namaste Friends?"

"Twice actually. I picked up a Tibetan singing bowl and have been using it while practicing meditation."

She stares at me like I just pulled a warthog out of my hat, then says, "Okaaaay."

"So, Ben," Lacey interrupts, "As you know, we here at *Wake Up America!* have been completely fascinated with you and Serafina. And we're not the only ones, because we haven't had so much fan mail since Backstreet Boys performed in short shorts. It seems that more than half of our viewers are desperate to see you two back together."

"What do the other half want?" I ask nervously.

"Seventy percent of the other half want Serafina to kick you to the curb, and the other thirty percent want to see the resurgence of boy bands," Hal says.

"Since the majority wins, we've invited some guests here today to try to talk some sense into the two of you. Maybe we can give America the happily ever after we've all been waiting for."

"Look around, Ben; you might recognize a few faces in our studio audience," Lacey adds as the lights in the audience come up. "Your mom and her two best friends, Lita and Lynda, are here." Gesturing for them to stand, Lacey says, "Come on, Mom, stand up and show yourself."

Holy crap. They've flown my mom and her friends here?

My mom gets up, looking like she's going to burst into tears from all the excitement. She waves around the crowd like she was just crowned Miss America before sitting back down.

I'm totally stunned, which makes the shock that much

greater when Lacey calls out to my team from the office to stand up. Dev looks oddly pleased with himself, while Alec and Carla wave wildly. The rest of them look decidedly nervous.

Just when I'm sure they can't fit any more rings into this circus, Gwen and her aunt June stand up. Oh, dear. I have no idea what Hal, Lacey, and Charley have in mind, but I sure hope to hell everything works out. I say there's about a forty percent chance it will. Sixty percent goes to the crowd having me tarred and feathered in retribution.

"So, Dr. Ben, what do you have to say for yourself?" Lacey asks.

"I, um ... well ... I ..." My thoughts are whirling around so fast I can't seem to grab a hold of any of them. "I've never felt so bad about anything in my entire life. I was closed-minded and well, just awful, really." I look at Serafina the whole time I'm talking.

"The first step to fixing a problem is admitting you have one," Hal says wisely.

"That's right," I tell him. "After I lost Serafina and made such a mess of things with Gwen, I realized I needed to make some changes."

"Changes, like getting a new wardrobe?" Lacey asks.

"That's part of it. I was so fixated on proving Serafina wrong, I lost sight of what science is all about — which is the pursuit of truth. One can't just decide what truth is without being open to unknowns. For instance, scientists of old believed the Earth was flat. If Aristotle hadn't thought bigger, we'd still be terrified of falling off the edge of the planet while sailing."

"Are you saying that you believe in astrology now?" Lacey asks.

I shake my head, unwilling to lie. "No, but I am open

to finding out more about it and I'm willing to concede that if practiced responsibly, there might be some benefit to it."

Hal leans forward in his chair, wearing a Diane-Sawyer-interviewing-Britney-Spears expression. "I think there's something more you want to say, Ben."

"I want to take this opportunity to apologize — to Serafina, to Gwen and her family — specifically her Aunt June who I never should have called a meddling busy-body — and to my team at NASA." I scan the audience trying to make meaningful eye contact as I go. "I was so far over the line of human decency that I couldn't even see it from my high horse. I got so caught up in trying to prove I was right that I forgot about what's important — treating others with respect and generally being a decent human being."

Lacey stands during my apology and walks off the stage, reappearing in the studio audience with a micro-phone. She walks over to the L-Triad and asks, "Which one of you is Ben's mom?"

"I am," my mom tells her, holding up one hand. "Lydia Williams."

"Why do you think your son got so sidetracked by the need to be right?"

My mom tears up a little before saying, "It's my fault. I have a horrible track record with men, and I think it's turned Ben into someone who's suspicious of everyone he meets."

"Mom, it's not your fault," I tell her, wishing we were having this conversation anywhere but here.

"No, it is," she says, shaking her head. She looks over at Lacey and says, "Ben's dad took off on us when Ben was seven. Then Geoff, he's the one who took our cat, Dr.

Pepper, when Ben was nine. Phil stole all my money and my car..."

Lita leans over and yells, "Phil Dewitt of Portland, Oregon, if you're out there, I'm coming for you!"

Lacey's eyes grow wide, then Lita looks at me. "And you, get your head out of your keister. And come visit once in a while."

"Thanks, Aunt Lita," I say as flames of embarrassment lick my face. Then louder, I add, "None of this is my mom's fault. She was a wonderful parent who tried to teach me to be open-minded and kind. I failed her along with everyone else here in the audience..." I glance at Serafina. "And on stage too."

"The truth is, you hurt us all," Hal says. "We have viewers promising not to watch us anymore if you don't come back."

Lacey is now standing in the aisle next to Gwen and her aunt. "Stand up, you two." When they do as she asks, Lacey says, "America, I'd like to introduce you to Ben's former friend, pediatric dentist Gwen Phalen, and her aunt June. I think we all remember how Ben outed his sham of a relationship with Gwen right here on *Wake Up America!*"

The audience gives them a round of applause, then they wait to see what's going to go down next.

"Gwen, you must have been absolutely humiliated by Ben's last appearance on our show," Lacey says, before holding the mic up to Gwen's mouth.

"I was very angry at Ben. But I just want to point out that I didn't do anything wrong by taking him to my cousin's engagement party. People go out as friends all the time."

"I don't know," Lacey tells her. "You did lie to your family about Ben being your boyfriend."

Gwen's face turns red. "Sometimes you have to stretch the truth when people won't stay out of your personal business." She glares at her aunt.

June pulls the microphone to her and loudly declares, "We've forgiven Gwen. In fact, I may have been a little ... pushy about setting her up with my chiropractor, Dr. Kwak."

"I know you only had my happiness in mind, Aunt June." Gwen pulls her aunt in for a hug.

"What do you say, Gwen? Do you forgive Ben?" Lacey interjects.

I give her a pleading look before she finally says, "Yes, I do. Ben's been trying to make it up to me ever since that episode and I don't think a jerk would go to all that trouble."

"It's true," June says. "He sent lovely flowers, then he had a most interesting singing telegram come by the house. The tallest woman I've ever seen dressed like Cher. She even let me video her on my camera so we can enjoy her performance again and again."

"So, you forgive him too?" Lacey asks June.

"I do," she answers with a nod. Smiling up at me, she says, "I think you've learned your lesson, young man."

Gwen cuts in with, "Lacey, I'd like to clarify something. Ben and I went on one date, but we both agreed that what we had was the beginning of a great friendship. When I asked him to go with me to the engagement party, it was only as a friend, even though we did mislead my family."

Lacey turns back to the stage. "What do you think about that, Serafina? Does that change anything for you?"

My heart stops while I wait for her to answer. The entire studio goes completely silent as she parts her lips. She doesn't speak right away, though. Instead, she looks at me and gives me the tiniest nod I think I've ever seen. Then she says, "I made some mistakes, too. I should have stuck around when Mr. Spock got sick, and I should have told the truth about being the one to give him Cheez Whiz. On that note, I shouldn't have sprayed Cheez Whiz all over the coffee table. I also should have never looked at Ben's phone without his permission."

Relief fills my body, making me feel like a helium balloon lifting off. "I should never have signed up for your dating app. And I should have told you that I did the moment things between us shifted from colleagues to, well, something more." I continue, "Serafina, I miss you so much. I can hardly breathe, as corny as that sounds. I can't sleep, I can't eat, I certainly can't laugh without you. I've spent the last two weeks pretty much positive that I ruined my only shot at happiness, because even though statistically there should be several thousand women I'd be compatible with in New York, I'm convinced that you're the only one who could ever make me feel so alive and so happy. You're the only one I've ever fallen so wonderfully, stupidly, in love with."

The audience lets out a collective "Awwww ..." then someone shouts, "Kiss him!"

Serafina smiles at me, but she still looks worried. "I don't know, Ben. It's one thing to dress up in that outfit and say nice things, but you wanted to ruin my business. I just don't know if I can trust you."

Swallowing hard, I tell her, "I wouldn't trust me either, which is why I contacted Charley and asked if I could help run a few numbers for you regarding your dating app."

I smile at Charley, who's sitting in the audience. She looks at Serafina, gives her a shrug, then shouts, "Turns out, he's really good at math."

"Not to toot my own horn, but I really am. And what I discovered, based on the beta testing of your dating app, is that couples who participated had a fourteen percent chance of finding someone compatible, which is remarkable given the small sample size. When I compared the questionnaire you designed to those of the top five dating sites — not including those intended for hookups — I discovered that yours creates a much more comprehensive picture of each person than the usual sites. Setting aside star signs, your questions manage to get to the heart of who a person is, what their beliefs are, and what their quote-unquote love languages are. You and Charley have created what could become the most effective means of finding love ever—"

I've never wooed someone with my math skills, but I know I've succeeded when Serafina jumps up and throws herself into my arms. After spinning her around, I reach up so I can hold her cheeks in both hands and kiss her with everything in me. I only pull back long enough to say, "This is an I'm sorry, I love you, I missed you, and I want to be with you forever kiss."

The first few bars of "If I Could Turn Back Time" suddenly blare over the speakers. Serafina and I step back and watch as a giant man in drag struts out onto the stage. This must be Madonna from Drag-o-Grams. All I can say is, wow!

When she turns to the audience and serenades them

in a pitch-perfect Cher impersonation, it isn't long before everyone is singing along with her.

I lean down and whisper in Serafina's ear, "I guess this is our song."

"It's a little strange, but it really can't be helped, can it?" She smiles back at me.

"Nope, there's nothing we can do about it."

"You do realize the odds are very high that we are it for each other. I crunched the numbers and came up with ninety-eight point six nine five percent, actually."

"Nerd," she says while snuggling into me.

"And proud of it."

EPILOGUE

Serafina

"Ben, the timer on your oven just went off!" I call out to my fabulous boyfriend of three months. We've been practically inseparable since we made up on *Wake Up America!* So much so, that even Mr. Spock lets me snuggle with him. When a cat you've inadvertently almost exploded doesn't hold a grudge, that's a pretty good sign.

If I had to guess, I'd say that Mr. Spock is an Aquarius. This insight has helped me understand his innate needs. Traditionally of a water sign, Aquarians don't hold a single clear shape and they defy categorization. Simply knowing this quirk helps make it easier to accept their moods.

My relationship with Ben's cat has started me on a path of exploring a new category for my app, *Your Pet and Their Star Sign*. I've even spoken with Ben's workmate Carla several times about her dog Chewy's anal sac situation. When I found out Chewy was born on July 10th, making him a Cancer, so many parts of his personality became clear. Cancers demand a lot of attention in their relationships. Chewy was smart enough to discover that when he dragged his bum against the carpet, he got a lot more attention. So, Carla learned to ignore the behavior and now gives him lots of love just for lying quietly on his bed.

Ben comes sauntering into the kitchen with the phone pressed up against his ear. "That sounds great, Dev, and while I'd love to be at the launch, Serafina and I have already booked tickets to Florence during that week."

He nuzzles up against my side and starts to nibble on my ear. I can hear Dev saying, "Put me on speakerphone and stop kissing each other long enough for me to tell you my news."

Ben pushes the speaker button and then puts the phone down onto the counter before pulling me into his arms to kiss me properly. Neither of us pays any attention to Dev until he practically yells, "Are either of you listening to me?"

"Sorry, Dev," I say with a laugh. "What was that?"

"I just heard from NASA that they want Ben at the launch because they are considering him for a spot on the Mars team. That's the mothership, man! You've got to go!"

Ben doesn't even pause. He just says, "But Serafina lives in New York, so while I'm flattered, I can't take the job, even if they offer it to me."

"What?!" Dev and I yell at the same time.

Ben shrugs. "I need to be where you are. You're my happiness."

"I'm gonna throw up," Dev says.

I pull Ben into my arms. "I work from home. I can do that as easily from Florida as I can from New York."

"But you love New York," Ben says.

"I love you more." Then, I add, "Plus, I'd love to spend as much time with my grandparents as I can while they're still around."

Holding me tightly, Ben says, "We're going to have to get a big enough place so they can both have their own bedroom and bathroom ... maybe their own wing now that I think about it."

"Why, Ben Williams, are you asking me to move in with you?" I ask as a wave of delight pours through me.

He drops down on one knee in front of me and says, "I'm asking you to marry me. What do you say, my beautiful, fiery Libra? Do you want to make an honest man out of this Gemini?"

I jump up and down and clap while answering, "I do, I really do!"

Dev speaks up, sounding super choked up. "This is so sweet. Can you send me a picture of the ring? You did get her a ring didn't you, Ben?"

"Of course I got her a ring," he says, pulling a small bag of Tempty cat treats out of his pocket.

I narrow my eyes at them, hoping he doesn't expect me to dig around in the Chicken Delites. But thankfully, instead of handing the bag to me, he shakes it and Mr. Spock comes running. Around his neck is a ribbon with one heck of a glittery diamond ring hanging from it.

"Aww, Mr. Spock? Are you in on the proposal?"

"Tell me you didn't tie the ring around your cat's neck, Ben," Dev says.

"He did," I tell him, tears filling my eyes. "And I absolutely love that Mr. Spock's okay with having me as his furless mom."

Ben tugs at the bow and the ribbon falls off. He deftly

catches the ring in his left hand and holds it up to me while Dev says, "Okay, well as long as you love it, that's the important thing. I think it's a bit cheesy, but..." When we don't answer him, because we've started kissing again, he says, "I'm going to hang up. This is kind of getting awkward."

If being an astrology aficionado has taught me one thing, it's this. When the stars are in the right alignment, there is nothing that can get in the way of your success. Don't tell Ben, but I had both of our natal charts done and we were absolutely meant for each other. As long as none of our kids are Taurus, we should be good to go.

COMING SOON...

Text in Show: An Accidentally in Love Story, Book 4

It's a dog text dog world...

Autumn Jones is at a crossroads. With no job offers in sight, she can either return to Koshkonong, Wisconsin to work at her dad's feed store or she can move to New York and help her older sister Helen coordinate the Manhattan Kennel Club Show. She and Helen may fight like cats and dogs, but Autumn would rather live with a thousand Helens than go home after seven years of college.

Jack Campbell is the veterinarian to Manhattan's elite. Despite their adoration, he does not love them back. In fact, he's vowed never to date anyone who walks through the front door of his clinic. He spends his days caring for pampered poodles sporting diamond encrusted collars and placating their high maintenance owners. When he meets Autumn, he assumes she's going to be another client with more money than brains.

Autumn is thrown into a bizarre world of highly competitive rich women who will do anything to win the coveted title of Best in Show at Manhattan's most exclusive competition. With her haughty sister breathing down her neck, and a high-strung poodle following her everywhere she goes, she doesn't have time for love, even if she does find herself face-to-face with America's hottest vet every day.

Will Autumn run back to Wisconsin with her tail between her legs? Will Jack find out that appearances can be deceiving? Will Helen's dog Fifi win Best in Show? Find out in the hysterical fourth edition of the Accidentally in Love Series, Text in Show.

GET IT HERE

AFTERWORD

A Note from Melanie and Whitney:

Thank you so much for taking the time to read Ben and Sera's story! If you enjoyed it, please take a moment to leave a review. Reviews are a true gift to writers. They are the best way for other readers to find our work.

If you aren't already signed up for our newsletters, please do so! This way we can keep you apprised of new releases, promotions, etc.

Whitney Dineen
Melanie Summers

ABOUT THE AUTHORS

WHITNEY DINEEN

USA Today Bestseller Whitney Dineen is a rock star in her own head. While delusional about her singing abilities, there's been a plethora of validation that she's a fairly decent author (AMAZING!!!). After winning many writing awards and selling nearly a kabillion books (math may not be her forte, either), she's decided to let the voices in her head say whatever they want (sorry, Mom). She also won a fourth-place ribbon in a fifth-grade swim meet in backstroke. So, there's that.

Whitney loves to play with her kids (a.k.a. dazzle them with her amazing flossing abilities), bake stuff, eat stuff, and write books for people who "get" her. She thinks french fries are the perfect food and Mrs. Roper is her spirit animal.

MELANIE SUMMERS

Melanie Summers lives in Edmonton, Canada, with her husband, three kiddos, and two cuddly dogs. When she's not writing, she loves reading (obviously), snuggling up on the couch with her family for movie night (which would not be complete without lots of popcorn and milkshakes), and long walks in the woods near her house. Melanie also loves shutting down restaurants with her girlfriends. Well, not

literally shutting them down, like calling the health inspector or something. More like just staying until they turn the lights off.

.